LAST TIME IN

12-year-old Armand Jones was having a bad day. The school bully was on his case. His homework was in the trash. And to top it off, he'd forgotten it was Class Picture day. Armand figured there was no way things could get worse...

That is, until he was "Zapt" across the galaxy and inducted into the ranks of P.O.O.P. [the Pan-Galactic Order Of Police]!

Now, in between gym class and history, Armand's zapping across the universe fighting off invading alien hordes and giant space slugs. His first major challenge pitted him against Thaddeus, a renegade ex-P.O.O.P. Op out for revenge. But an even bigger threat to the galaxy has been Gongar "The Peeved," a hulking warlord bent on interstellar domination.

For the time being, Thaddeus is in P.O.O.P. prison. But Gongar is still out there. Somewhere in the cosmos, he plots his next move...

CONTENTS
VOL. 02

PROLOGUE: BOY, AM I POOPED!

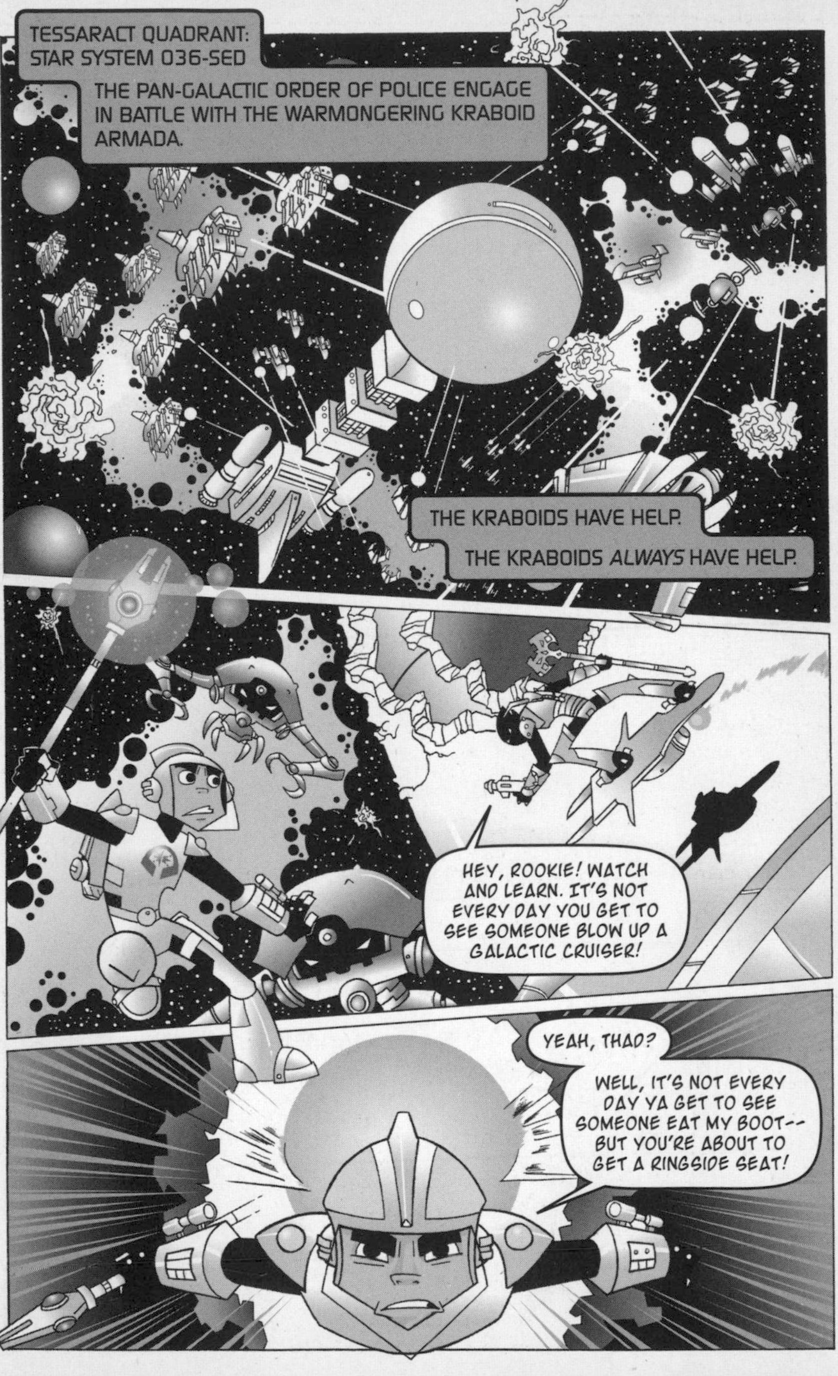
TESSARACT QUADRANT: STAR SYSTEM 036-SED
THE PAN-GALACTIC ORDER OF POLICE ENGAGE IN BATTLE WITH THE WARMONGERING KRABOID ARMADA.
THE KRABOIDS HAVE HELP.
THE KRABOIDS *ALWAYS* HAVE HELP.
HEY, ROOKIE! WATCH AND LEARN. IT'S NOT EVERY DAY YOU GET TO SEE SOMEONE BLOW UP A GALACTIC CRUISER!
YEAH, THAD?
WELL, IT'S NOT EVERY DAY YA GET TO SEE SOMEONE EAT MY BOOT-- BUT YOU'RE ABOUT TO GET A RINGSIDE SEAT!

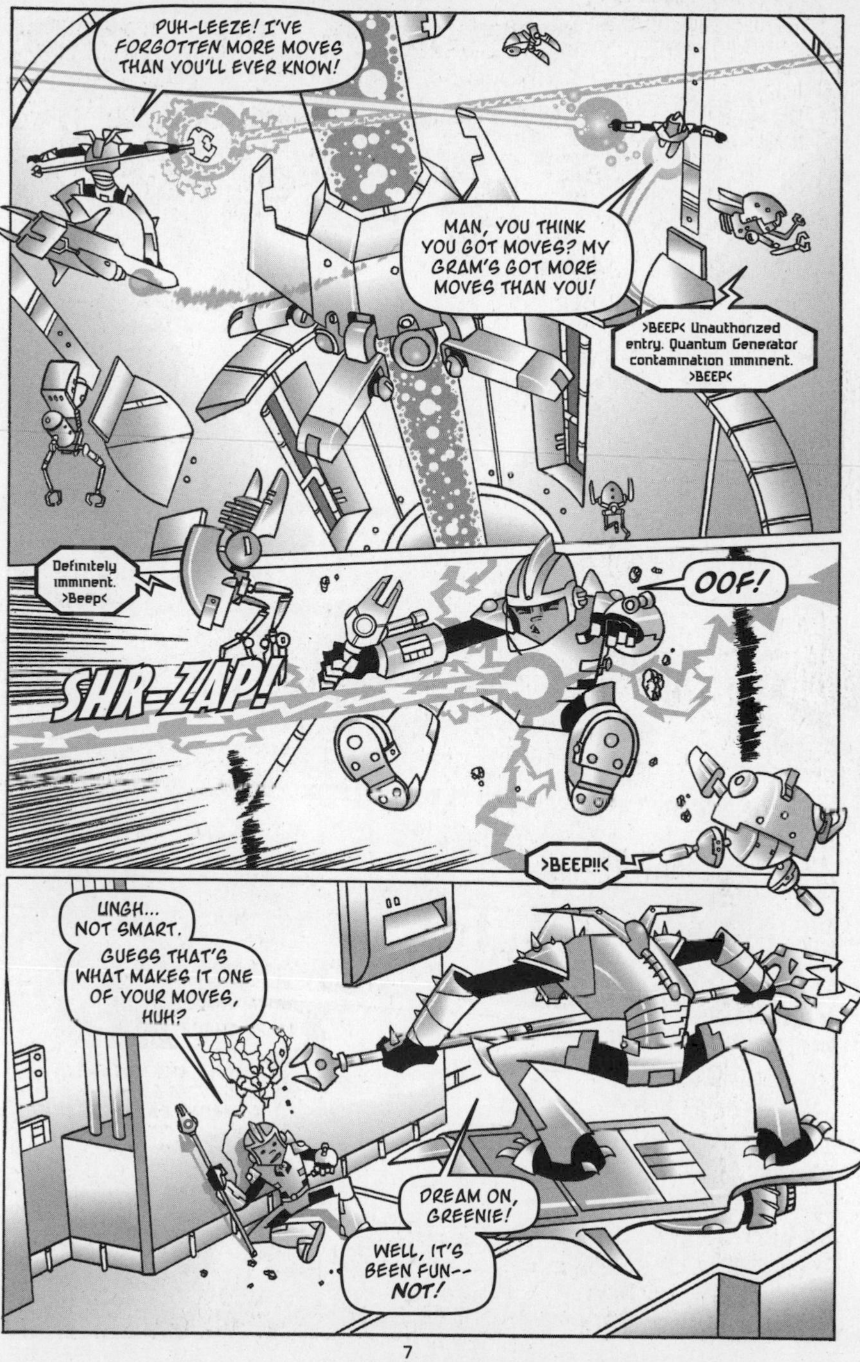
PUH-LEEZE! I'VE FORGOTTEN MORE MOVES THAN YOU'LL EVER KNOW!
MAN, YOU THINK YOU GOT MOVES? MY GRAM'S GOT MORE MOVES THAN YOU!
>BEEP< Unauthorized entry. Quantum Generator contamination imminent. >BEEP<
Definitely imminent. >Beep<
OOF!
SHR-ZAP!
>BEEP!!<
UNGH... NOT SMART.
GUESS THAT'S WHAT MAKES IT ONE OF YOUR MOVES, HUH?
DREAM ON, GREENIE!
WELL, IT'S BEEN FUN-- NOT!

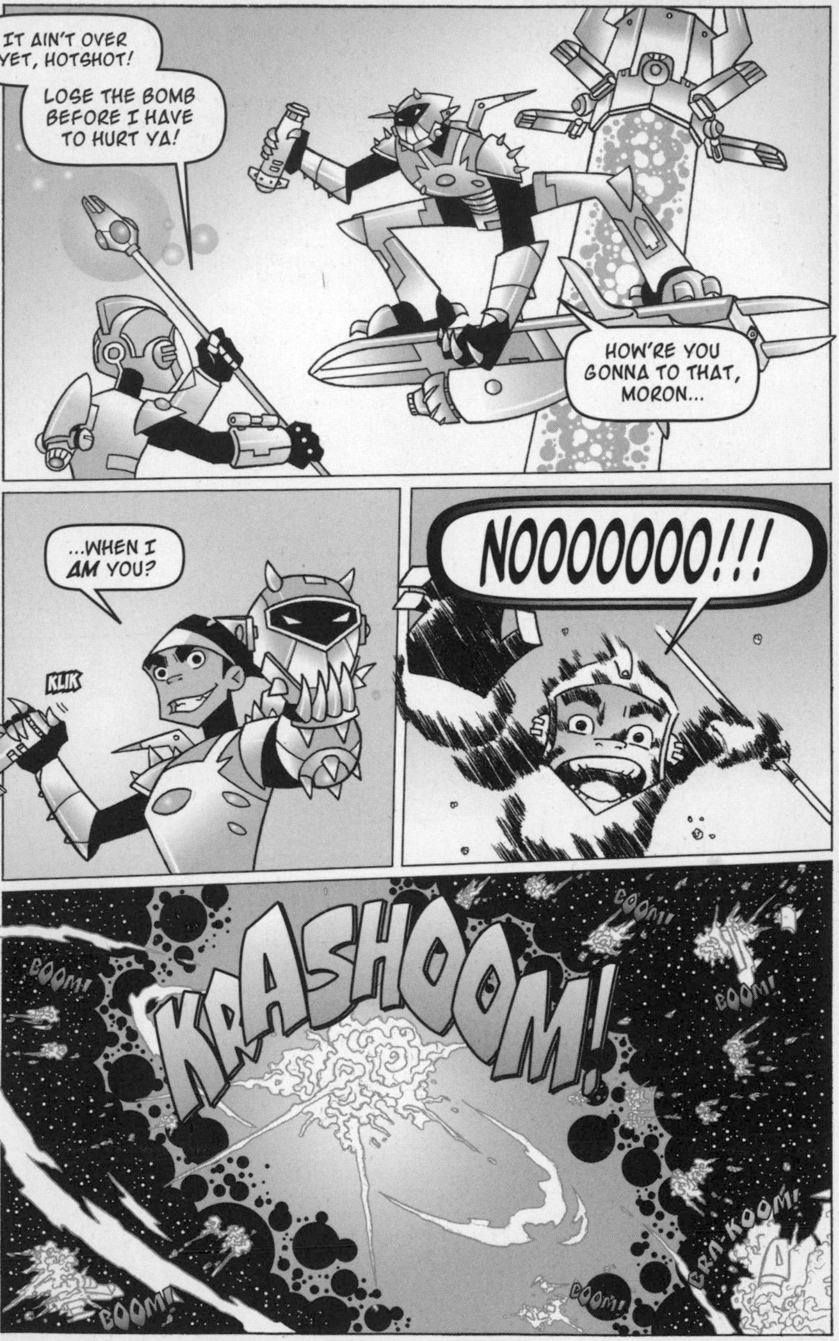
IT AIN'T OVER YET, HOTSHOT!
LOSE THE BOMB BEFORE I HAVE TO HURT YA!
HOW'RE YOU GONNA TO THAT, MORON...
...WHEN I AM YOU?
KLIK
NOOOOOOO!!!
KRASHOOM!
BOOM!
BOOM!
BOOM!
BOOM!
BOOM!
CRA-KOOM!

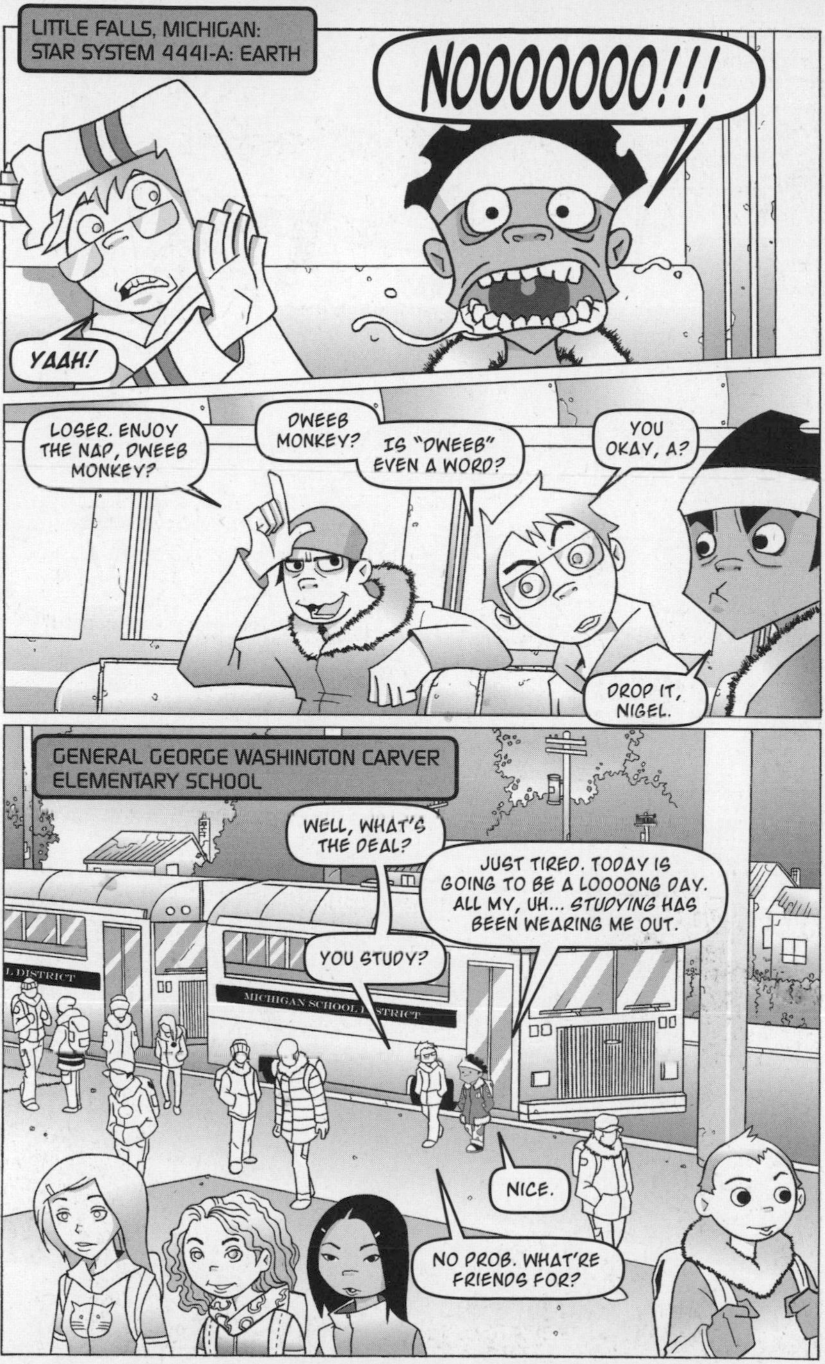
LITTLE FALLS, MICHIGAN:
STAR SYSTEM 4441-A: EARTH
NOOOOOOO!!!
YAAH!
LOSER. ENJOY THE NAP, DWEEB MONKEY?
DWEEB MONKEY?
IS "DWEEB" EVEN A WORD?
YOU OKAY, A?
DROP IT, NIGEL.
GENERAL GEORGE WASHINGTON CARVER ELEMENTARY SCHOOL
WELL, WHAT'S THE DEAL?
JUST TIRED. TODAY IS GOING TO BE A LOOOONG DAY. ALL MY, UH... STUDYING HAS BEEN WEARING ME OUT.
YOU STUDY?
MICHIGAN SCHOOL DISTRICT
NICE.
NO PROB. WHAT'RE FRIENDS FOR?

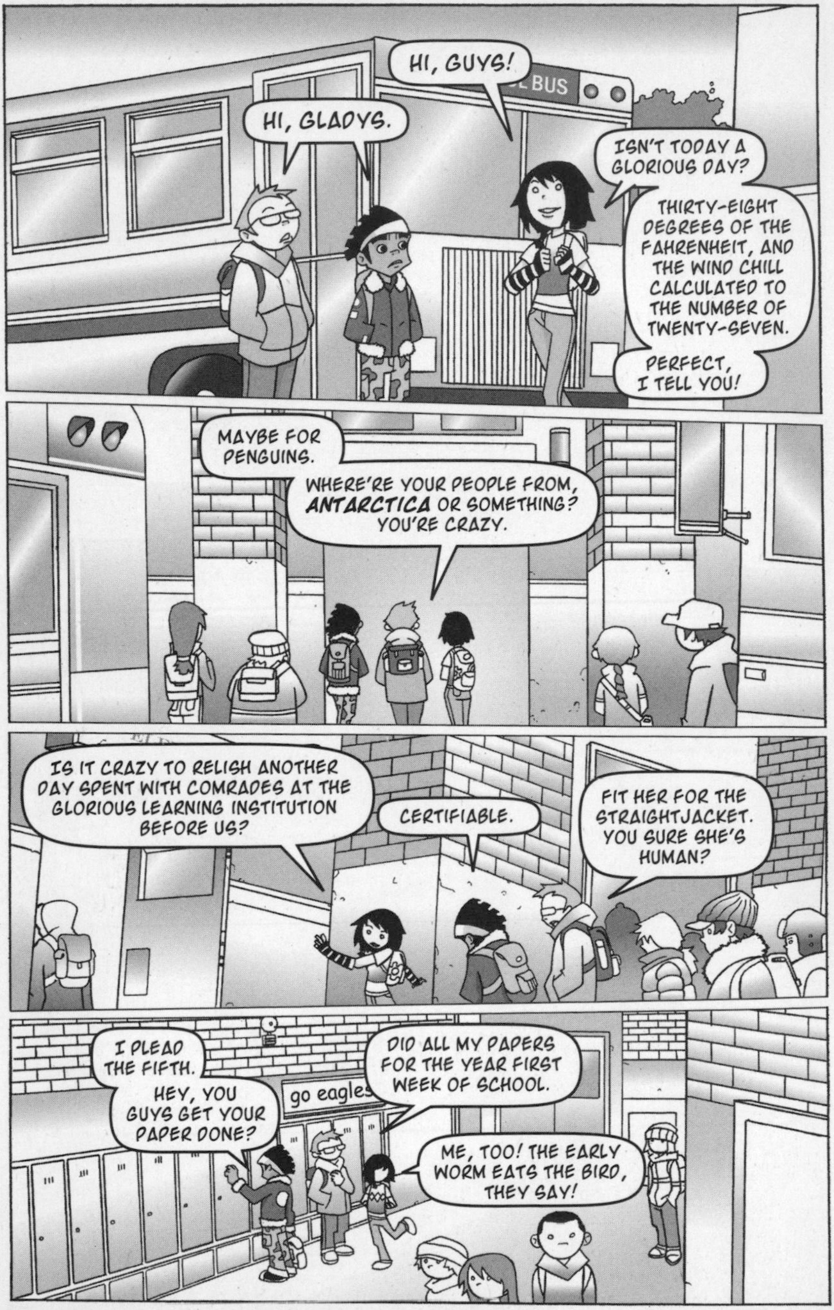
HI, GUYS!
BUS
HI, GLADYS.
ISN'T TODAY A GLORIOUS DAY?
THIRTY-EIGHT DEGREES OF THE FAHRENHEIT, AND THE WIND CHILL CALCULATED TO THE NUMBER OF TWENTY-SEVEN.
PERFECT, I TELL YOU!
MAYBE FOR PENGUINS.
WHERE'RE YOUR PEOPLE FROM, ANTARCTICA OR SOMETHING? YOU'RE CRAZY.
IS IT CRAZY TO RELISH ANOTHER DAY SPENT WITH COMRADES AT THE GLORIOUS LEARNING INSTITUTION BEFORE US?
CERTIFIABLE.
FIT HER FOR THE STRAIGHTJACKET. YOU SURE SHE'S HUMAN?
I PLEAD THE FIFTH.
HEY, YOU GUYS GET YOUR PAPER DONE?
go eagles
DID ALL MY PAPERS FOR THE YEAR FIRST WEEK OF SCHOOL.
ME, TOO! THE EARLY WORM EATS THE BIRD, THEY SAY!

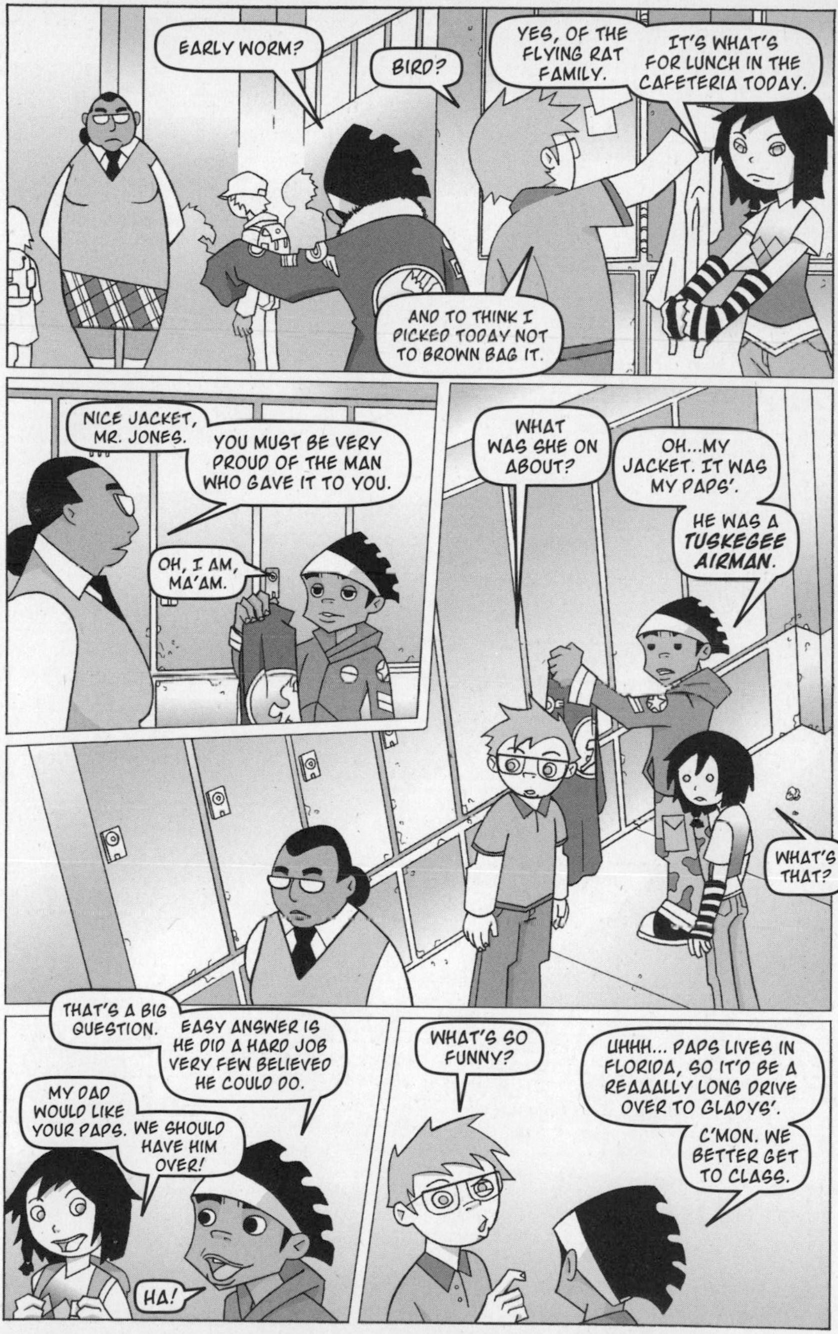
EARLY WORM?
BIRD?
YES, OF THE FLYING RAT FAMILY.
IT'S WHAT'S FOR LUNCH IN THE CAFETERIA TODAY.
AND TO THINK I PICKED TODAY NOT TO BROWN BAG IT.
NICE JACKET, MR. JONES.
YOU MUST BE VERY PROUD OF THE MAN WHO GAVE IT TO YOU.
OH, I AM, MA'AM.
WHAT WAS SHE ON ABOUT?
OH...MY JACKET. IT WAS MY PAPS'.
HE WAS A ***TUSKEGEE AIRMAN***.
WHAT'S THAT?
THAT'S A BIG QUESTION.
EASY ANSWER IS HE DID A HARD JOB VERY FEW BELIEVED HE COULD DO.
MY DAD WOULD LIKE YOUR PAPS. WE SHOULD HAVE HIM OVER!
HA!
WHAT'S SO FUNNY?
UHHH... PAPS LIVES IN FLORIDA, SO IT'D BE A REAAALLY LONG DRIVE OVER TO GLADYS'.
C'MON. WE BETTER GET TO CLASS.

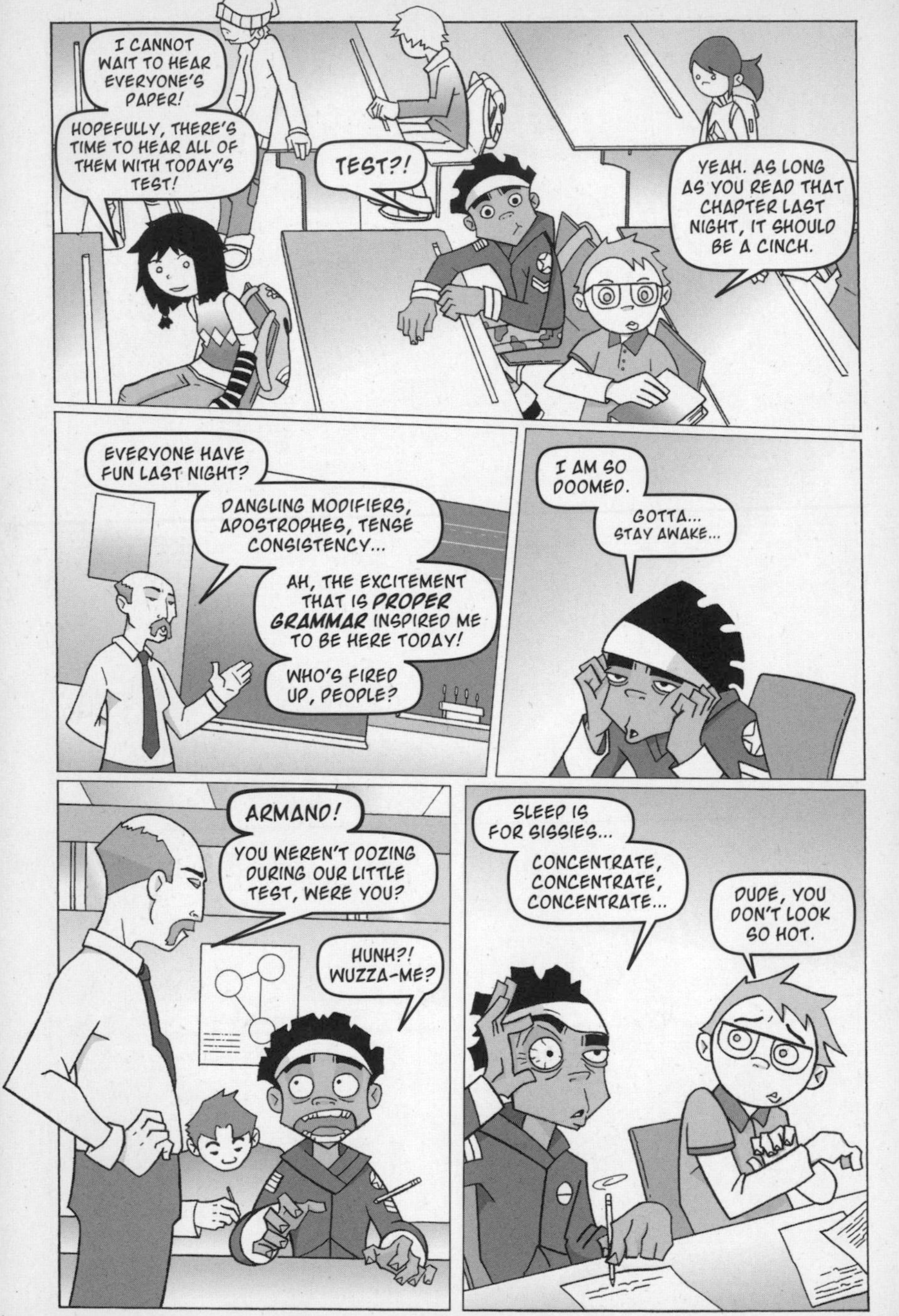
I CANNOT WAIT TO HEAR EVERYONE'S PAPER!
HOPEFULLY, THERE'S TIME TO HEAR ALL OF THEM WITH TODAY'S TEST!
TEST?!
YEAH. AS LONG AS YOU READ THAT CHAPTER LAST NIGHT, IT SHOULD BE A CINCH.
EVERYONE HAVE FUN LAST NIGHT?
DANGLING MODIFIERS, APOSTROPHES, TENSE CONSISTENCY...
AH, THE EXCITEMENT THAT IS PROPER GRAMMAR INSPIRED ME TO BE HERE TODAY!
WHO'S FIRED UP, PEOPLE?
I AM SO DOOMED.
GOTTA... STAY AWAKE...
ARMANDO!
YOU WEREN'T DOZING DURING OUR LITTLE TEST, WERE YOU?
HUNH?! WUZZA-ME?
SLEEP IS FOR SISSIES...
CONCENTRATE, CONCENTRATE, CONCENTRATE...
DUDE, YOU DON'T LOOK SO HOT.

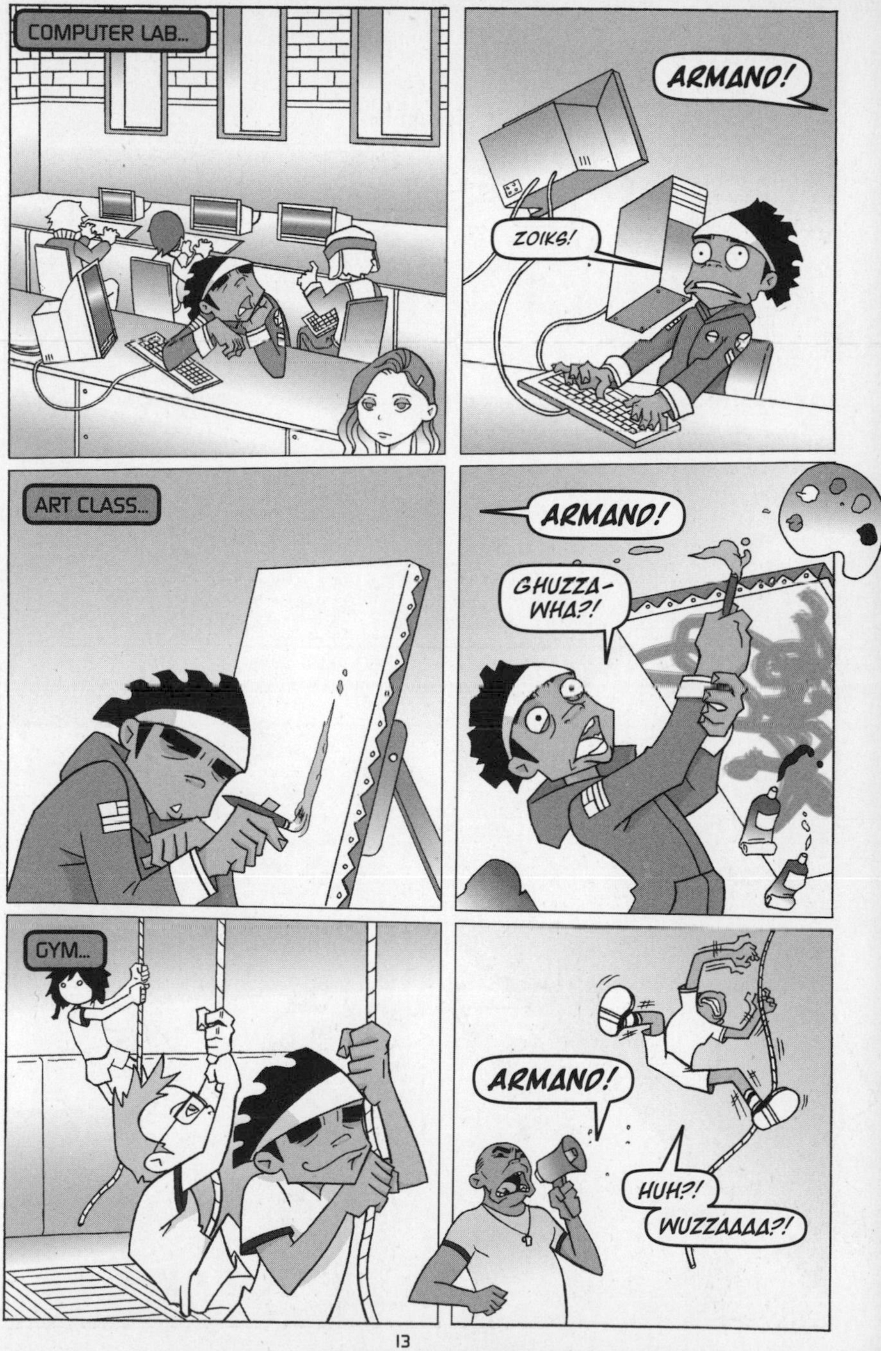
COMPUTER LAB...
ARMAND!
ZOIKS!
ART CLASS...
ARMAND!
GHUZZA-WHA?!
GYM...
ARMAND!
HUH?!
WUZZAAAA?!

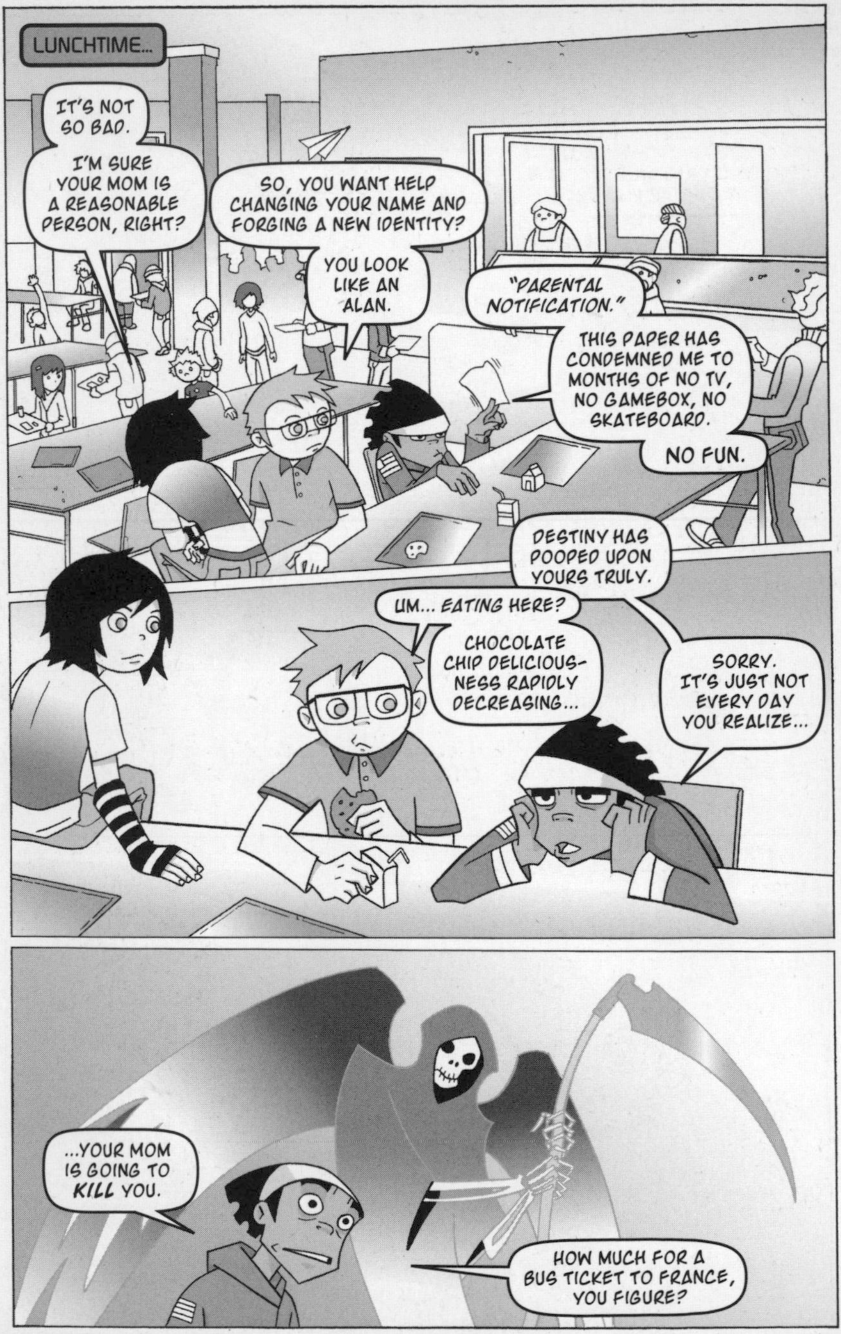
LUNCHTIME...
IT'S NOT SO BAD.
I'M SURE YOUR MOM IS A REASONABLE PERSON, RIGHT?
SO, YOU WANT HELP CHANGING YOUR NAME AND FORGING A NEW IDENTITY?
YOU LOOK LIKE AN ALAN.
"PARENTAL NOTIFICATION."
THIS PAPER HAS CONDEMNED ME TO MONTHS OF NO TV, NO GAMEBOX, NO SKATEBOARD.
NO FUN.
DESTINY HAS POOPED UPON YOURS TRULY.
UM... EATING HERE?
CHOCOLATE CHIP DELICIOUS-NESS RAPIDLY DECREASING...
SORRY. IT'S JUST NOT EVERY DAY YOU REALIZE...
...YOUR MOM IS GOING TO KILL YOU.
HOW MUCH FOR A BUS TICKET TO FRANCE, YOU FIGURE?

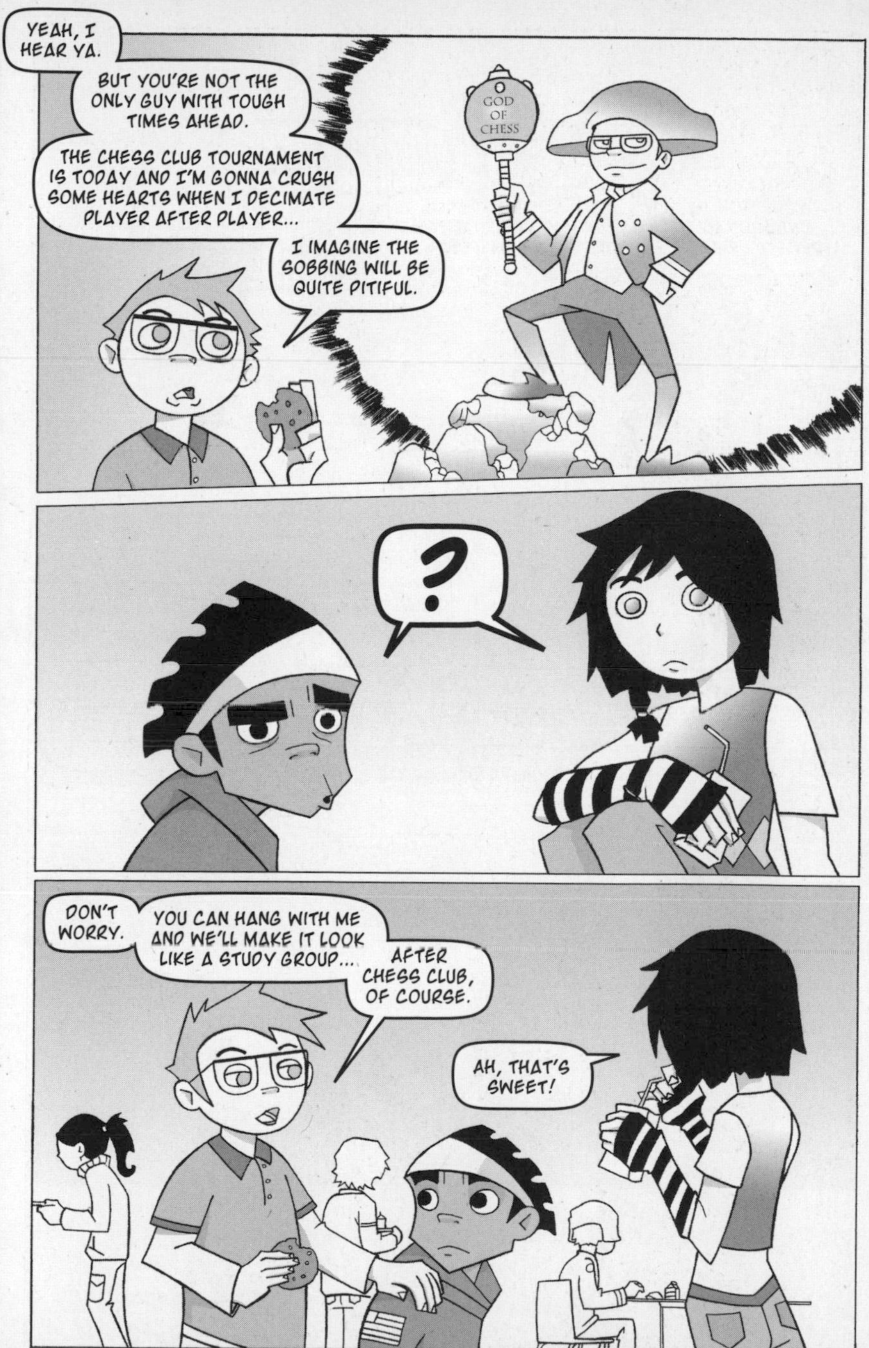
YEAH, I HEAR YA.
BUT YOU'RE NOT THE ONLY GUY WITH TOUGH TIMES AHEAD.
THE CHESS CLUB TOURNAMENT IS TODAY AND I'M GONNA CRUSH SOME HEARTS WHEN I DECIMATE PLAYER AFTER PLAYER...
I IMAGINE THE SOBBING WILL BE QUITE PITIFUL.
GOD OF CHESS
?
DON'T WORRY.
YOU CAN HANG WITH ME AND WE'LL MAKE IT LOOK LIKE A STUDY GROUP....
AFTER CHESS CLUB, OF COURSE.
AH, THAT'S SWEET!

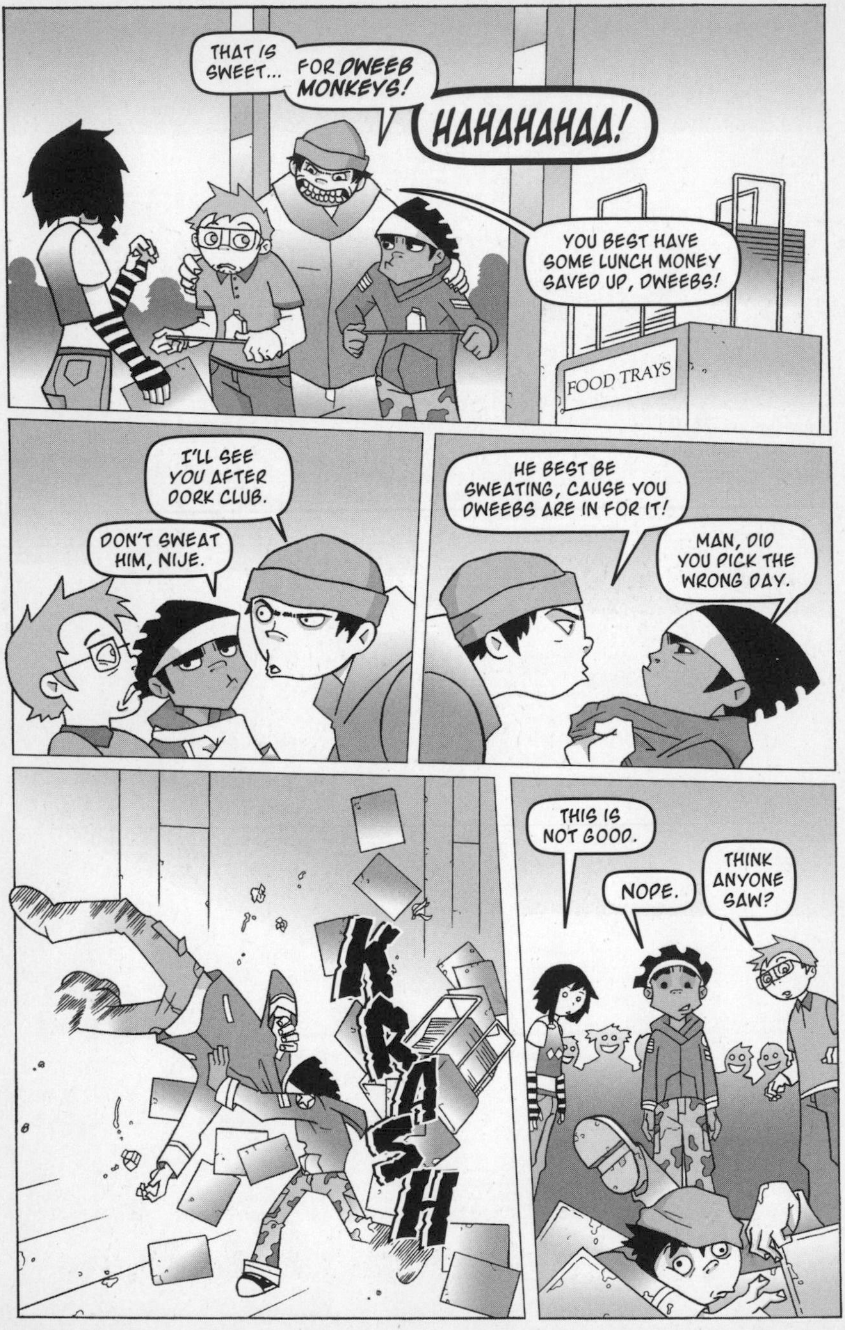
THAT IS SWEET...
FOR DWEEB MONKEYS!
HAHAHAHAHAA!
YOU BEST HAVE SOME LUNCH MONEY SAVED UP, DWEEBS!
FOOD TRAYS
I'LL SEE YOU AFTER DORK CLUB.
DON'T SWEAT HIM, NIJE.
HE BEST BE SWEATING, CAUSE YOU DWEEBS ARE IN FOR IT!
MAN, DID YOU PICK THE WRONG DAY.
KRASH
THIS IS NOT GOOD.
NOPE.
THINK ANYONE SAW?

ACT: 02

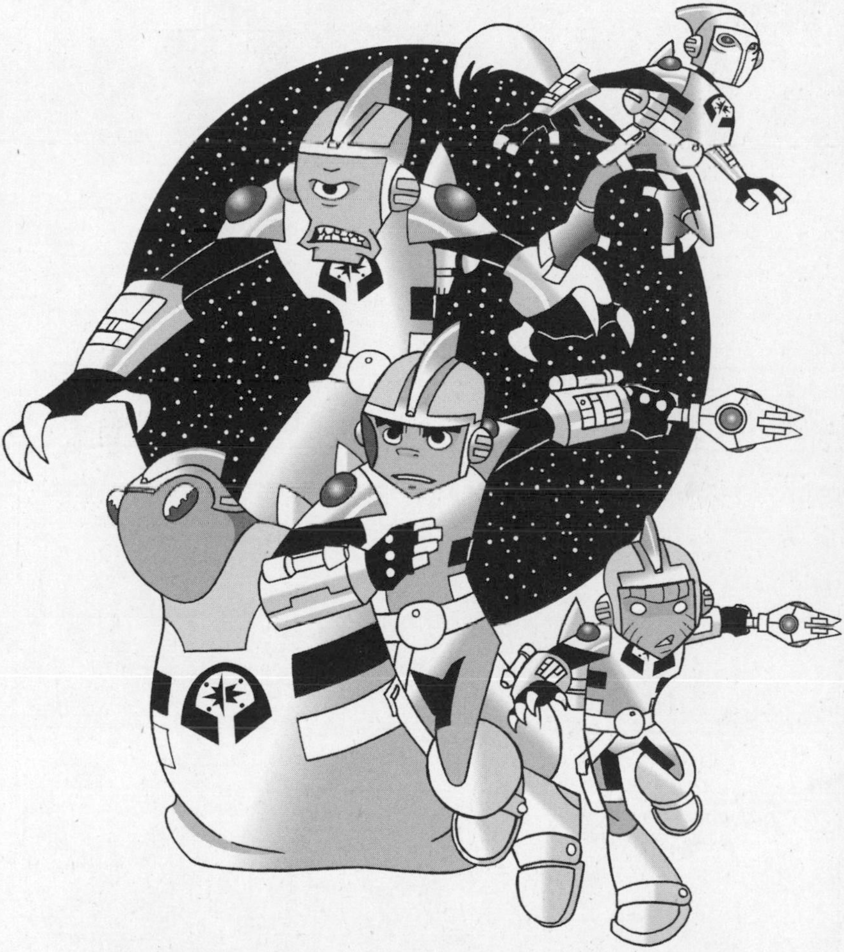

HE'S BAAACK!

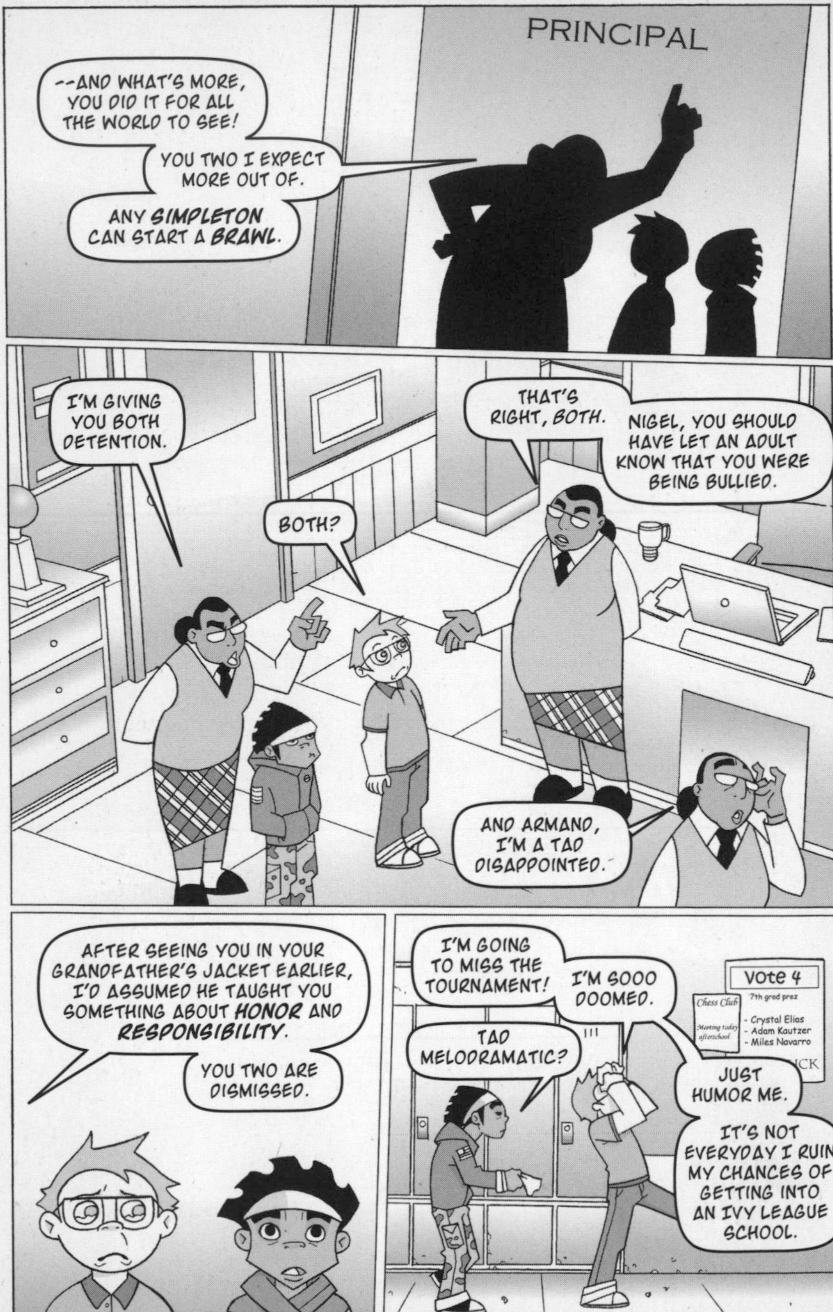
PRINCIPAL
--AND WHAT'S MORE, YOU DID IT FOR ALL THE WORLD TO SEE!
YOU TWO I EXPECT MORE OUT OF.
ANY SIMPLETON CAN START A BRAWL.
I'M GIVING YOU BOTH DETENTION.
BOTH?
THAT'S RIGHT, BOTH.
NIGEL, YOU SHOULD HAVE LET AN ADULT KNOW THAT YOU WERE BEING BULLIED.
AND ARMAND, I'M A TAD DISAPPOINTED.
AFTER SEEING YOU IN YOUR GRANDFATHER'S JACKET EARLIER, I'D ASSUMED HE TAUGHT YOU SOMETHING ABOUT HONOR AND RESPONSIBILITY.
YOU TWO ARE DISMISSED.
I'M GOING TO MISS THE TOURNAMENT!
I'M SOOO DOOMED.
TAD MELODRAMATIC?
Vote 4
7th grad prez
- Crystal Elias
- Adam Kautzer
- Miles Navarro
Chess Club
Meeting today afterschool
JUST HUMOR ME.
IT'S NOT EVERYDAY I RUIN MY CHANCES OF GETTING INTO AN IVY LEAGUE SCHOOL.

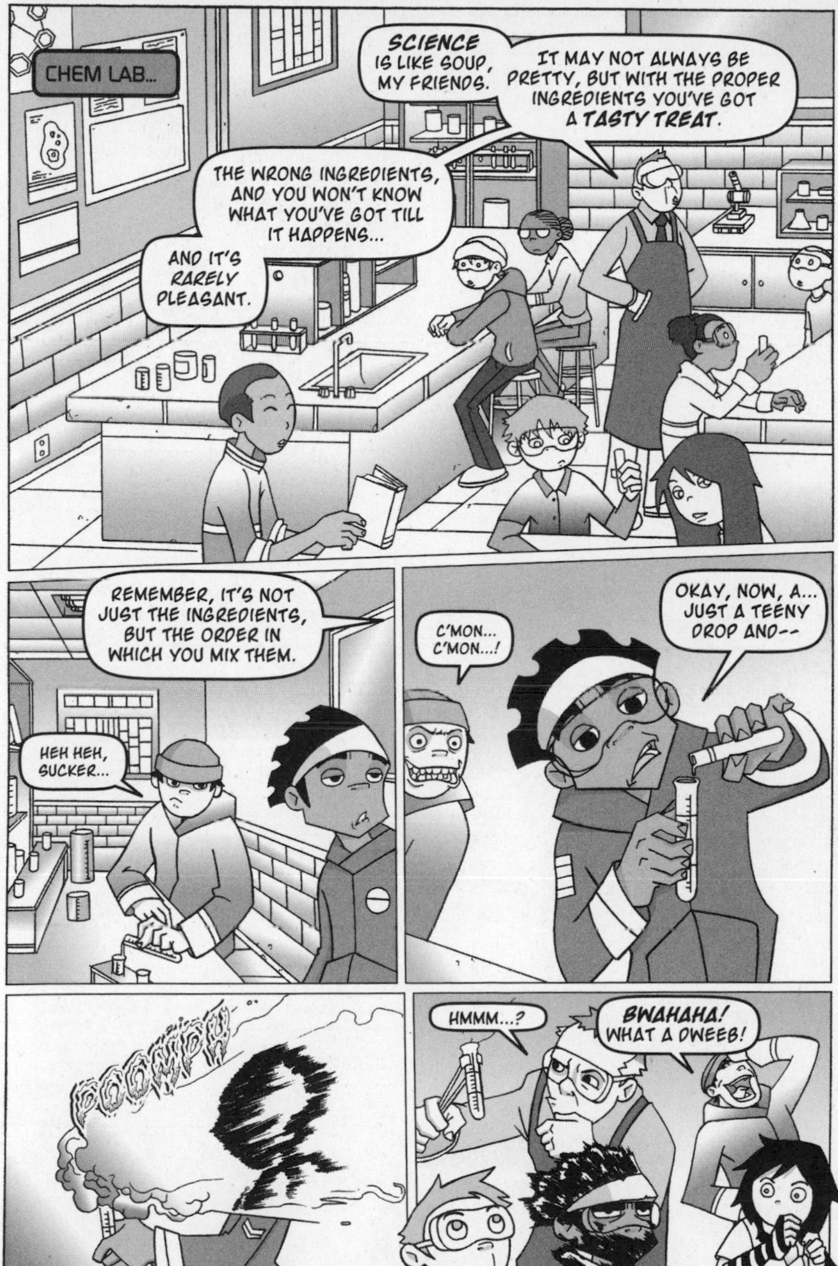
CHEM LAB...
SCIENCE IS LIKE SOUP, MY FRIENDS.
IT MAY NOT ALWAYS BE PRETTY, BUT WITH THE PROPER INGREDIENTS YOU'VE GOT A TASTY TREAT.
THE WRONG INGREDIENTS, AND YOU WON'T KNOW WHAT YOU'VE GOT TILL IT HAPPENS...
AND IT'S RARELY PLEASANT.
REMEMBER, IT'S NOT JUST THE INGREDIENTS, BUT THE ORDER IN WHICH YOU MIX THEM.
HEH HEH, SUCKER...
C'MON... C'MON...!
OKAY, NOW, A... JUST A TEENY DROP AND--
POOMPH
HMMM...?
BWAHAHA! WHAT A DWEEB!

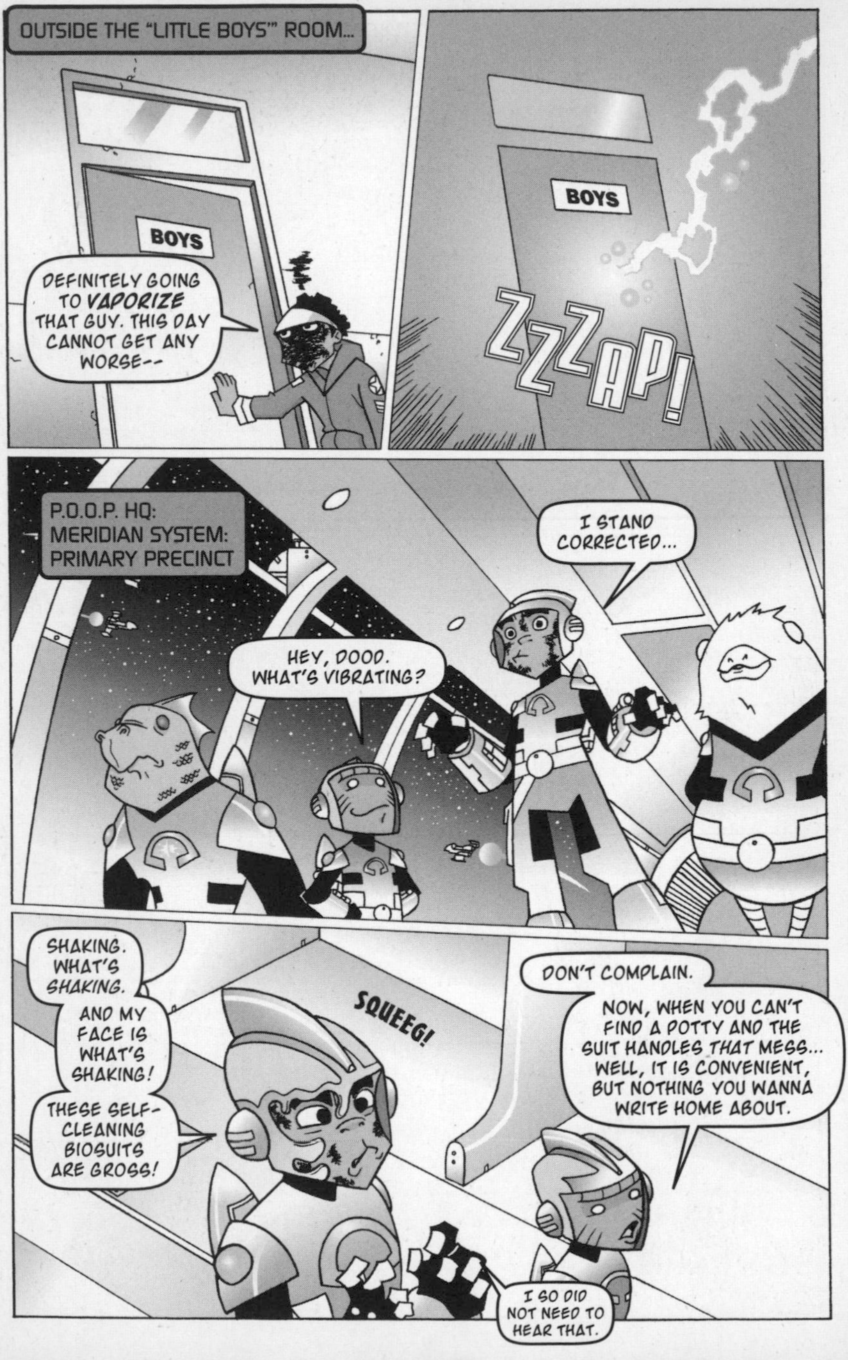
OUTSIDE THE "LITTLE BOYS'" ROOM...
BOYS
DEFINITELY GOING TO VAPORIZE THAT GUY. THIS DAY CANNOT GET ANY WORSE--
BOYS
ZZZAP!
P.O.O.P. HQ: MERIDIAN SYSTEM: PRIMARY PRECINCT
I STAND CORRECTED...
HEY, DOOD. WHAT'S VIBRATING?
SHAKING. WHAT'S SHAKING.
AND MY FACE IS WHAT'S SHAKING!
THESE SELF-CLEANING BIOSUITS ARE GROSS!
SQUEEG!
DON'T COMPLAIN.
NOW, WHEN YOU CAN'T FIND A POTTY AND THE SUIT HANDLES THAT MESS... WELL, IT IS CONVENIENT, BUT NOTHING YOU WANNA WRITE HOME ABOUT.
I SO DID NOT NEED TO HEAR THAT.

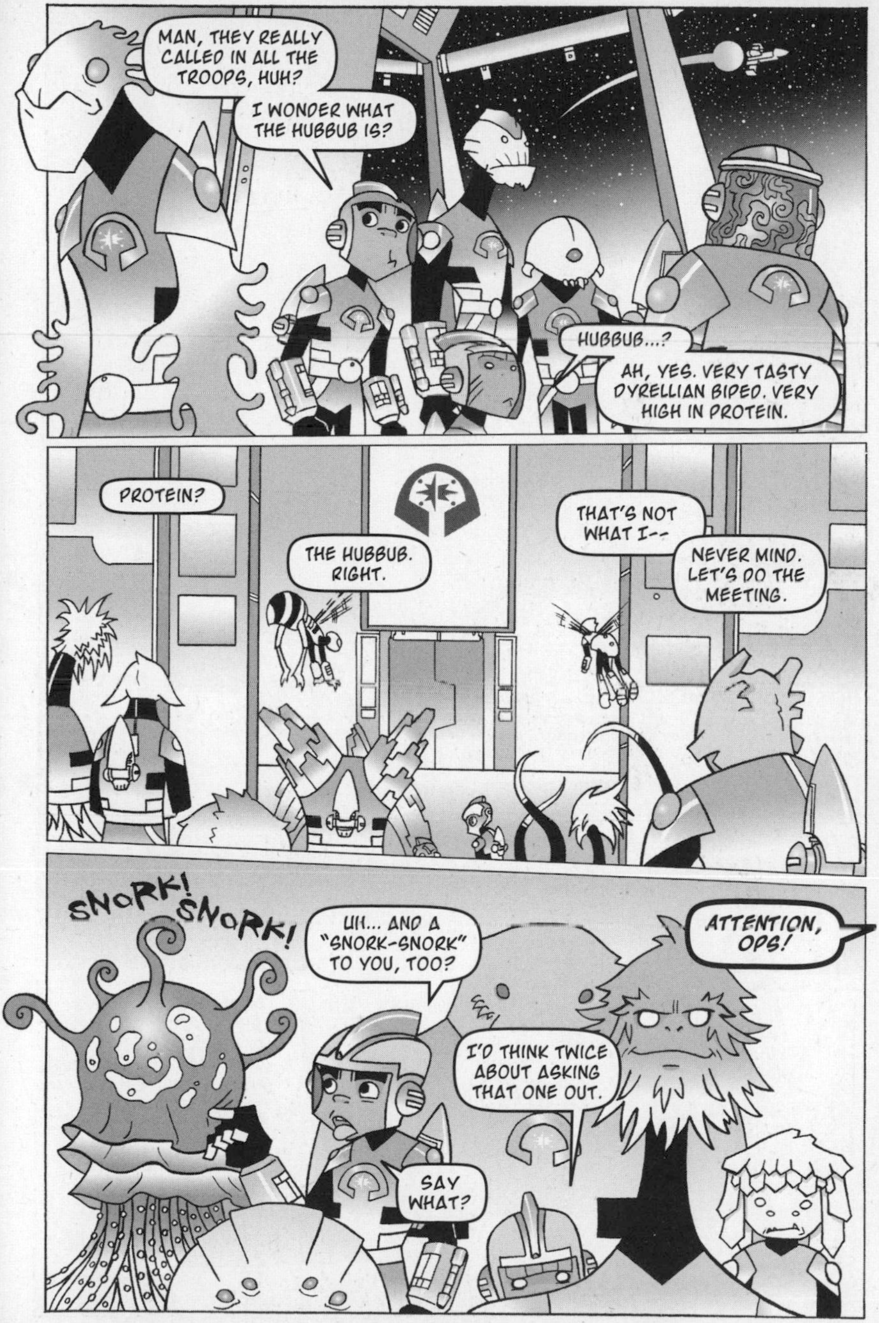
MAN, THEY REALLY CALLED IN ALL THE TROOPS, HUH?
I WONDER WHAT THE HUBBUB IS?
HUBBUB...?
AH, YES. VERY TASTY DYRELLIAN BIPED. VERY HIGH IN PROTEIN.
PROTEIN?
THE HUBBUB. RIGHT.
THAT'S NOT WHAT I--
NEVER MIND. LET'S DO THE MEETING.
SNORK! SNORK!
UH... AND A "SNORK-SNORK" TO YOU, TOO?
ATTENTION, OPS!
I'D THINK TWICE ABOUT ASKING THAT ONE OUT.
SAY WHAT?

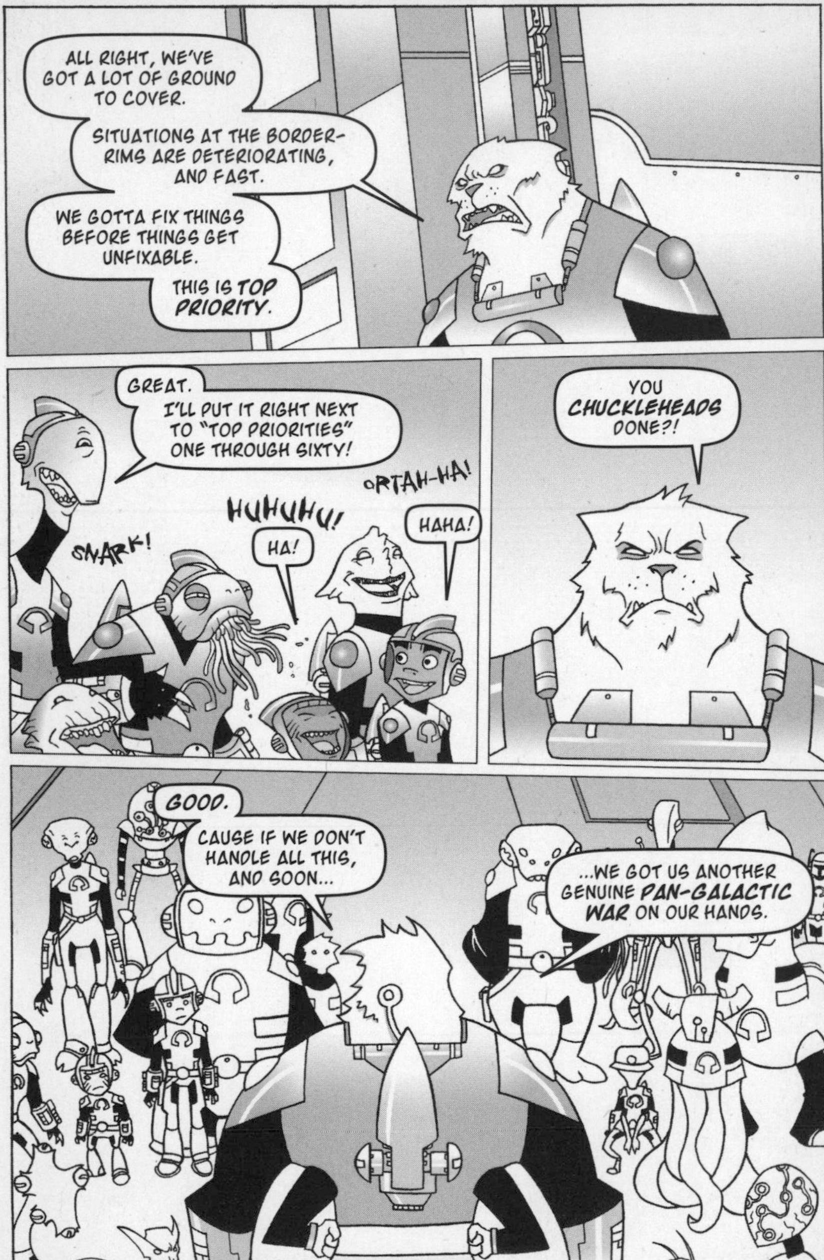
ALL RIGHT, WE'VE GOT A LOT OF GROUND TO COVER.
SITUATIONS AT THE BORDER-RIMS ARE DETERIORATING, AND FAST.
WE GOTTA FIX THINGS BEFORE THINGS GET UNFIXABLE.
THIS IS **TOP PRIORITY**.
GREAT.
I'LL PUT IT RIGHT NEXT TO "TOP PRIORITIES" ONE THROUGH SIXTY!
SNARK!
HUHUHU!
HA!
ORTAH-HA!
HAHA!
YOU **CHUCKLEHEADS** DONE?!
GOOD.
CAUSE IF WE DON'T HANDLE ALL THIS, AND SOON...
...WE GOT US ANOTHER GENUINE **PAN-GALACTIC WAR** ON OUR HANDS.

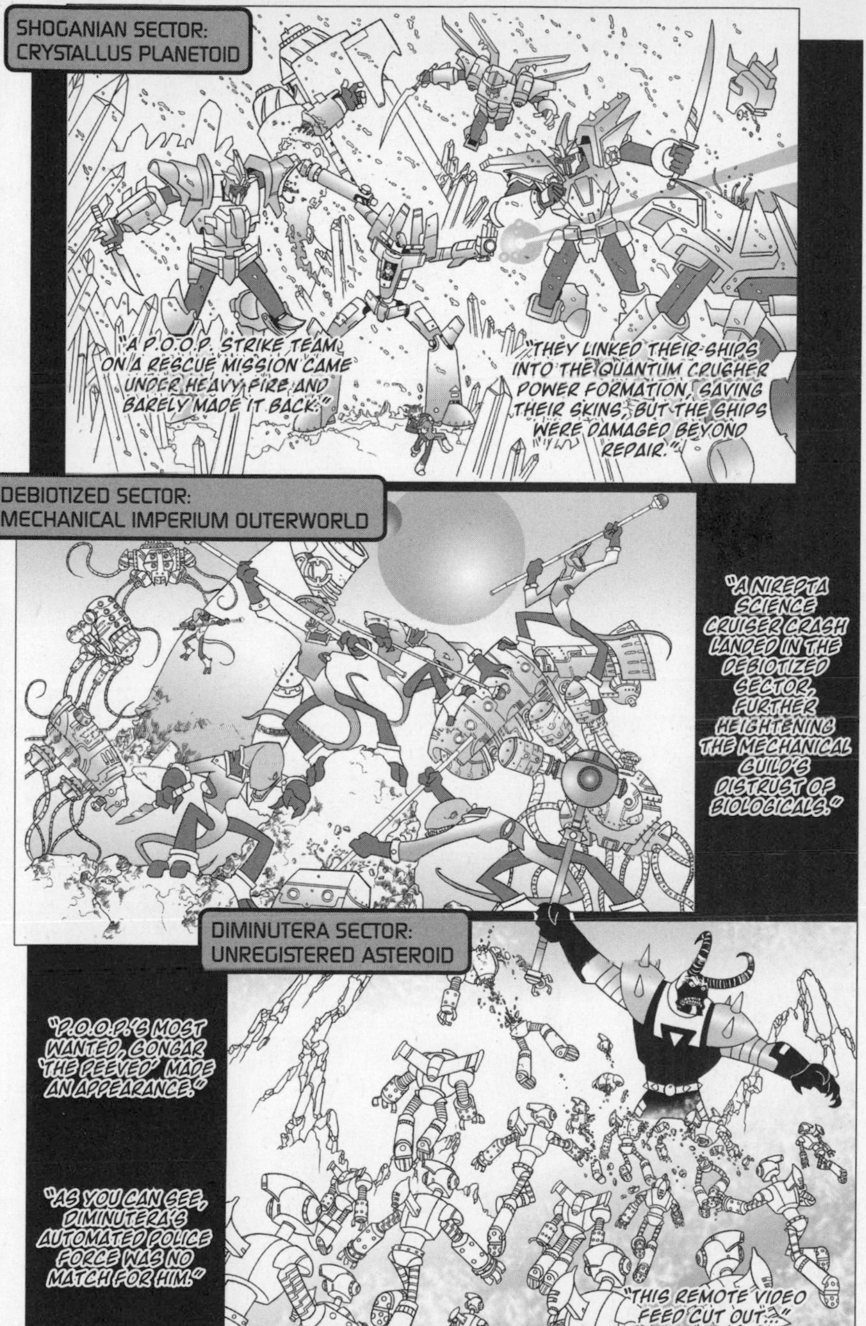
SHOGANIAN SECTOR: CRYSTALLUS PLANETOID
"A P.O.O.P. STRIKE TEAM ON A RESCUE MISSION CAME UNDER HEAVY FIRE AND BARELY MADE IT BACK."
"THEY LINKED THEIR SHIPS INTO THE QUANTUM CRUSHER POWER FORMATION, SAVING THEIR SKINS, BUT THE SHIPS WERE DAMAGED BEYOND REPAIR."
DEBIOTIZED SECTOR: MECHANICAL IMPERIUM OUTERWORLD
"A NIREPTA SCIENCE CRUISER CRASH LANDED IN THE DEBIOTIZED SECTOR, FURTHER HEIGHTENING THE MECHANICAL GUILD'S DISTRUST OF BIOLOGICALS."
DIMINUTERA SECTOR: UNREGISTERED ASTEROID
"P.O.O.P.'S MOST WANTED, GONGAR 'THE PEEVED' MADE AN APPEARANCE."
"AS YOU CAN SEE, DIMINUTERA'S AUTOMATED POLICE FORCE WAS NO MATCH FOR HIM."
"THIS REMOTE VIDEO FEED CUT OUT..."

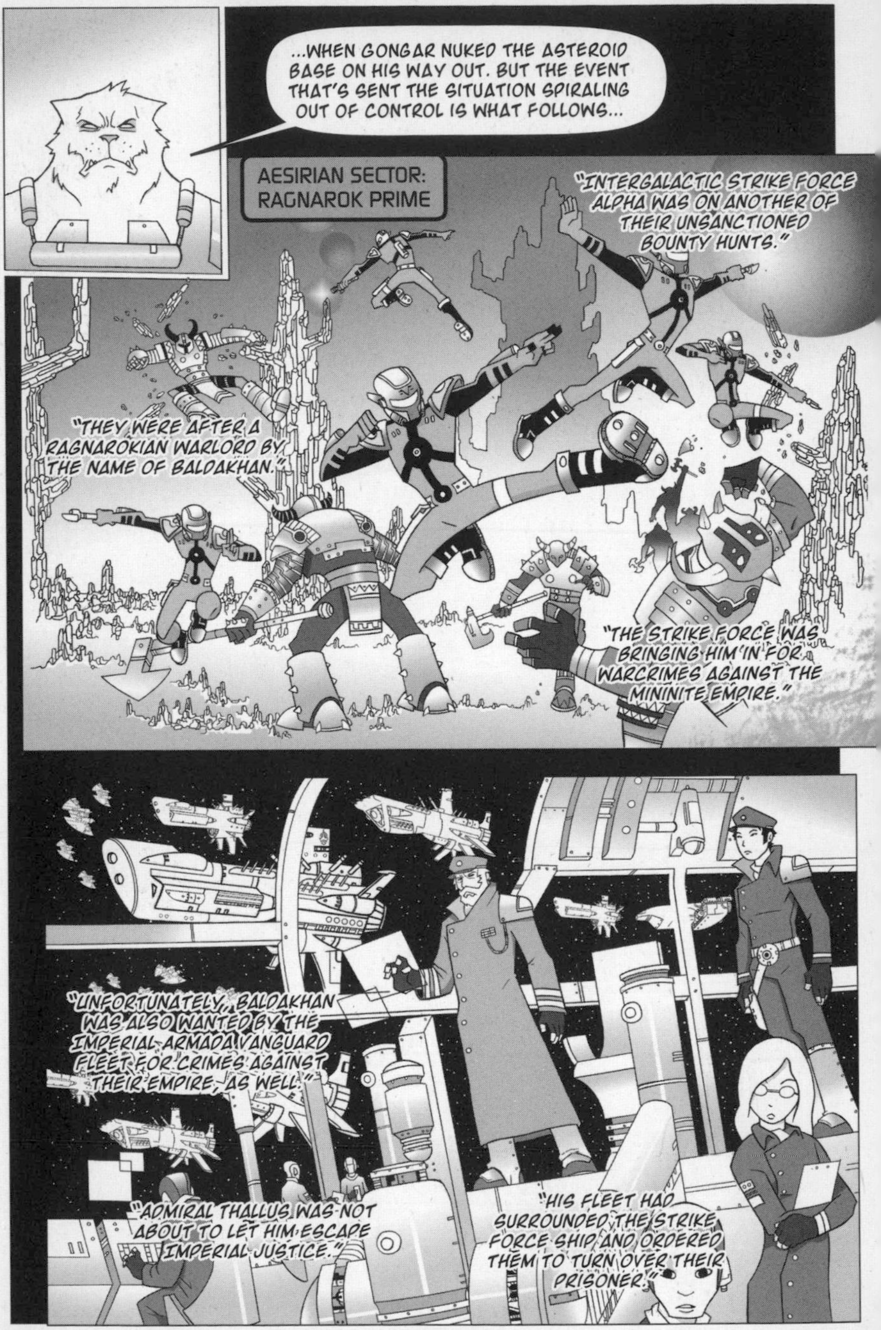
...WHEN GONGAR NUKED THE ASTEROID BASE ON HIS WAY OUT. BUT THE EVENT THAT'S SENT THE SITUATION SPIRALING OUT OF CONTROL IS WHAT FOLLOWS...
AESIRIAN SECTOR: RAGNAROK PRIME
"INTERGALACTIC STRIKE FORCE ALPHA WAS ON ANOTHER OF THEIR UNSANCTIONED BOUNTY HUNTS."
"THEY WERE AFTER A RAGNAROKIAN WARLORD BY THE NAME OF BALDAKHAN."
"THE STRIKE FORCE WAS BRINGING HIM IN FOR WARCRIMES AGAINST THE MININITE EMPIRE."
"UNFORTUNATELY, BALDAKHAN WAS ALSO WANTED BY THE IMPERIAL ARMADA VANGUARD FLEET FOR CRIMES AGAINST THEIR EMPIRE, AS WELL."
"ADMIRAL THALLUS WAS NOT ABOUT TO LET HIM ESCAPE IMPERIAL JUSTICE."
"HIS FLEET HAD SURROUNDED THE STRIKE FORCE SHIP AND ORDERED THEM TO TURN OVER THEIR PRISONER."

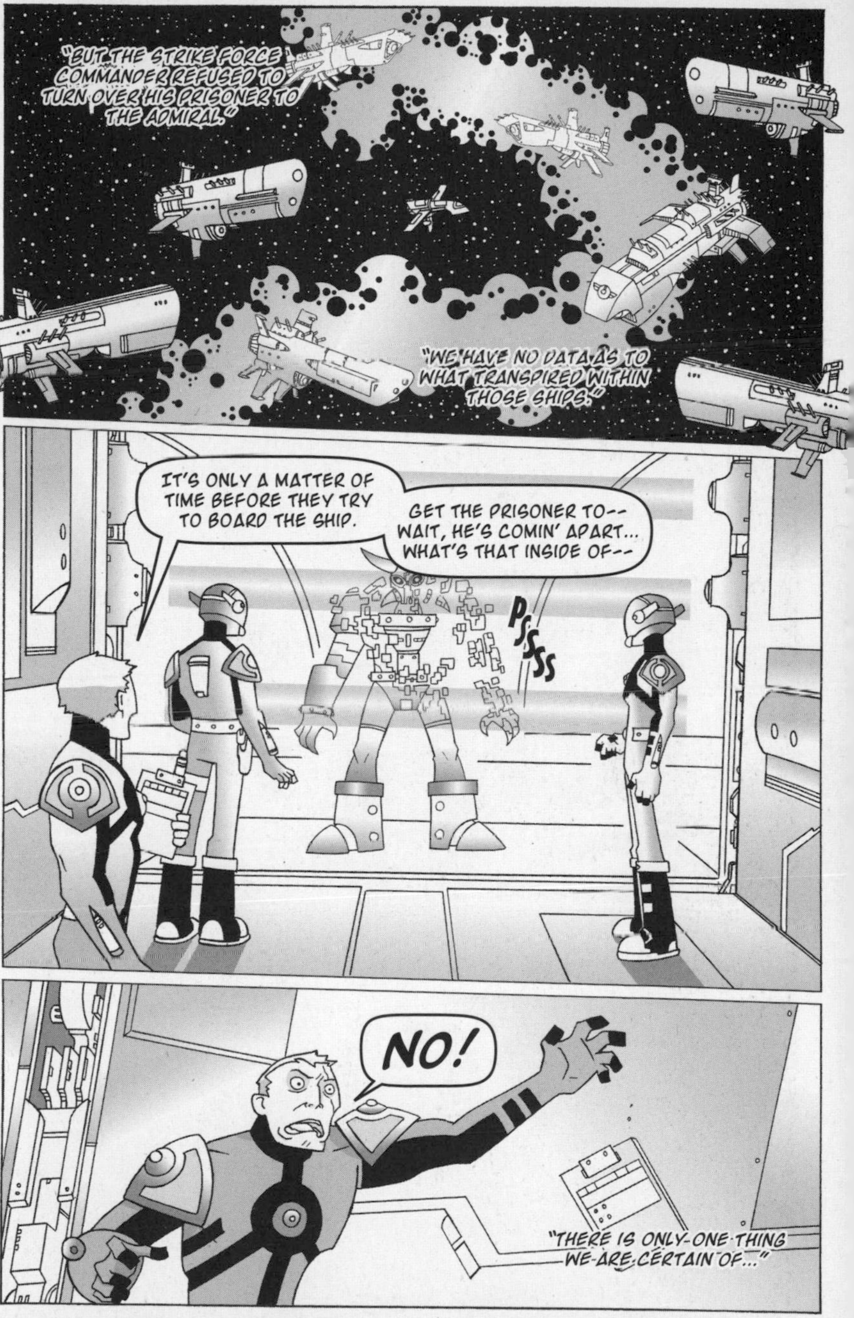
"BUT THE STRIKE FORCE COMMANDER REFUSED TO TURN OVER HIS PRISONER TO THE ADMIRAL."
"WE HAVE NO DATA AS TO WHAT TRANSPIRED WITHIN THOSE SHIPS."
IT'S ONLY A MATTER OF TIME BEFORE THEY TRY TO BOARD THE SHIP.
GET THE PRISONER TO-- WAIT, HE'S COMIN' APART... WHAT'S THAT INSIDE OF--
PSSSS
NO!
"THERE IS ONLY ONE THING WE ARE CERTAIN OF..."

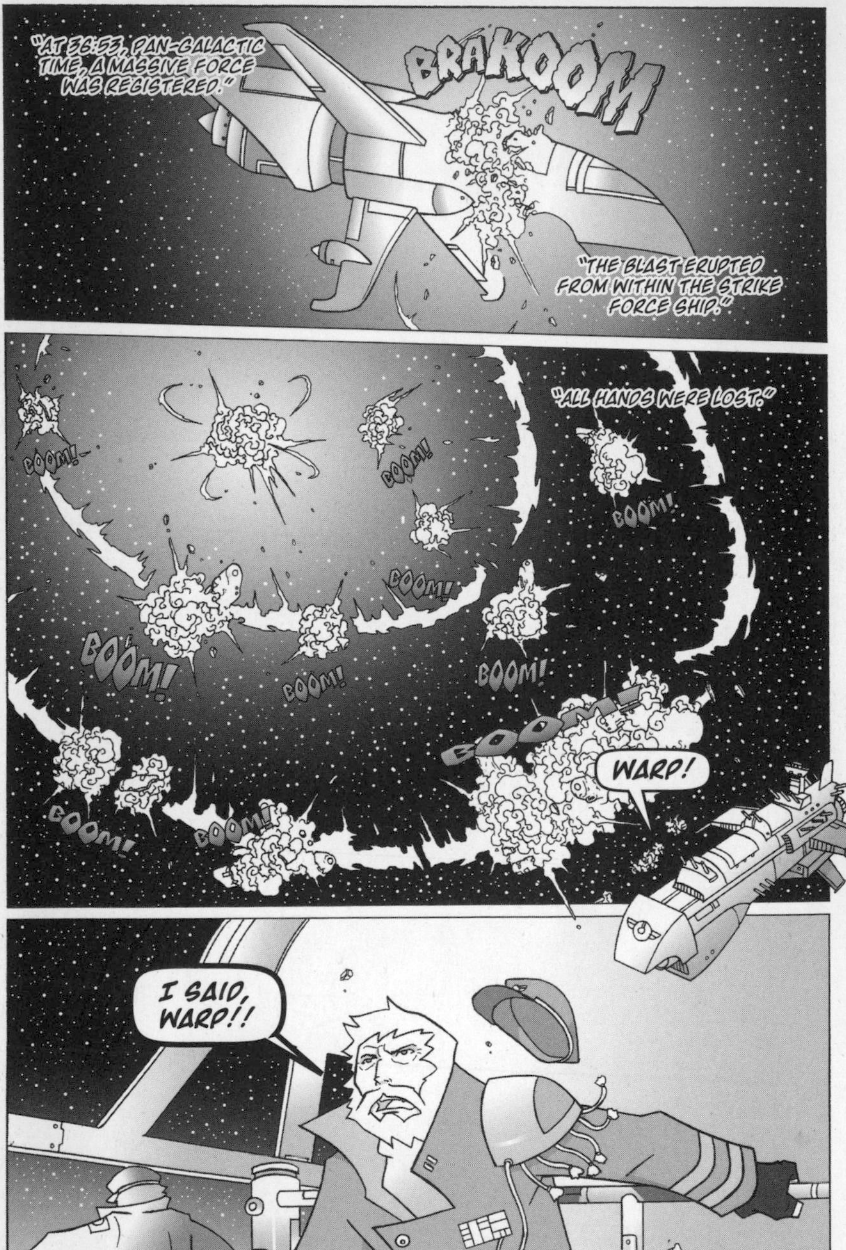
"AT 36:53, PAN-GALACTIC TIME, A MASSIVE FORCE WAS REGISTERED."
BRAKOOM
"THE BLAST ERUPTED FROM WITHIN THE STRIKE FORCE SHIP."
"ALL HANDS WERE LOST."
BOOM!
BOOM!
BOOM!
BOOM!
BOOM!
BOOM!
BOOM!
BOOM!
BOOM!
BOOOM!
WARP!
I SAID, WARP!!
"THE IMPERIAL VANGUARD FLEET IS NO MORE."

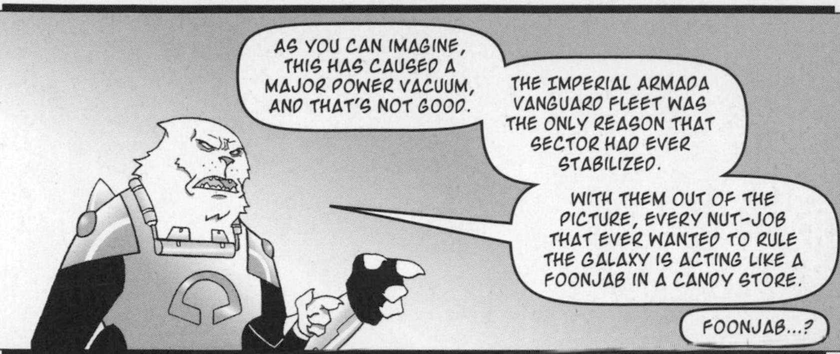
AS YOU CAN IMAGINE, THIS HAS CAUSED A MAJOR POWER VACUUM, AND THAT'S NOT GOOD.
THE IMPERIAL ARMADA VANGUARD FLEET WAS THE ONLY REASON THAT SECTOR HAD EVER STABILIZED.
WITH THEM OUT OF THE PICTURE, EVERY NUT-JOB THAT EVER WANTED TO RULE THE GALAXY IS ACTING LIKE A FOONJAB IN A CANDY STORE.
FOONJAB...?

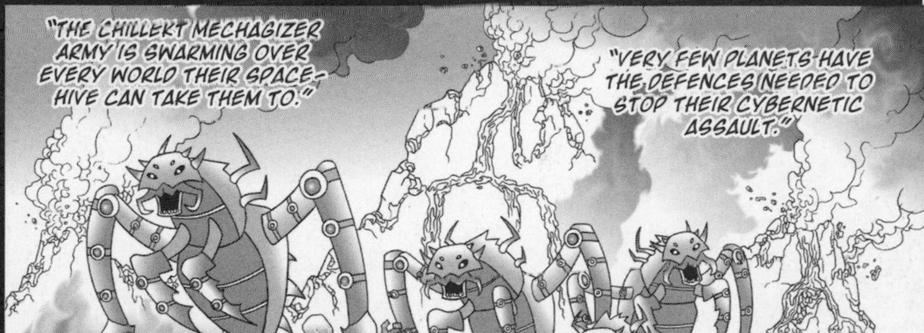
"THE CHILLEKT MECHAGIZER ARMY IS SWARMING OVER EVERY WORLD THEIR SPACE-HIVE CAN TAKE THEM TO."
"VERY FEW PLANETS HAVE THE DEFENCES NEEDED TO STOP THEIR CYBERNETIC ASSAULT."

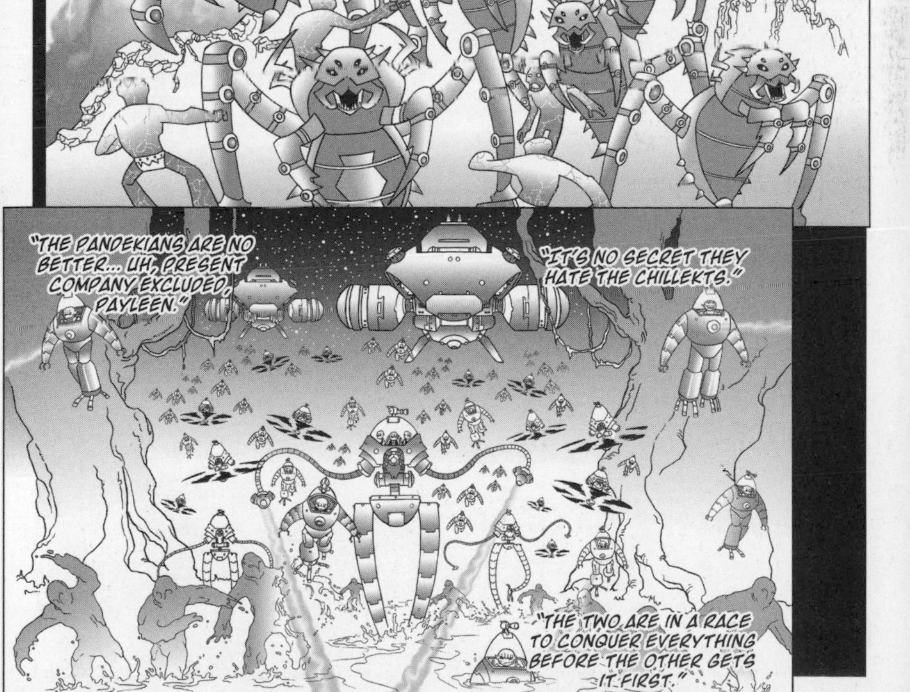
"THE PANDEKIANS ARE NO BETTER... UH, PRESENT COMPANY EXCLUDED, PAYLEEN."
"IT'S NO SECRET THEY HATE THE CHILLEKTS."
"THE TWO ARE IN A RACE TO CONQUER EVERYTHING BEFORE THE OTHER GETS IT FIRST."

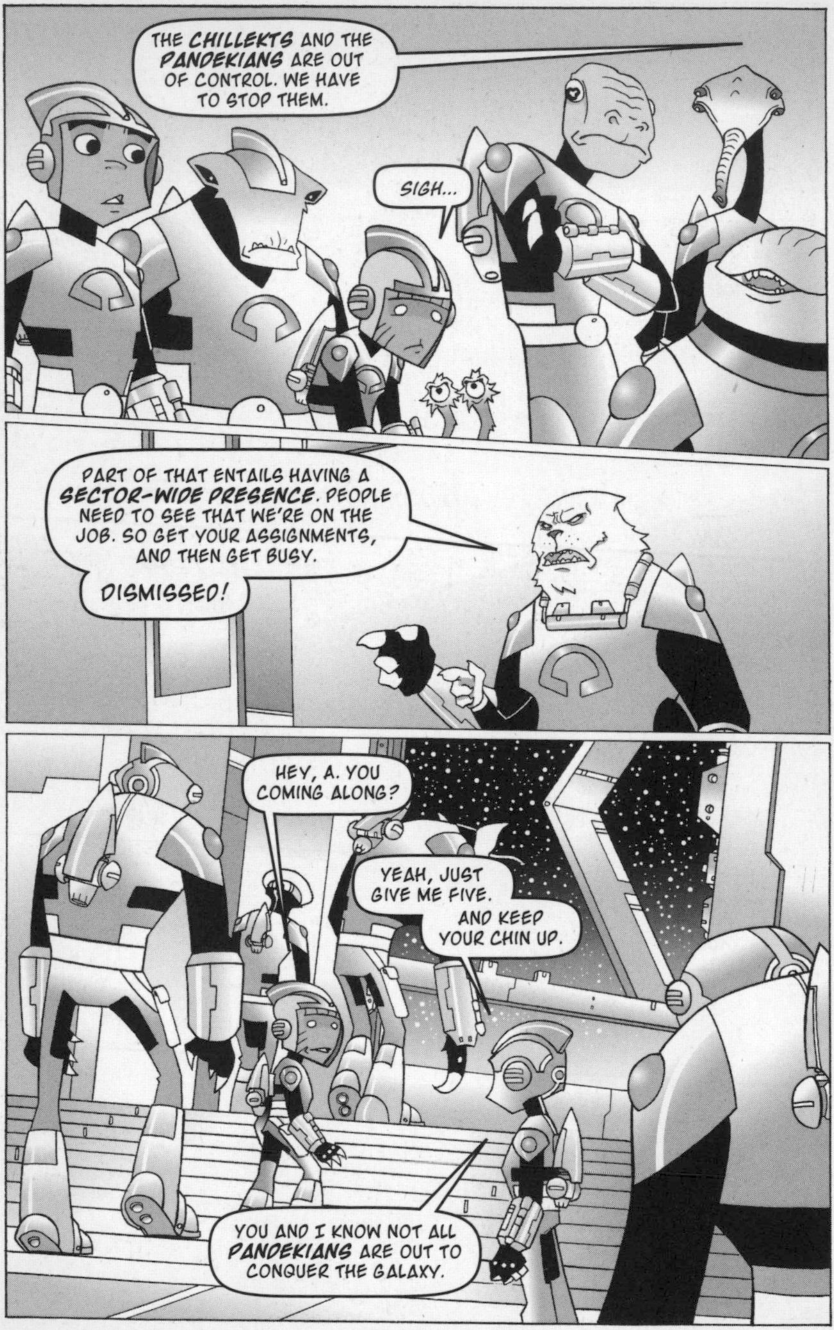
THE CHILLEKTS AND THE PANDEKIANS ARE OUT OF CONTROL. WE HAVE TO STOP THEM.
SIGH...
PART OF THAT ENTAILS HAVING A SECTOR-WIDE PRESENCE. PEOPLE NEED TO SEE THAT WE'RE ON THE JOB. SO GET YOUR ASSIGNMENTS, AND THEN GET BUSY.
DISMISSED!
HEY, A. YOU COMING ALONG?
YEAH, JUST GIVE ME FIVE.
AND KEEP YOUR CHIN UP.
YOU AND I KNOW NOT ALL PANDEKIANS ARE OUT TO CONQUER THE GALAXY.

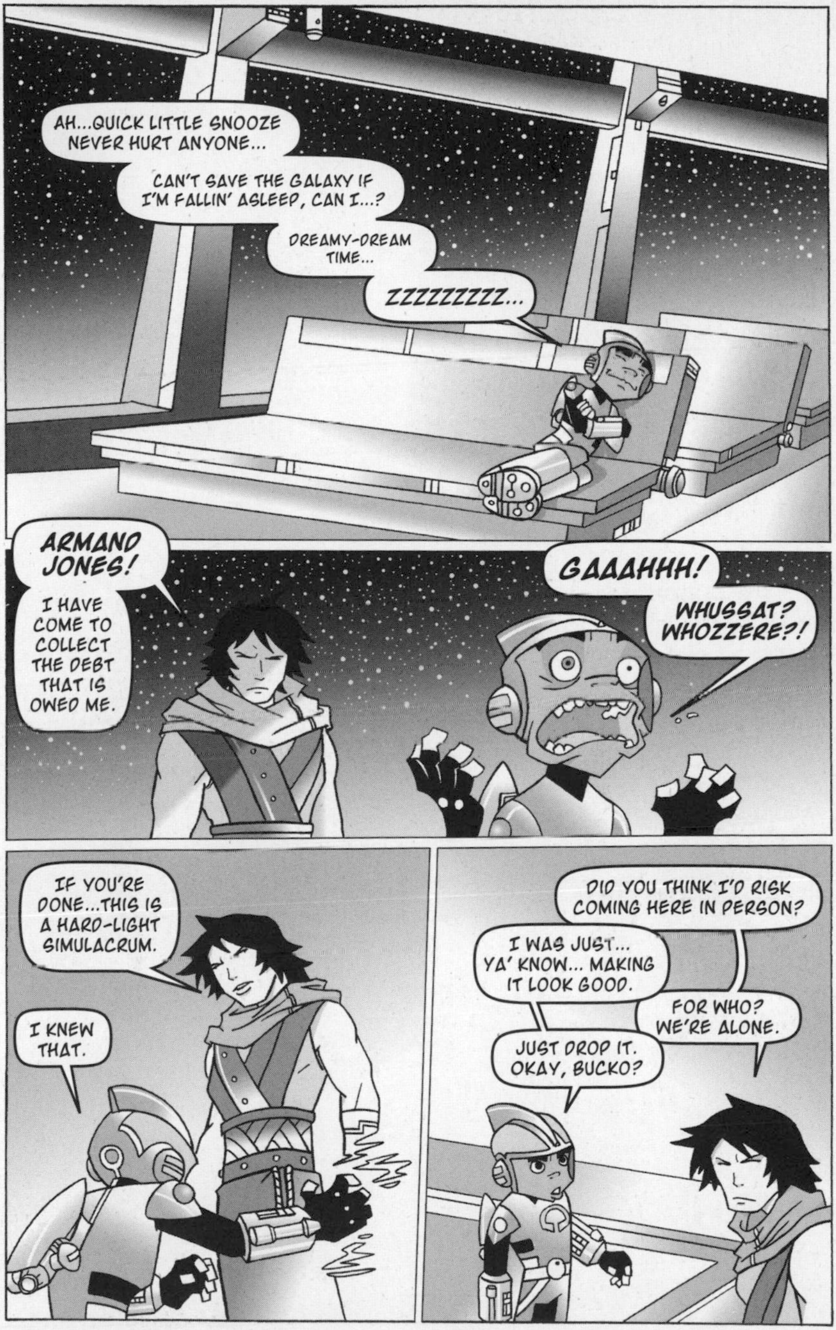
AH...QUICK LITTLE SNOOZE NEVER HURT ANYONE...
CAN'T SAVE THE GALAXY IF I'M FALLIN' ASLEEP, CAN I...?
DREAMY-DREAM TIME...
ZZZZZZZZZ...
ARMAND JONES!
I HAVE COME TO COLLECT THE DEBT THAT IS OWED ME.
GAAAHHH!
WHUSSAT? WHOZZERE?!
IF YOU'RE DONE...THIS IS A HARD-LIGHT SIMULACRUM.
I KNEW THAT.
DID YOU THINK I'D RISK COMING HERE IN PERSON?
I WAS JUST... YA' KNOW... MAKING IT LOOK GOOD.
FOR WHO? WE'RE ALONE.
JUST DROP IT. OKAY, BUCKO?

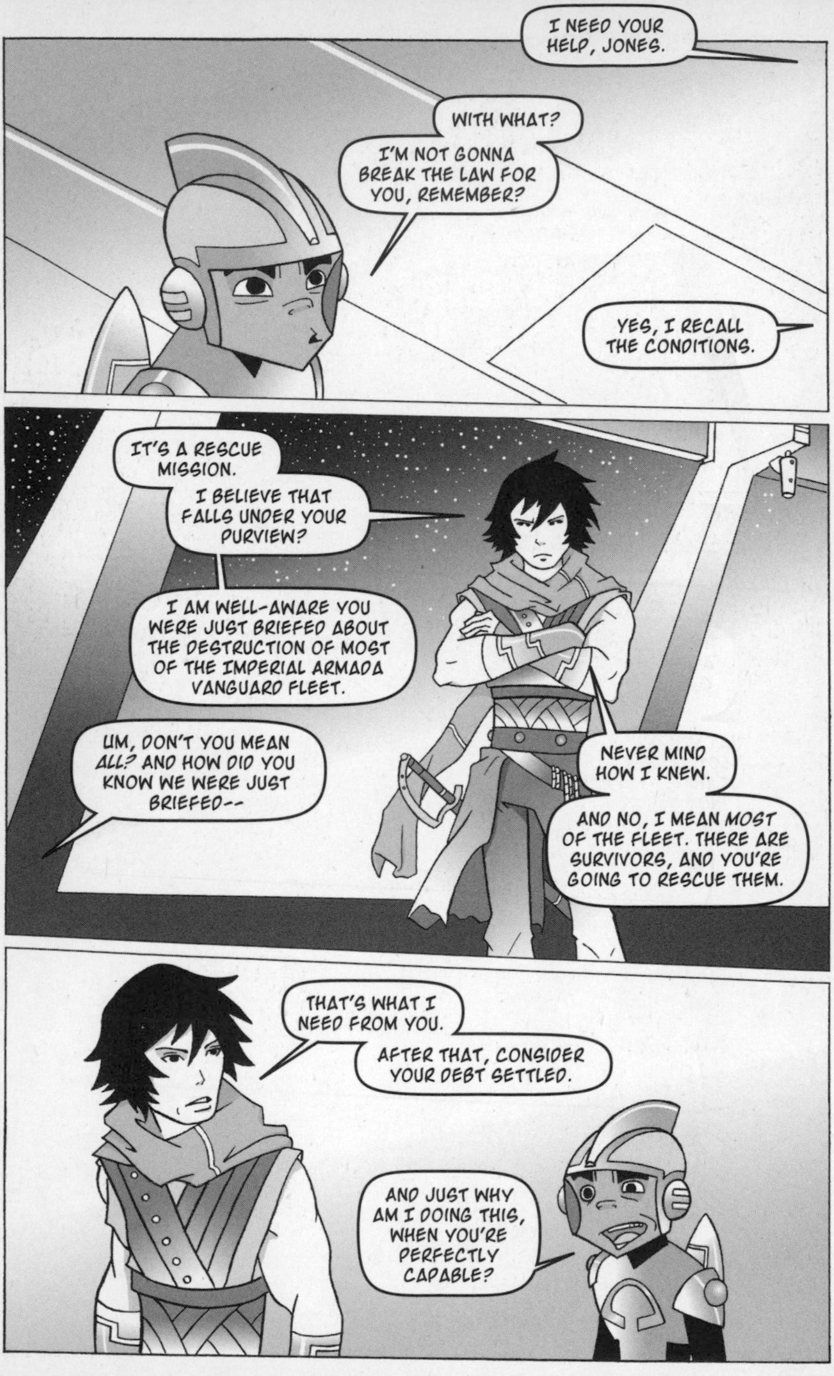
I NEED YOUR HELP, JONES.
WITH WHAT?
I'M NOT GONNA BREAK THE LAW FOR YOU, REMEMBER?
YES, I RECALL THE CONDITIONS.
IT'S A RESCUE MISSION.
I BELIEVE THAT FALLS UNDER YOUR PURVIEW?
I AM WELL-AWARE YOU WERE JUST BRIEFED ABOUT THE DESTRUCTION OF MOST OF THE IMPERIAL ARMADA VANGUARD FLEET.
UM, DON'T YOU MEAN ALL? AND HOW DID YOU KNOW WE WERE JUST BRIEFED--
NEVER MIND HOW I KNEW.
AND NO, I MEAN MOST OF THE FLEET. THERE ARE SURVIVORS, AND YOU'RE GOING TO RESCUE THEM.
THAT'S WHAT I NEED FROM YOU.
AFTER THAT, CONSIDER YOUR DEBT SETTLED.
AND JUST WHY AM I DOING THIS, WHEN YOU'RE PERFECTLY CAPABLE?

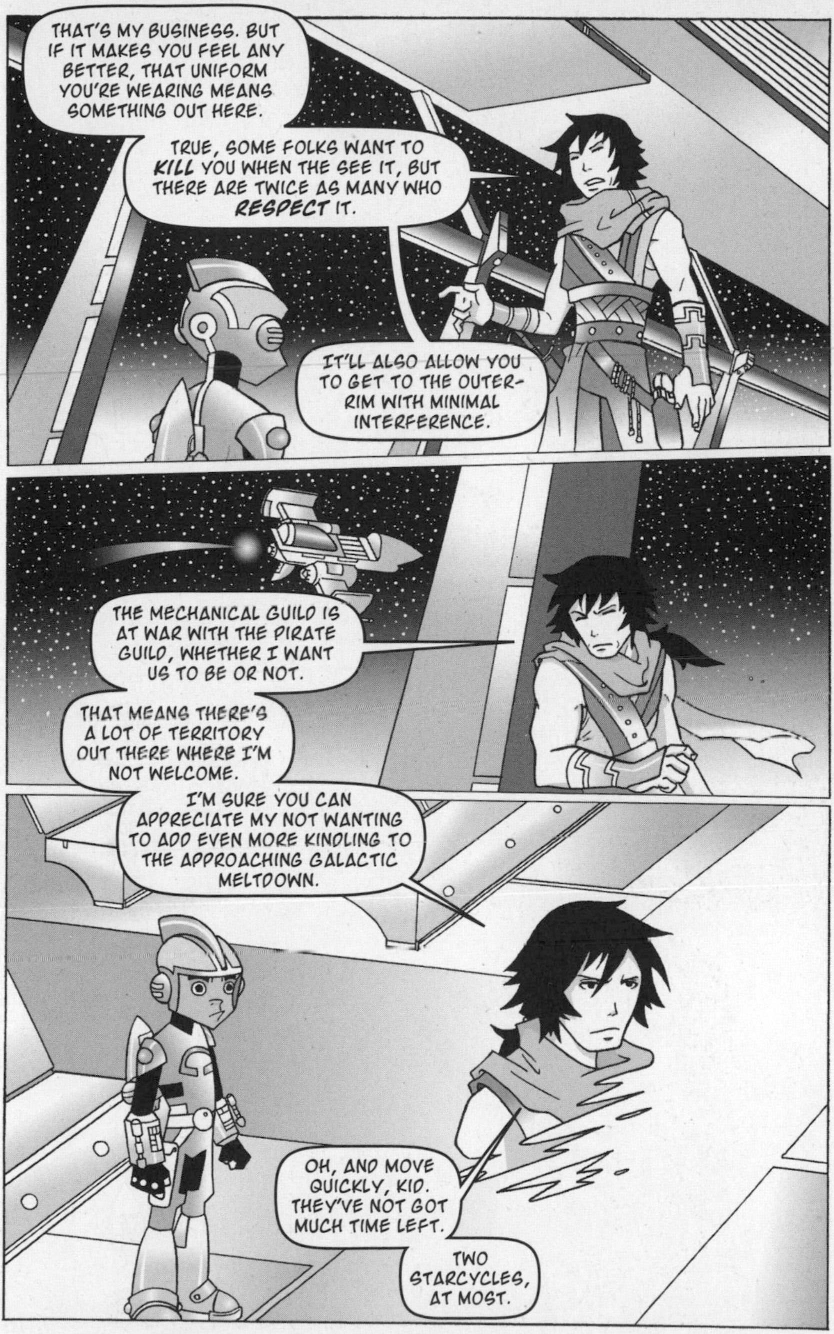
THAT'S MY BUSINESS. BUT IF IT MAKES YOU FEEL ANY BETTER, THAT UNIFORM YOU'RE WEARING MEANS SOMETHING OUT HERE.
TRUE, SOME FOLKS WANT TO *KILL* YOU WHEN THE SEE IT, BUT THERE ARE TWICE AS MANY WHO *RESPECT* IT.
IT'LL ALSO ALLOW YOU TO GET TO THE OUTER-RIM WITH MINIMAL INTERFERENCE.
THE MECHANICAL GUILD IS AT WAR WITH THE PIRATE GUILD, WHETHER I WANT US TO BE OR NOT.
THAT MEANS THERE'S A LOT OF TERRITORY OUT THERE WHERE I'M NOT WELCOME.
I'M SURE YOU CAN APPRECIATE MY NOT WANTING TO ADD EVEN MORE KINDLING TO THE APPROACHING GALACTIC MELTDOWN.
OH, AND MOVE QUICKLY, KID. THEY'VE NOT GOT MUCH TIME LEFT.
TWO STARCYCLES, AT MOST.

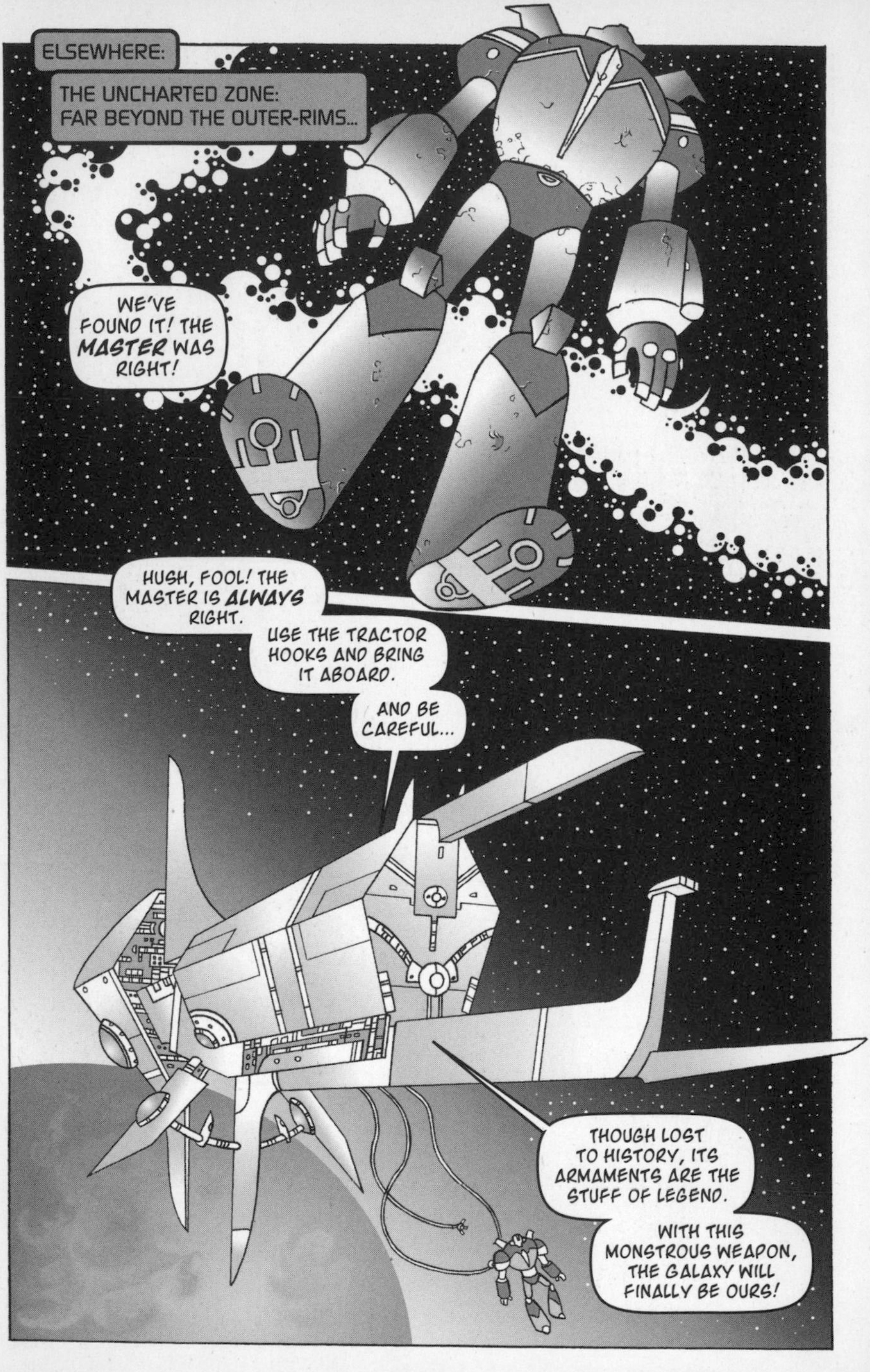
ELSEWHERE:
THE UNCHARTED ZONE: FAR BEYOND THE OUTER-RIMS...
WE'VE FOUND IT! THE MASTER WAS RIGHT!
HUSH, FOOL! THE MASTER IS ALWAYS RIGHT.
USE THE TRACTOR HOOKS AND BRING IT ABOARD.
AND BE CAREFUL...
THOUGH LOST TO HISTORY, ITS ARMAMENTS ARE THE STUFF OF LEGEND.
WITH THIS MONSTROUS WEAPON, THE GALAXY WILL FINALLY BE OURS!

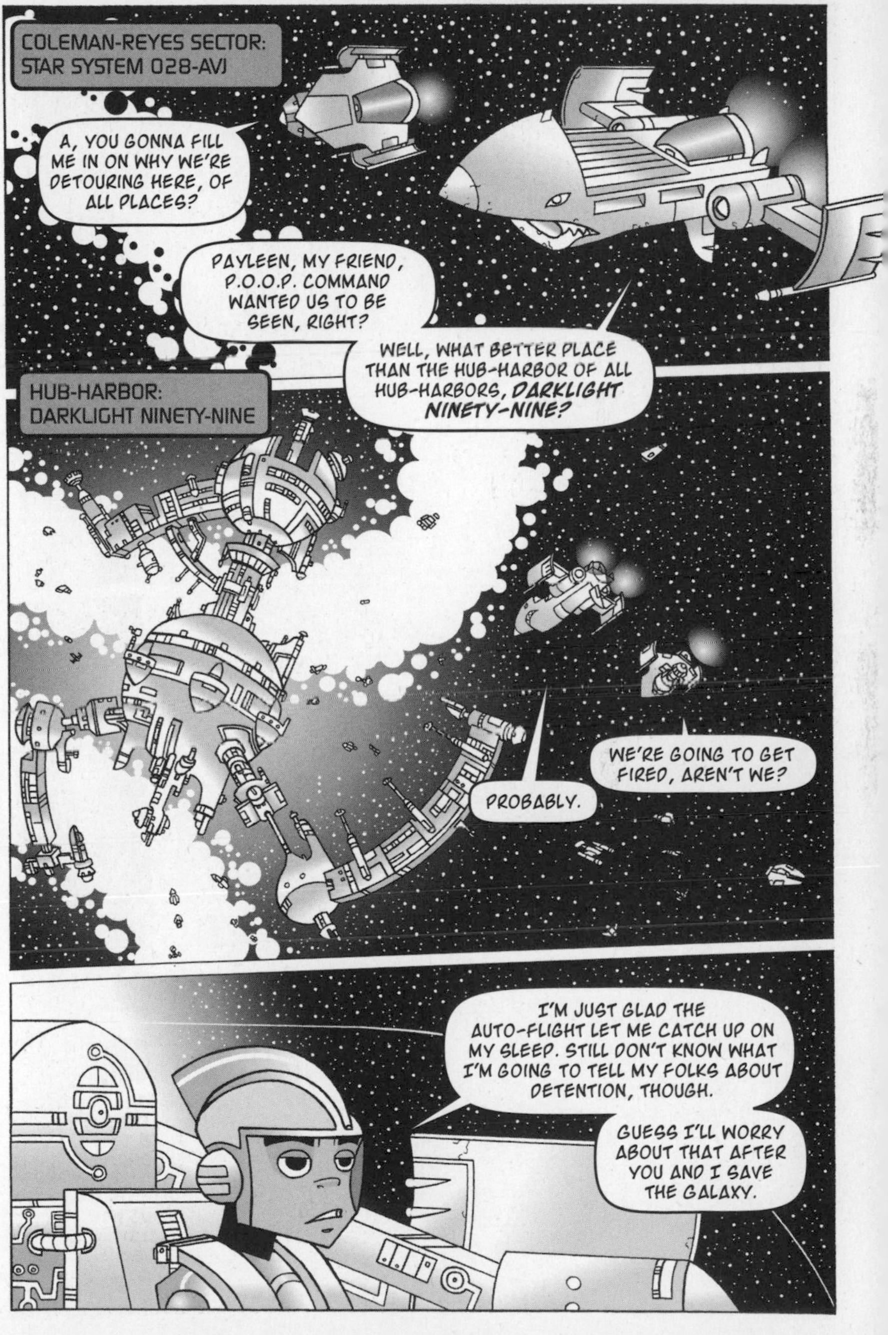
COLEMAN-REYES SECTOR: STAR SYSTEM 028-AVJ
A, YOU GONNA FILL ME IN ON WHY WE'RE DETOURING HERE, OF ALL PLACES?
PAYLEEN, MY FRIEND, P.O.O.P. COMMAND WANTED US TO BE SEEN, RIGHT?
WELL, WHAT BETTER PLACE THAN THE HUB-HARBOR OF ALL HUB-HARBORS, DARKLIGHT NINETY-NINE?
HUB-HARBOR: DARKLIGHT NINETY-NINE
WE'RE GOING TO GET FIRED, AREN'T WE?
PROBABLY.
I'M JUST GLAD THE AUTO-FLIGHT LET ME CATCH UP ON MY SLEEP. STILL DON'T KNOW WHAT I'M GOING TO TELL MY FOLKS ABOUT DETENTION, THOUGH.
GUESS I'LL WORRY ABOUT THAT AFTER YOU AND I SAVE THE GALAXY.

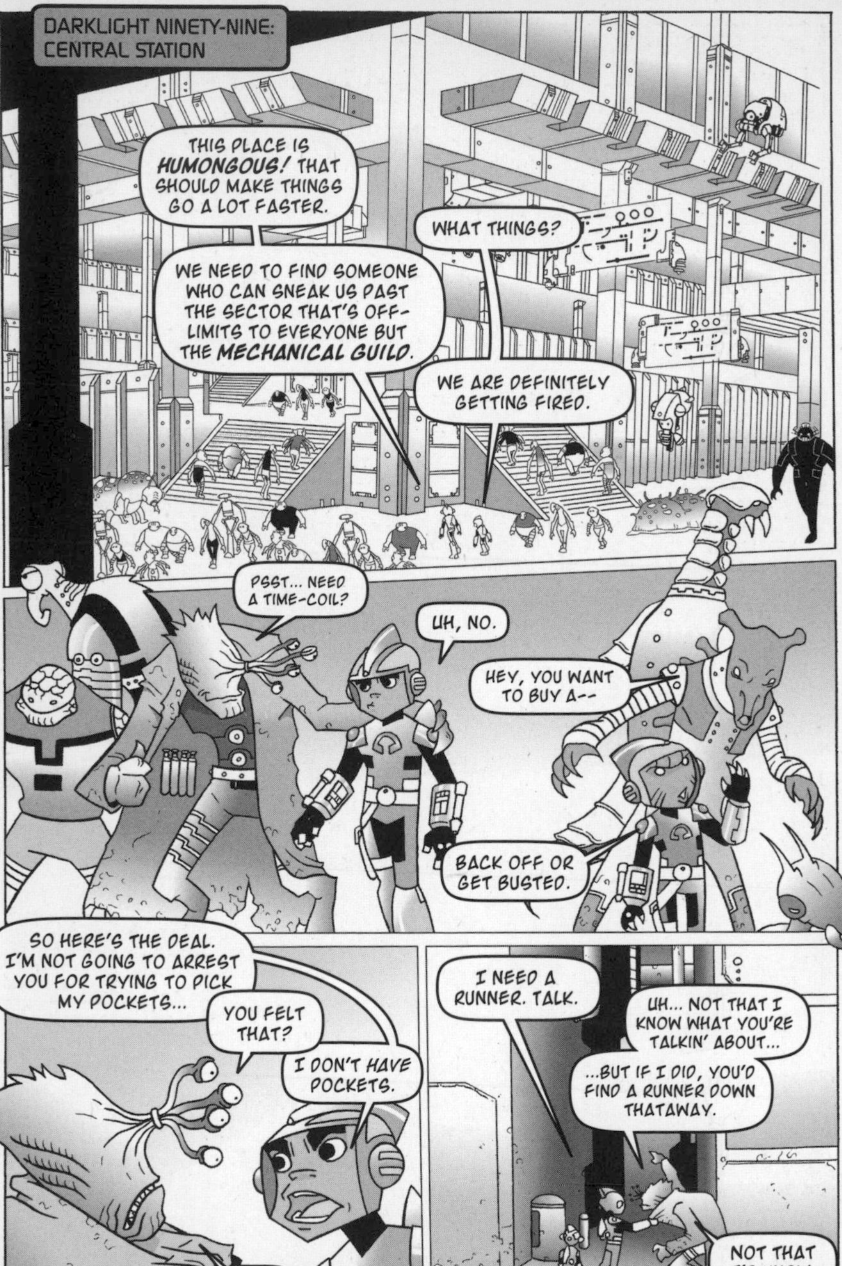
DARKLIGHT NINETY-NINE: CENTRAL STATION
THIS PLACE IS ***HUMONGOUS!*** THAT SHOULD MAKE THINGS GO A LOT FASTER.
WHAT THINGS?
WE NEED TO FIND SOMEONE WHO CAN SNEAK US PAST THE SECTOR THAT'S OFF-LIMITS TO EVERYONE BUT THE ***MECHANICAL GUILD***.
WE ARE DEFINITELY GETTING FIRED.
PSST... NEED A TIME-COIL?
UH, NO.
HEY, YOU WANT TO BUY A--
BACK OFF OR GET BUSTED.
SO HERE'S THE DEAL. I'M NOT GOING TO ARREST YOU FOR TRYING TO PICK MY POCKETS...
YOU FELT THAT?
I DON'T HAVE POCKETS.
OH.
I NEED A RUNNER. TALK.
UH... NOT THAT I KNOW WHAT YOU'RE TALKIN' ABOUT...
...BUT IF I DID, YOU'D FIND A RUNNER DOWN THATAWAY.
NOT THAT I'D KNOW.

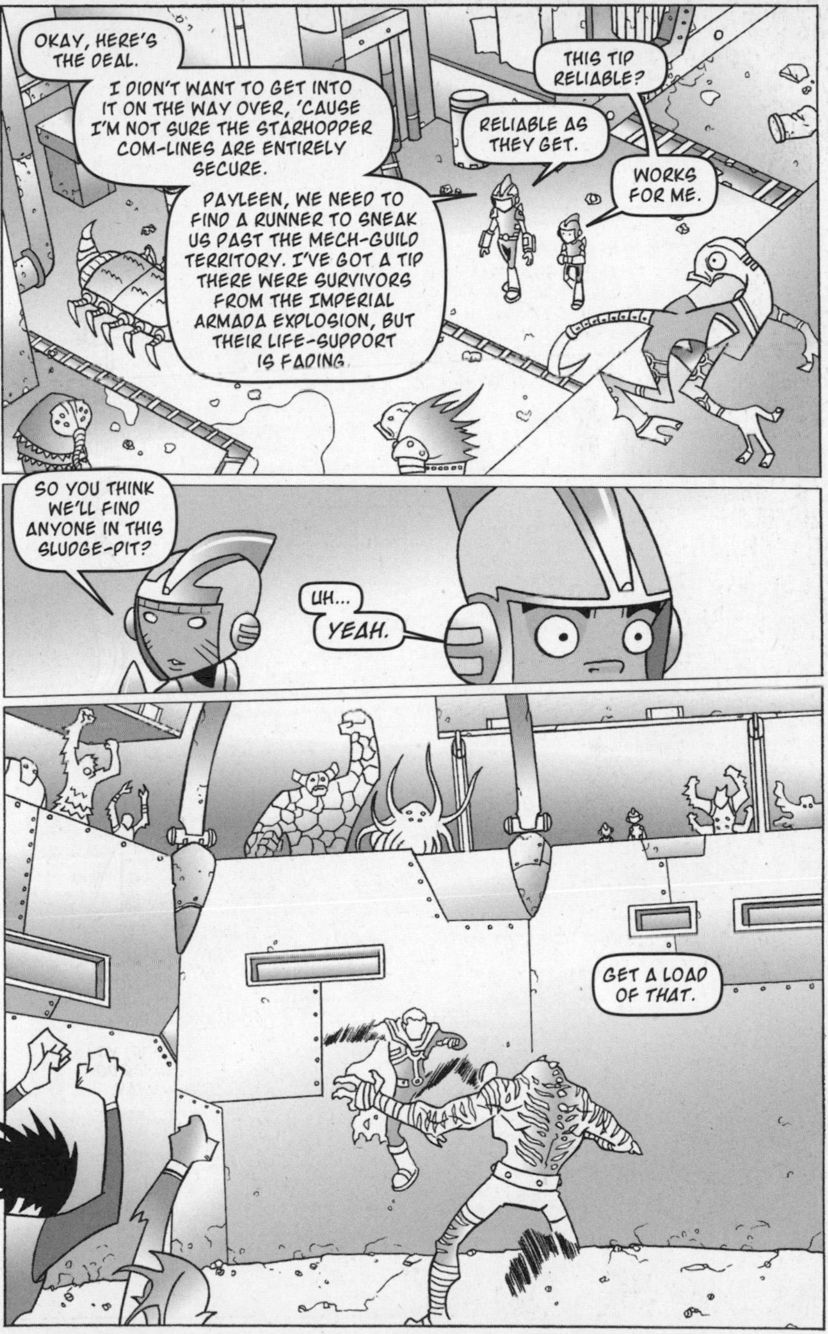
OKAY, HERE'S THE DEAL.
I DIDN'T WANT TO GET INTO IT ON THE WAY OVER, 'CAUSE I'M NOT SURE THE STARHOPPER COM-LINES ARE ENTIRELY SECURE.
PAYLEEN, WE NEED TO FIND A RUNNER TO SNEAK US PAST THE MECH-GUILD TERRITORY. I'VE GOT A TIP THERE WERE SURVIVORS FROM THE IMPERIAL ARMADA EXPLOSION, BUT THEIR LIFE-SUPPORT IS FADING.
THIS TIP RELIABLE?
RELIABLE AS THEY GET.
WORKS FOR ME.
SO YOU THINK WE'LL FIND ANYONE IN THIS SLUDGE-PIT?
UH... YEAH.
GET A LOAD OF THAT.

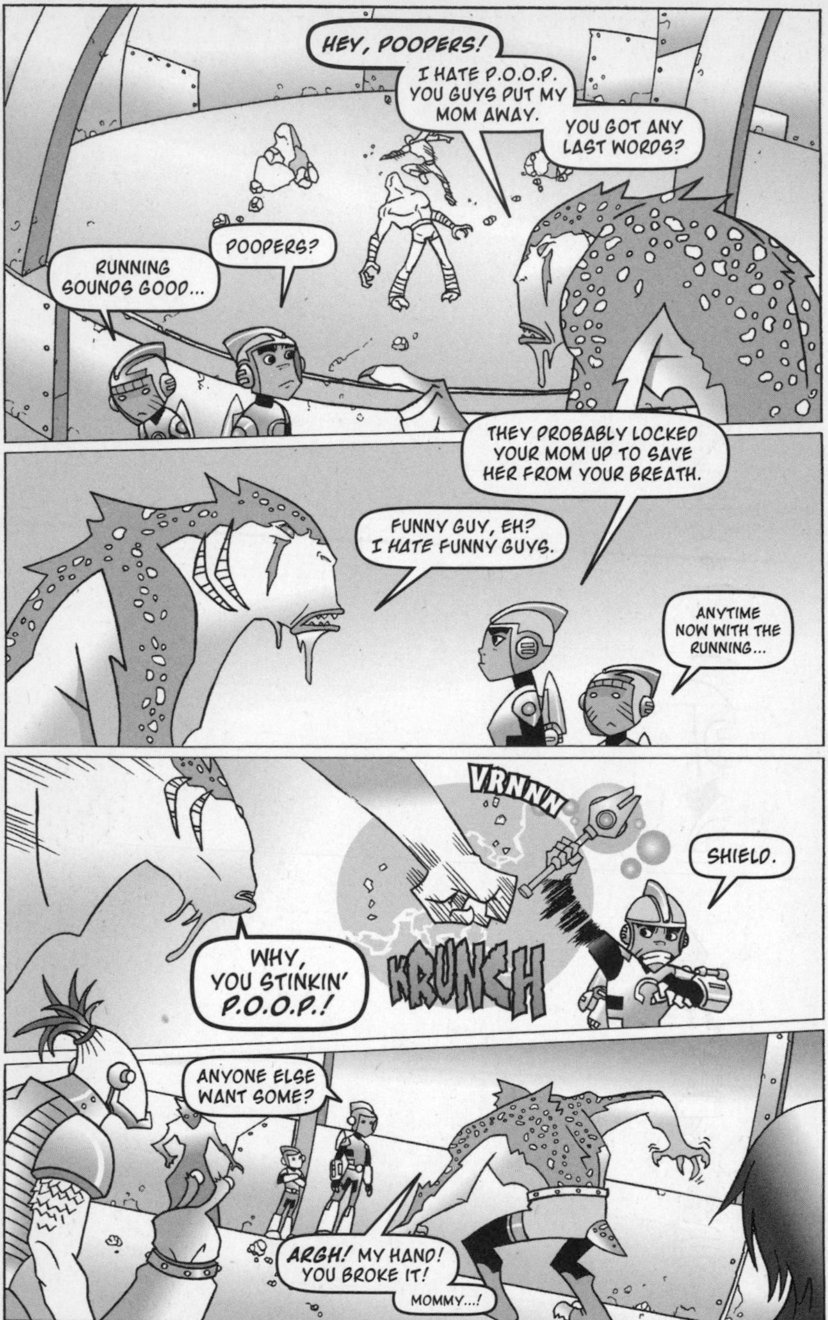
HEY, POOPERS!
I HATE P.O.O.P. YOU GUYS PUT MY MOM AWAY.
YOU GOT ANY LAST WORDS?
RUNNING SOUNDS GOOD...
POOPERS?
THEY PROBABLY LOCKED YOUR MOM UP TO SAVE HER FROM YOUR BREATH.
FUNNY GUY, EH? I HATE FUNNY GUYS.
ANYTIME NOW WITH THE RUNNING...
VRNNN
SHIELD.
WHY, YOU STINKIN' P.O.O.P.!
KRUNCH
ANYONE ELSE WANT SOME?
ARGH! MY HAND! YOU BROKE IT!
MOMMY...!

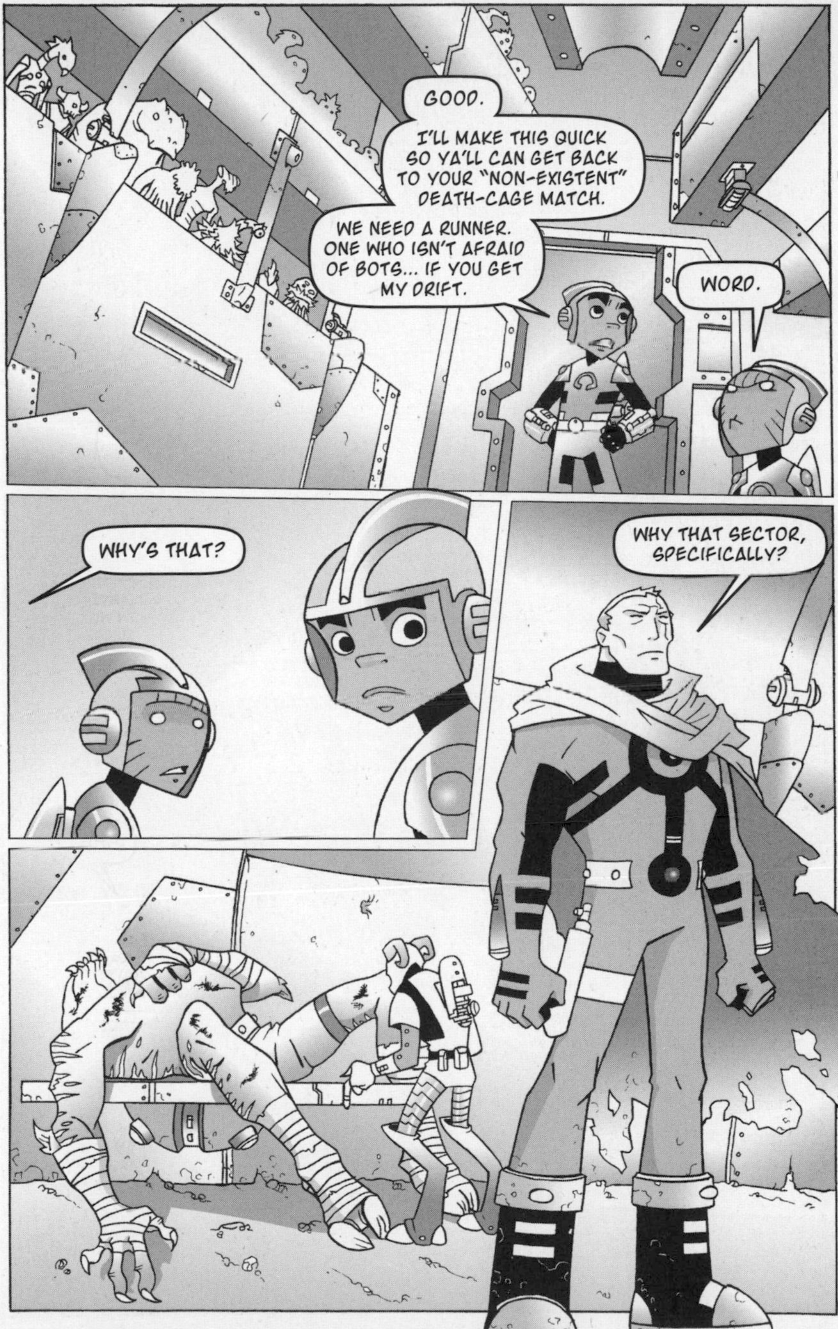
GOOD.
I'LL MAKE THIS QUICK SO YA'LL CAN GET BACK TO YOUR "NON-EXISTENT" DEATH-CAGE MATCH.
WE NEED A RUNNER. ONE WHO ISN'T AFRAID OF BOTS... IF YOU GET MY DRIFT.
WORD.
WHY'S THAT?
WHY THAT SECTOR, SPECIFICALLY?

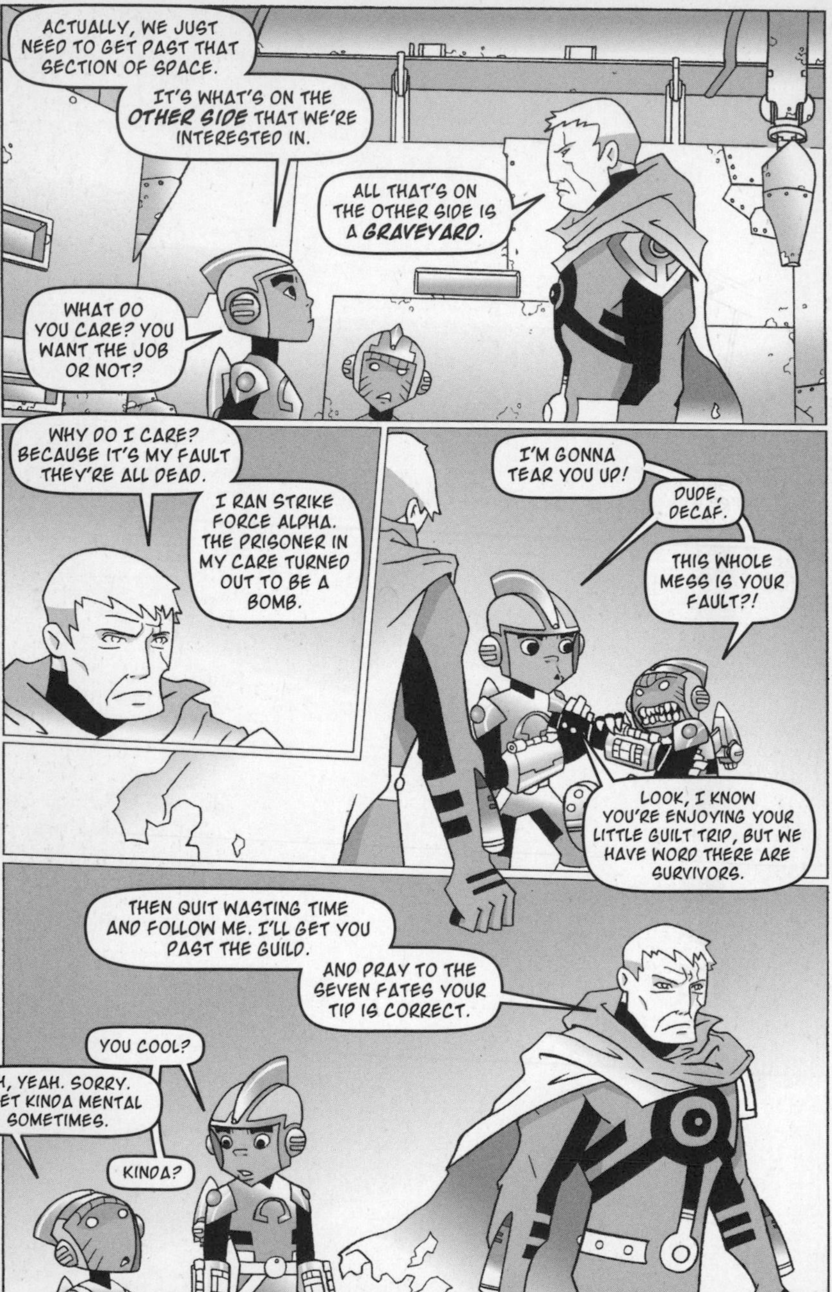
ACTUALLY, WE JUST NEED TO GET PAST THAT SECTION OF SPACE.
IT'S WHAT'S ON THE *OTHER SIDE* THAT WE'RE INTERESTED IN.
ALL THAT'S ON THE OTHER SIDE IS A *GRAVEYARD*.
WHAT DO YOU CARE? YOU WANT THE JOB OR NOT?
WHY DO I CARE? BECAUSE IT'S MY FAULT THEY'RE ALL DEAD.
I RAN STRIKE FORCE ALPHA. THE PRISONER IN MY CARE TURNED OUT TO BE A BOMB.
I'M GONNA TEAR YOU UP!
DUDE, DECAF.
THIS WHOLE MESS IS YOUR FAULT?!
LOOK, I KNOW YOU'RE ENJOYING YOUR LITTLE GUILT TRIP, BUT WE HAVE WORD THERE ARE SURVIVORS.
THEN QUIT WASTING TIME AND FOLLOW ME. I'LL GET YOU PAST THE GUILD.
AND PRAY TO THE SEVEN FATES YOUR TIP IS CORRECT.
YOU COOL?
UH, YEAH. SORRY. I GET KINDA MENTAL SOMETIMES.
KINDA?

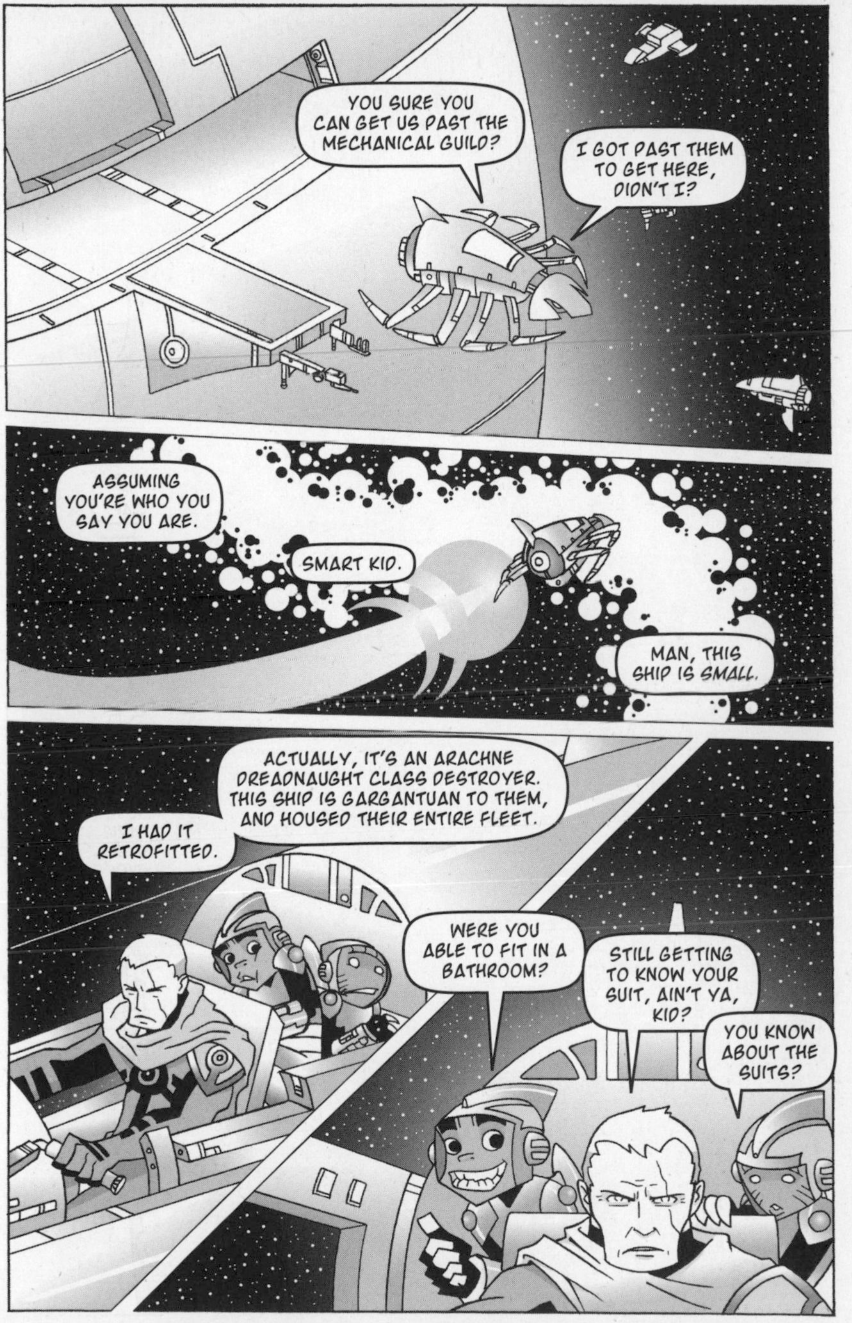
YOU SURE YOU CAN GET US PAST THE MECHANICAL GUILD?
I GOT PAST THEM TO GET HERE, DIDN'T I?
ASSUMING YOU'RE WHO YOU SAY YOU ARE.
SMART KID.
MAN, THIS SHIP IS SMALL.
I HAD IT RETROFITTED.
ACTUALLY, IT'S AN ARACHNE DREADNAUGHT CLASS DESTROYER. THIS SHIP IS GARGANTUAN TO THEM, AND HOUSED THEIR ENTIRE FLEET.
WERE YOU ABLE TO FIT IN A BATHROOM?
STILL GETTING TO KNOW YOUR SUIT, AIN'T YA, KID?
YOU KNOW ABOUT THE SUITS?

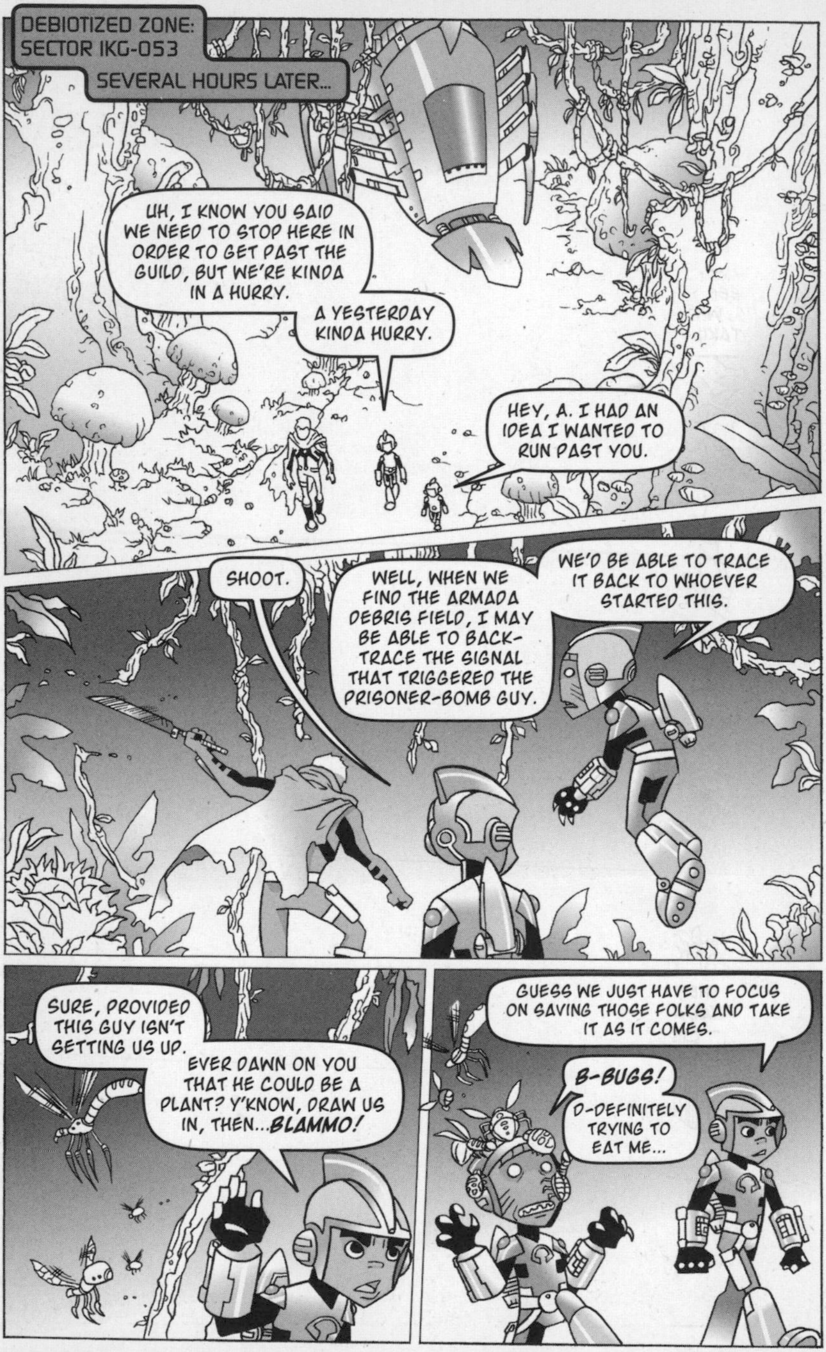
DEBIOTIZED ZONE: SECTOR IKG-053
SEVERAL HOURS LATER...
UH, I KNOW YOU SAID WE NEED TO STOP HERE IN ORDER TO GET PAST THE GUILD, BUT WE'RE KINDA IN A HURRY.
A YESTERDAY KINDA HURRY.
HEY, A. I HAD AN IDEA I WANTED TO RUN PAST YOU.
SHOOT.
WELL, WHEN WE FIND THE ARMADA DEBRIS FIELD, I MAY BE ABLE TO BACK-TRACE THE SIGNAL THAT TRIGGERED THE PRISONER-BOMB GUY.
WE'D BE ABLE TO TRACE IT BACK TO WHOEVER STARTED THIS.
SURE, PROVIDED THIS GUY ISN'T SETTING US UP.
EVER DAWN ON YOU THAT HE COULD BE A PLANT? Y'KNOW, DRAW US IN, THEN...BLAMMO!
GUESS WE JUST HAVE TO FOCUS ON SAVING THOSE FOLKS AND TAKE IT AS IT COMES.
B-BUGS!
D-DEFINITELY TRYING TO EAT ME...

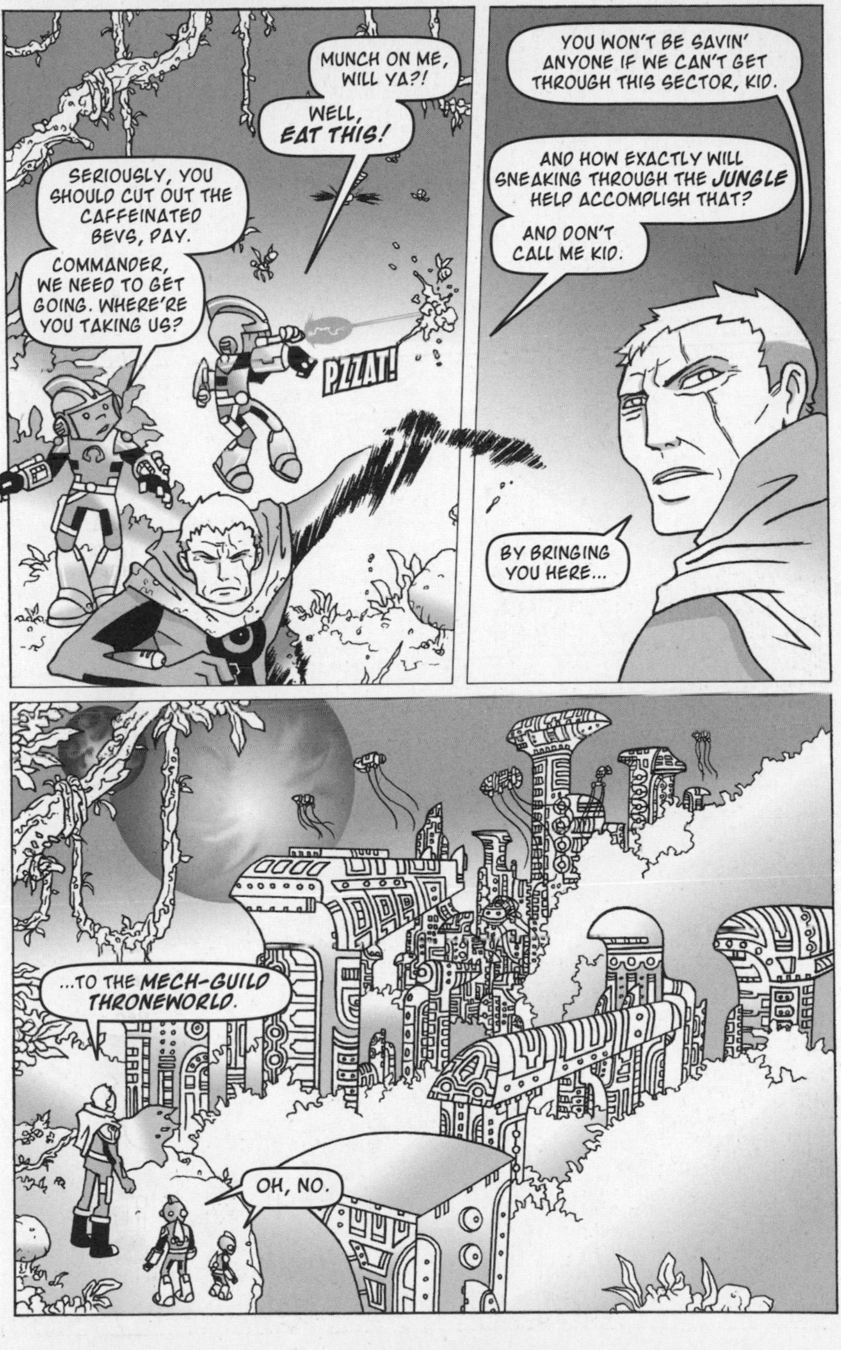
MUNCH ON ME, WILL YA?!
WELL, EAT THIS!
SERIOUSLY, YOU SHOULD CUT OUT THE CAFFEINATED BEVS, PAY.
COMMANDER, WE NEED TO GET GOING. WHERE'RE YOU TAKING US?
PZZAT!
YOU WON'T BE SAVIN' ANYONE IF WE CAN'T GET THROUGH THIS SECTOR, KID.
AND HOW EXACTLY WILL SNEAKING THROUGH THE JUNGLE HELP ACCOMPLISH THAT?
AND DON'T CALL ME KID.
BY BRINGING YOU HERE...
...TO THE MECH-GUILD THRONEWORLD.
OH, NO.

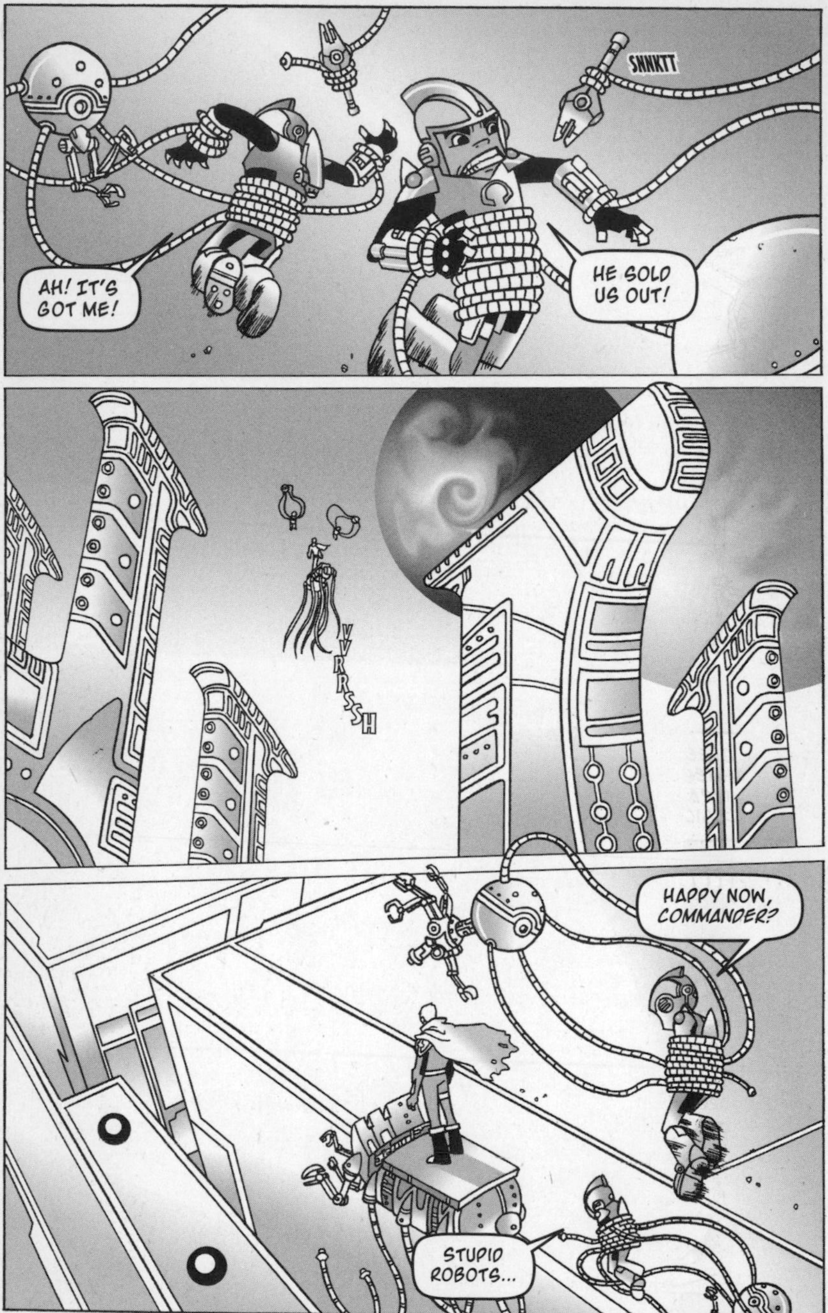
SNNKTT
AH! IT'S GOT ME!
HE SOLD US OUT!
VVRRSSH
HAPPY NOW, COMMANDER?
STUPID ROBOTS...

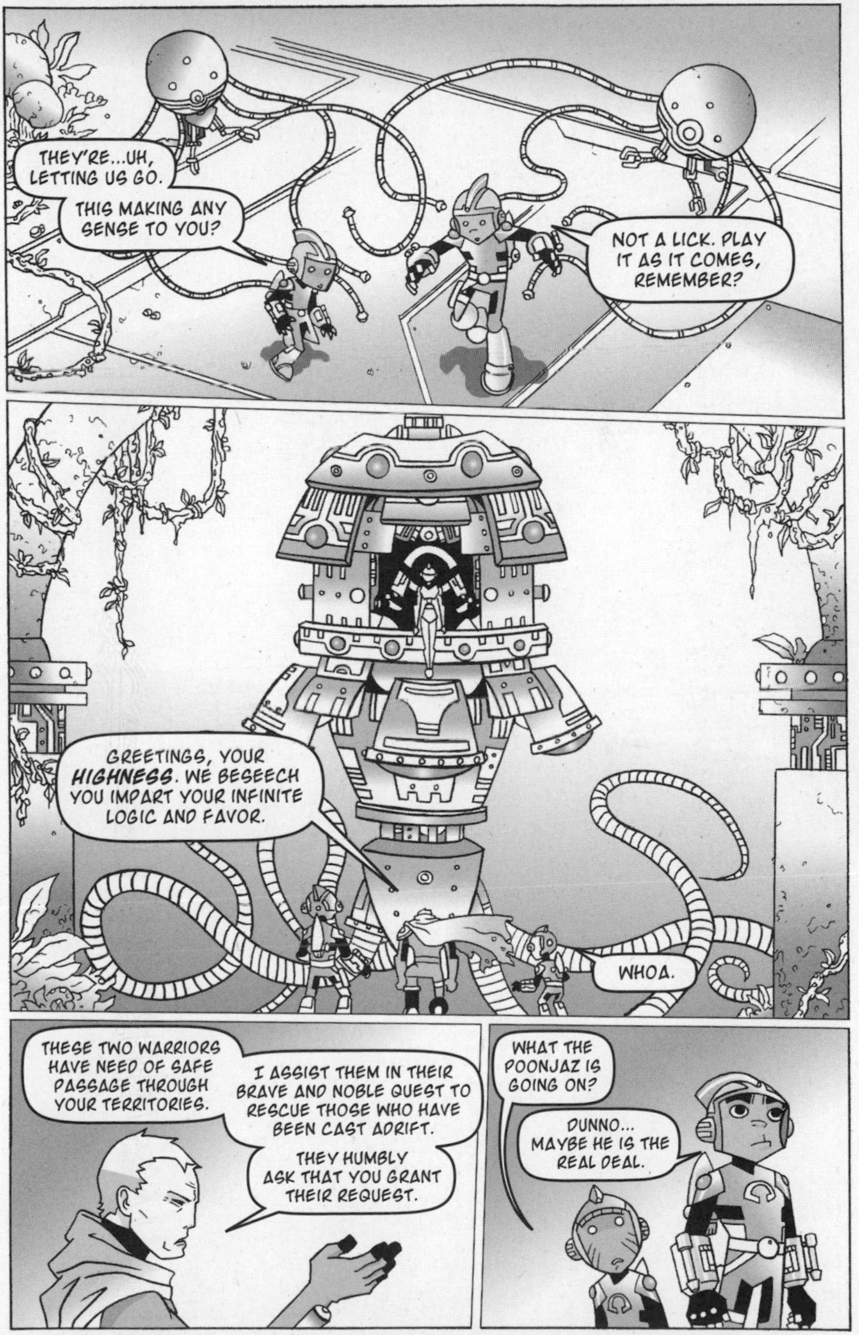
THEY'RE...UH, LETTING US GO.
THIS MAKING ANY SENSE TO YOU?
NOT A LICK. PLAY IT AS IT COMES, REMEMBER?
GREETINGS, YOUR **HIGHNESS**. WE BESEECH YOU IMPART YOUR INFINITE LOGIC AND FAVOR.
WHOA.
THESE TWO WARRIORS HAVE NEED OF SAFE PASSAGE THROUGH YOUR TERRITORIES.
I ASSIST THEM IN THEIR BRAVE AND NOBLE QUEST TO RESCUE THOSE WHO HAVE BEEN CAST ADRIFT.
THEY HUMBLY ASK THAT YOU GRANT THEIR REQUEST.
WHAT THE POONJAZ IS GOING ON?
DUNNO... MAYBE HE IS THE REAL DEAL.

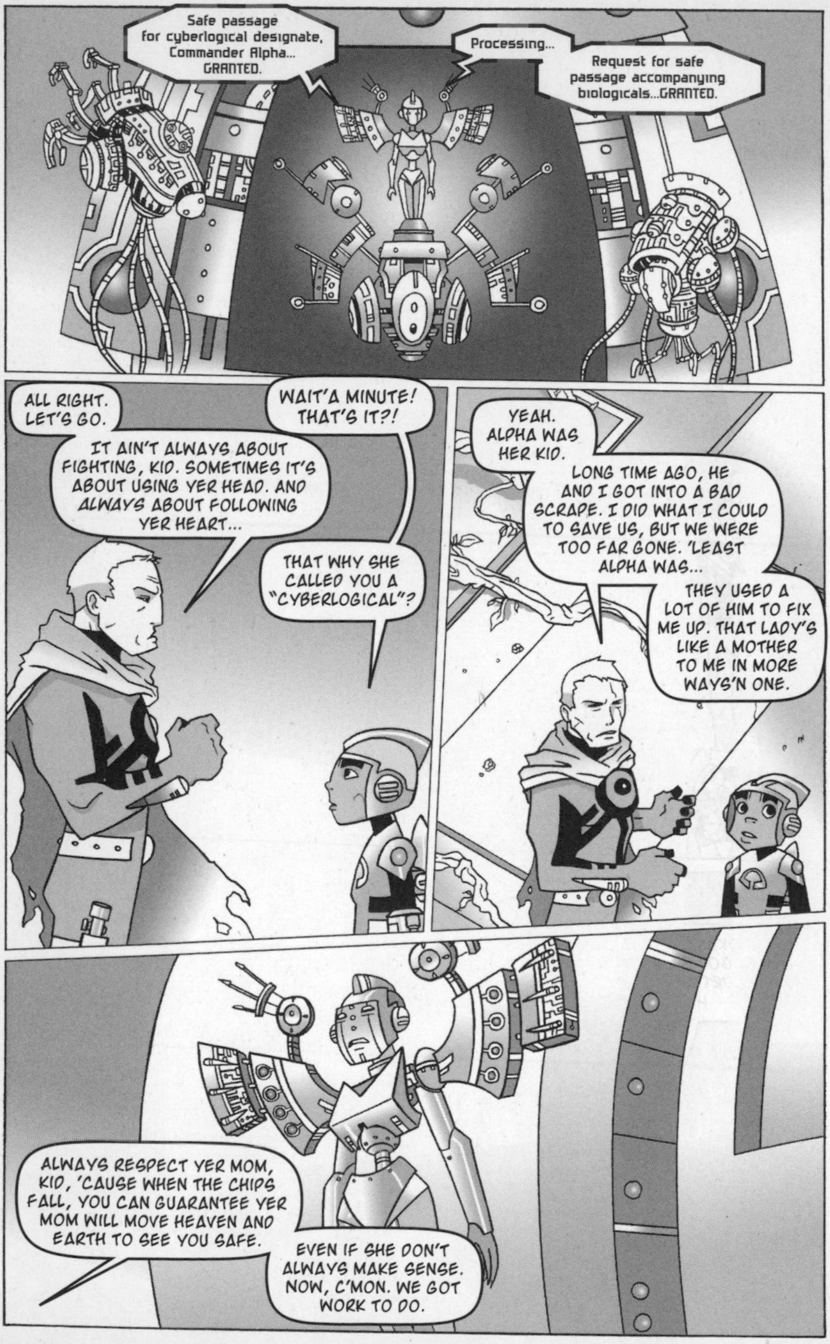
Safe passage for cyberlogical designate, Commander Alpha... GRANTED.
Processing...
Request for safe passage accompanying biologicals...GRANTED.
ALL RIGHT. LET'S GO.
IT AIN'T ALWAYS ABOUT FIGHTING, KID. SOMETIMES IT'S ABOUT USING YER HEAD. AND ALWAYS ABOUT FOLLOWING YER HEART...
WAIT'A MINUTE! THAT'S IT?!
THAT WHY SHE CALLED YOU A "CYBERLOGICAL"?
YEAH. ALPHA WAS HER KID.
LONG TIME AGO, HE AND I GOT INTO A BAD SCRAPE. I DID WHAT I COULD TO SAVE US, BUT WE WERE TOO FAR GONE. 'LEAST ALPHA WAS...
THEY USED A LOT OF HIM TO FIX ME UP. THAT LADY'S LIKE A MOTHER TO ME IN MORE WAYS'N ONE.
ALWAYS RESPECT YER MOM, KID, 'CAUSE WHEN THE CHIPS FALL, YOU CAN GUARANTEE YER MOM WILL MOVE HEAVEN AND EARTH TO SEE YOU SAFE.
EVEN IF SHE DON'T ALWAYS MAKE SENSE. NOW, C'MON. WE GOT WORK TO DO.

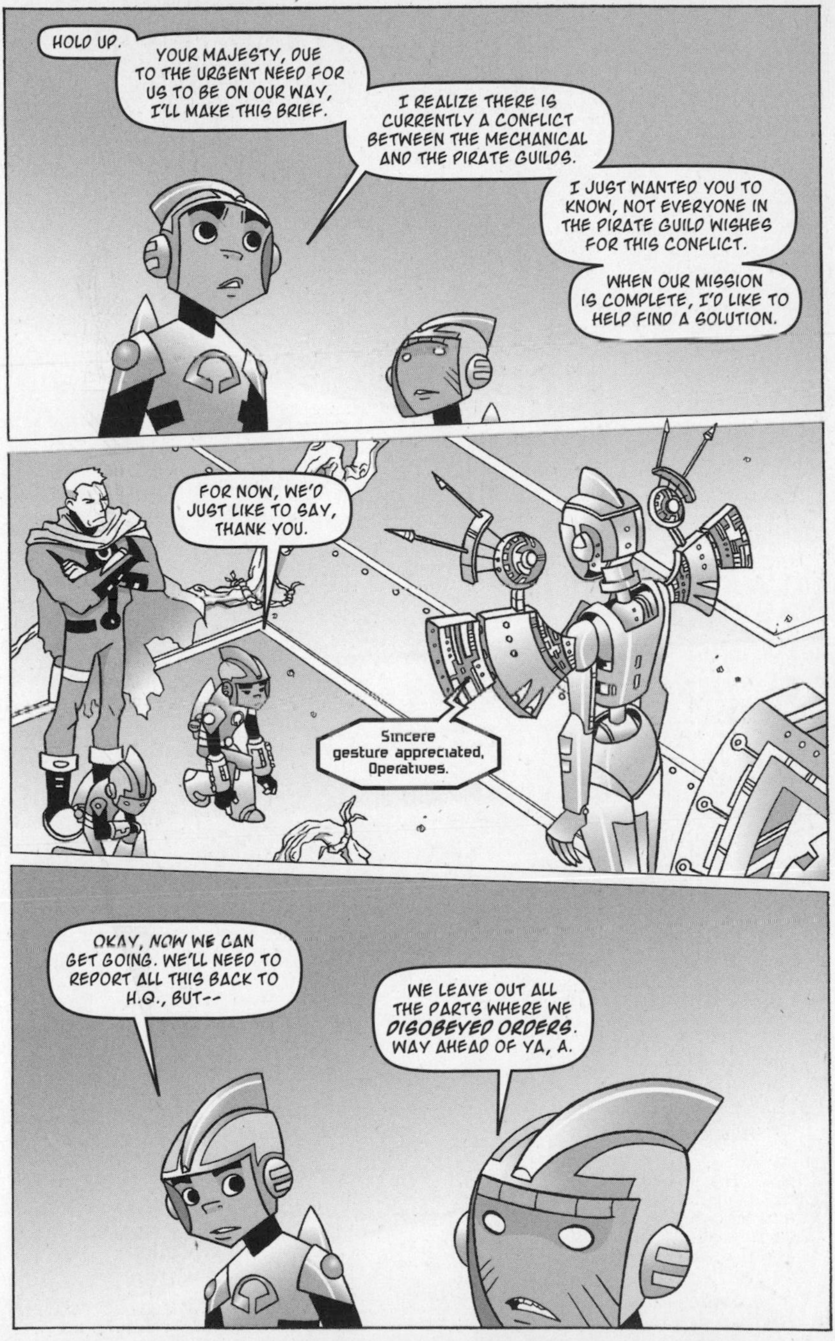
HOLD UP.
YOUR MAJESTY, DUE TO THE URGENT NEED FOR US TO BE ON OUR WAY, I'LL MAKE THIS BRIEF.
I REALIZE THERE IS CURRENTLY A CONFLICT BETWEEN THE MECHANICAL AND THE PIRATE GUILDS.
I JUST WANTED YOU TO KNOW, NOT EVERYONE IN THE PIRATE GUILD WISHES FOR THIS CONFLICT.
WHEN OUR MISSION IS COMPLETE, I'D LIKE TO HELP FIND A SOLUTION.
FOR NOW, WE'D JUST LIKE TO SAY, THANK YOU.
Sincere gesture appreciated, Operatives.
OKAY, NOW WE CAN GET GOING. WE'LL NEED TO REPORT ALL THIS BACK TO H.Q., BUT--
WE LEAVE OUT ALL THE PARTS WHERE WE DISOBEYED ORDERS. WAY AHEAD OF YA, A.

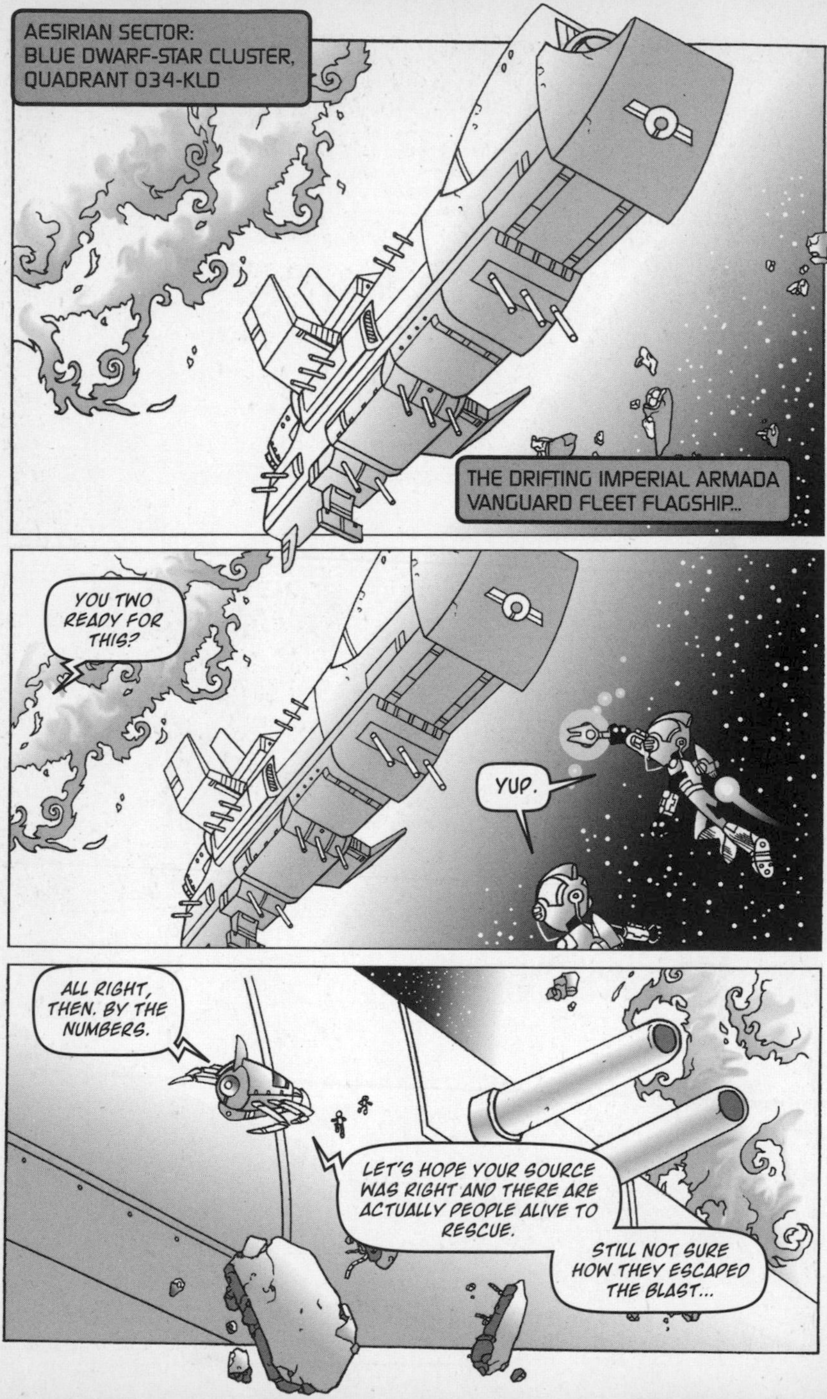
AESIRIAN SECTOR: BLUE DWARF-STAR CLUSTER, QUADRANT 034-KLD
THE DRIFTING IMPERIAL ARMADA VANGUARD FLEET FLAGSHIP...
YOU TWO READY FOR THIS?
YUP.
ALL RIGHT, THEN. BY THE NUMBERS.
LET'S HOPE YOUR SOURCE WAS RIGHT AND THERE ARE ACTUALLY PEOPLE ALIVE TO RESCUE.
STILL NOT SURE HOW THEY ESCAPED THE BLAST...

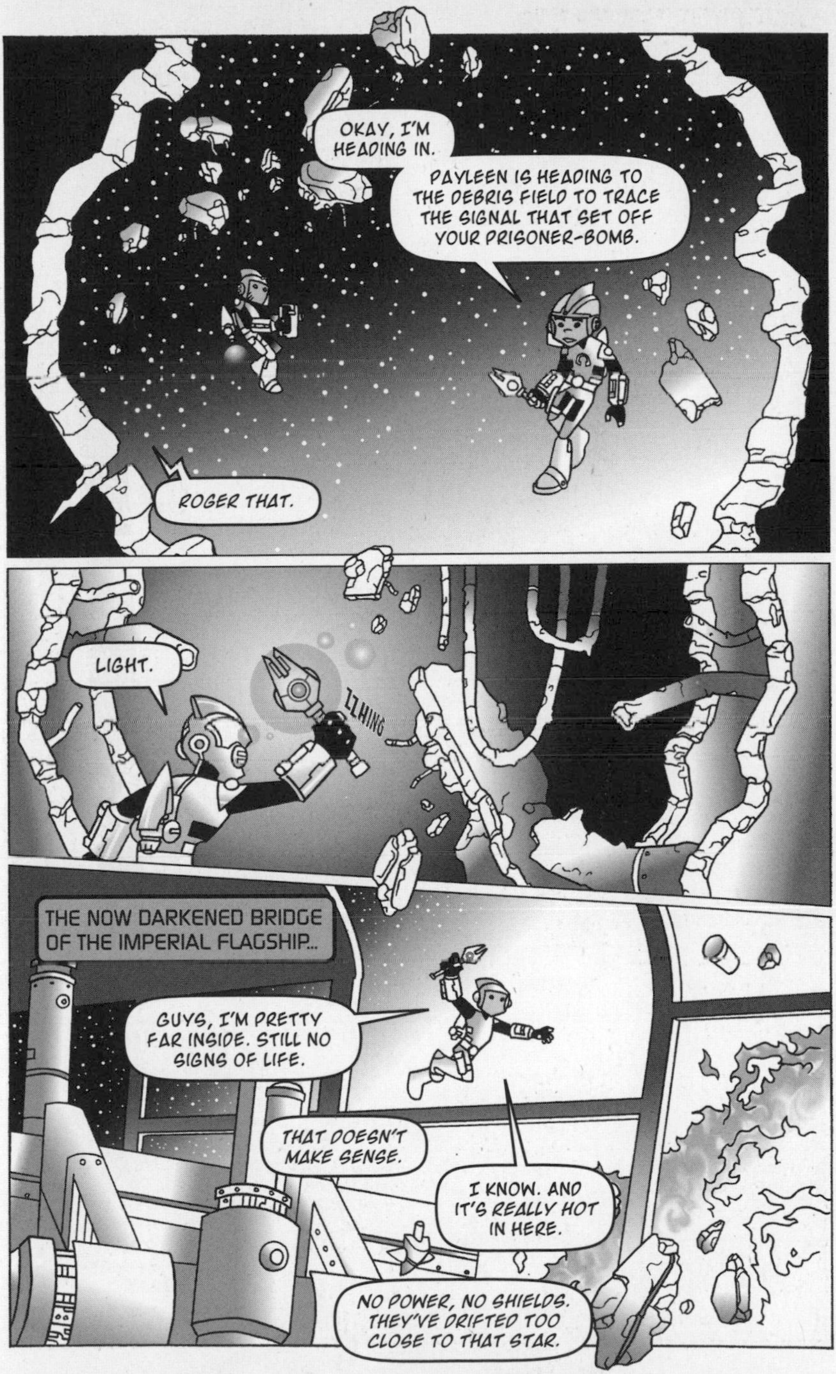
OKAY, I'M HEADING IN.
PAYLEEN IS HEADING TO THE DEBRIS FIELD TO TRACE THE SIGNAL THAT SET OFF YOUR PRISONER-BOMB.
ROGER THAT.
LIGHT.
ZZHING
THE NOW DARKENED BRIDGE OF THE IMPERIAL FLAGSHIP...
GUYS, I'M PRETTY FAR INSIDE. STILL NO SIGNS OF LIFE.
THAT DOESN'T MAKE SENSE.
I KNOW. AND IT'S REALLY HOT IN HERE.
NO POWER, NO SHIELDS. THEY'VE DRIFTED TOO CLOSE TO THAT STAR.

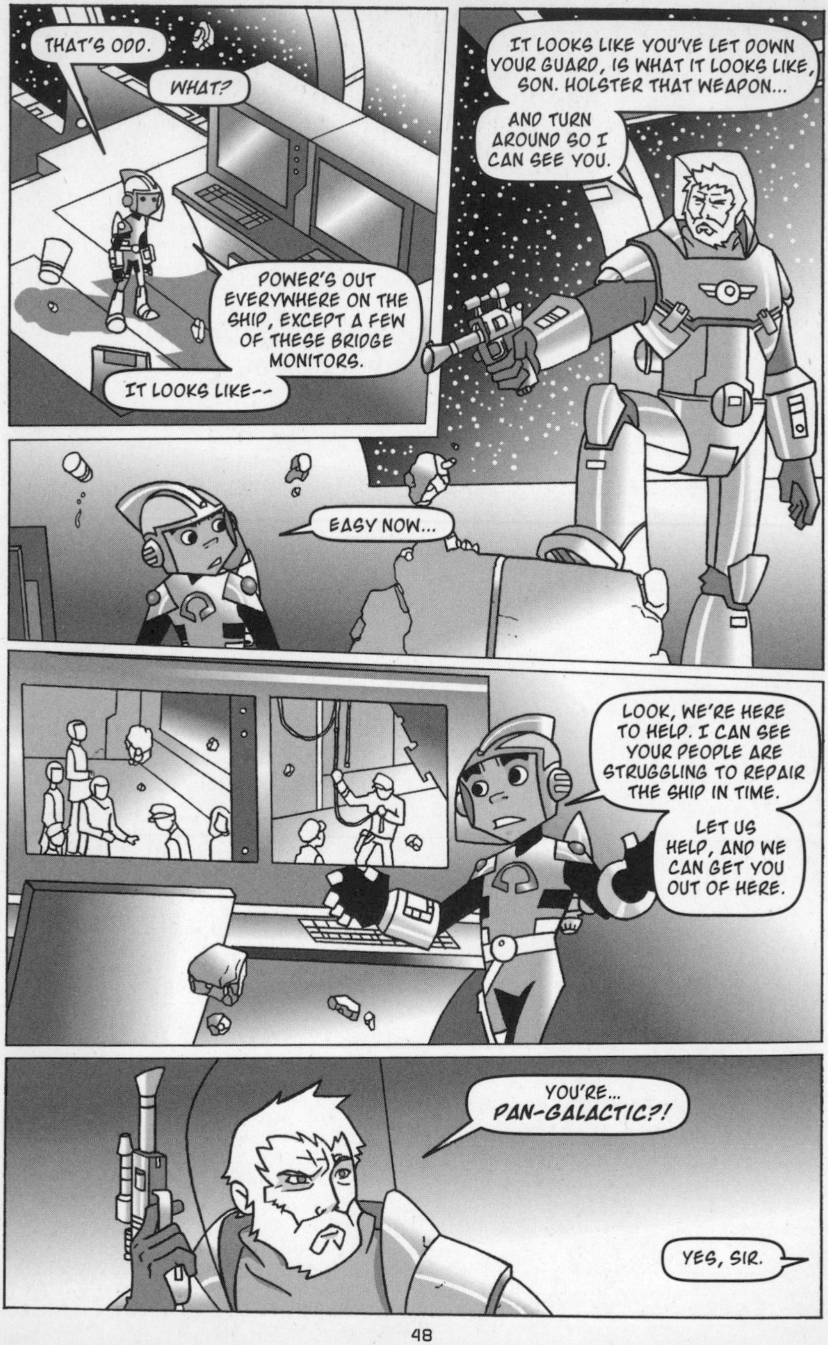
THAT'S ODD.
WHAT?
POWER'S OUT EVERYWHERE ON THE SHIP, EXCEPT A FEW OF THESE BRIDGE MONITORS.
IT LOOKS LIKE--
IT LOOKS LIKE YOU'VE LET DOWN YOUR GUARD, IS WHAT IT LOOKS LIKE, SON. HOLSTER THAT WEAPON...
AND TURN AROUND SO I CAN SEE YOU.
EASY NOW...
LOOK, WE'RE HERE TO HELP. I CAN SEE YOUR PEOPLE ARE STRUGGLING TO REPAIR THE SHIP IN TIME.
LET US HELP, AND WE CAN GET YOU OUT OF HERE.
YOU'RE... PAN-GALACTIC?!
YES, SIR.

WE GOT A TIP YOU GUYS WERE OUT HERE. THE INITIAL AUTOMATED SEARCH DIDN'T DETECT YOUR SHIP.

LUCKILY, SOMEONE PICKED UP YOUR S.O.S.

NOT LIKELY. IT'S A SECURE CHANNEL. I DIDN'T BROADCAST IT TO ANYONE OUTSIDE THE FLEET.

WE JUMPED INTO WARPSPACE TO AVOID THE BLAST.

DIDN'T HAVE TIME TO VECTOR IN AN EXIT POINT, SO WE POPPED OUT HERE.

SO WHO PICKED UP OUR S.O.S.?

HE'S ASKED TO REMAIN ANONYMOUS.

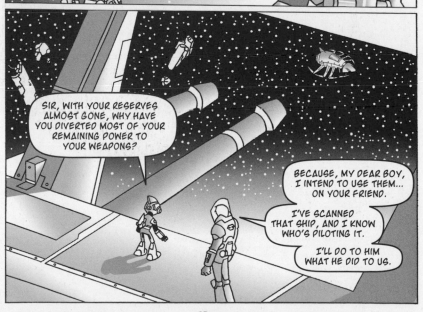

SIR, WITH YOUR RESERVES ALMOST GONE, WHY HAVE YOU DIVERTED MOST OF YOUR REMAINING POWER TO YOUR WEAPONS?

BECAUSE, MY DEAR BOY, I INTEND TO USE THEM... ON YOUR FRIEND.

I'VE SCANNED THAT SHIP, AND I KNOW WHO'S PILOTING IT.

I'LL DO TO HIM WHAT HE DID TO US.

49

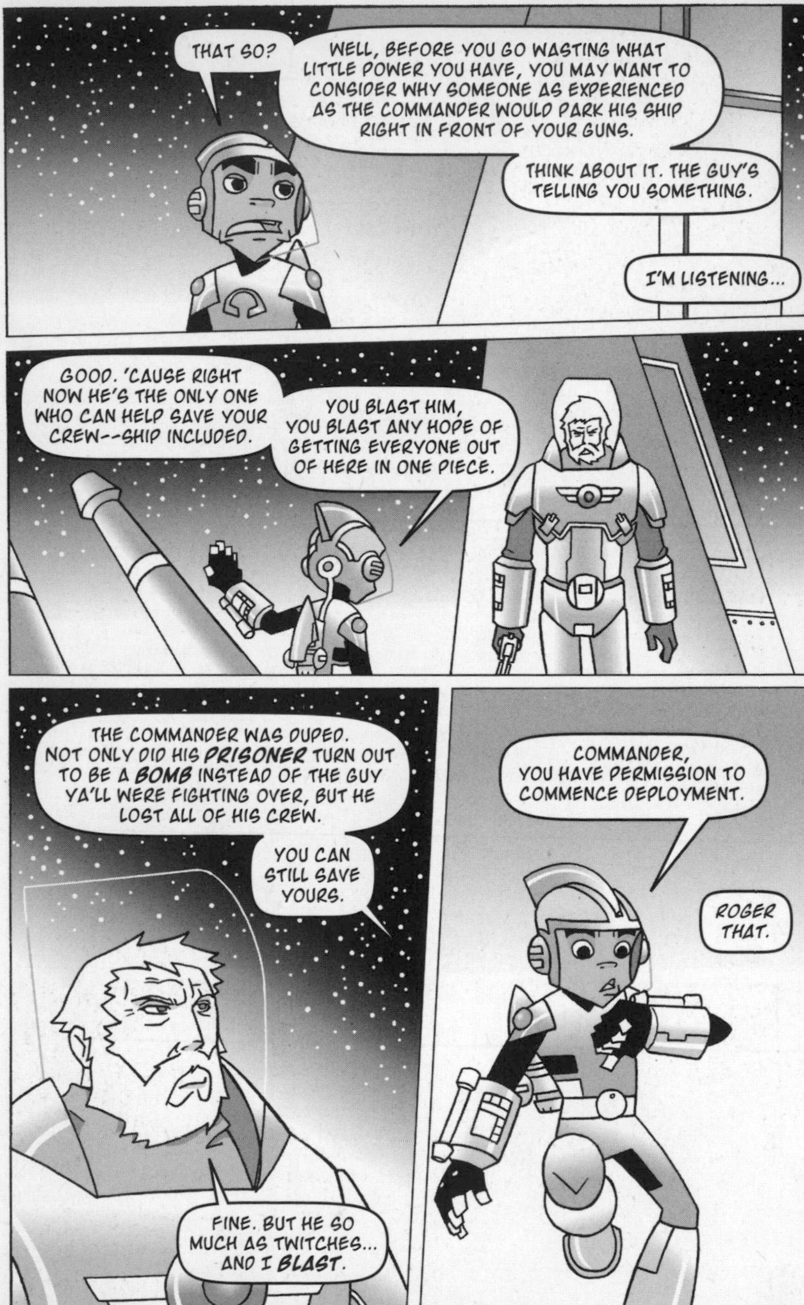
THAT SO?
WELL, BEFORE YOU GO WASTING WHAT LITTLE POWER YOU HAVE, YOU MAY WANT TO CONSIDER WHY SOMEONE AS EXPERIENCED AS THE COMMANDER WOULD PARK HIS SHIP RIGHT IN FRONT OF YOUR GUNS.
THINK ABOUT IT. THE GUY'S TELLING YOU SOMETHING.
I'M LISTENING...
GOOD. 'CAUSE RIGHT NOW HE'S THE ONLY ONE WHO CAN HELP SAVE YOUR CREW--SHIP INCLUDED.
YOU BLAST HIM, YOU BLAST ANY HOPE OF GETTING EVERYONE OUT OF HERE IN ONE PIECE.
THE COMMANDER WAS DUPED. NOT ONLY DID HIS *PRISONER* TURN OUT TO BE A *BOMB* INSTEAD OF THE GUY YA'LL WERE FIGHTING OVER, BUT HE LOST ALL OF HIS CREW.
YOU CAN STILL SAVE YOURS.
FINE. BUT HE SO MUCH AS TWITCHES... AND I *BLAST*.
COMMANDER, YOU HAVE PERMISSION TO COMMENCE DEPLOYMENT.
ROGER THAT.

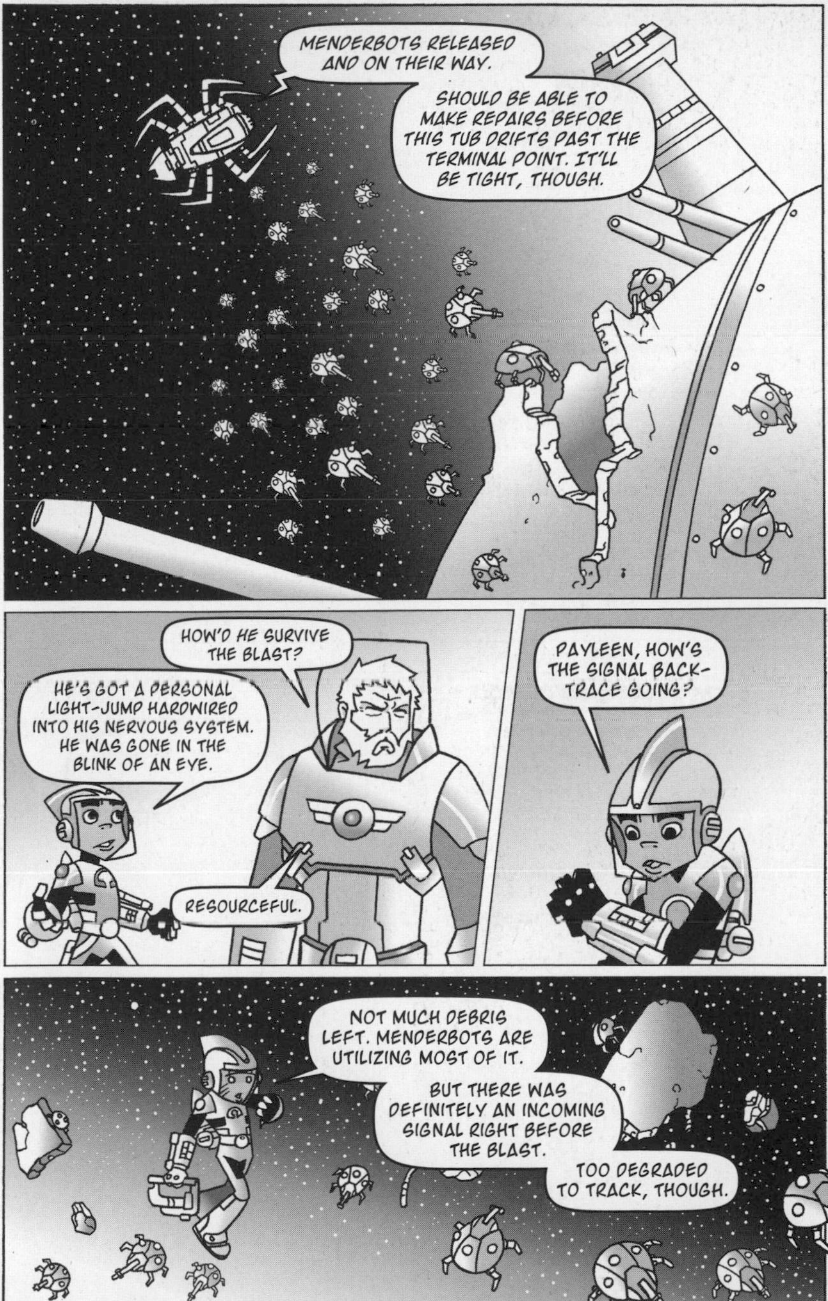
MENDERBOTS RELEASED AND ON THEIR WAY.
SHOULD BE ABLE TO MAKE REPAIRS BEFORE THIS TUB DRIFTS PAST THE TERMINAL POINT. IT'LL BE TIGHT, THOUGH.
HOW'D HE SURVIVE THE BLAST?
HE'S GOT A PERSONAL LIGHT-JUMP HARDWIRED INTO HIS NERVOUS SYSTEM. HE WAS GONE IN THE BLINK OF AN EYE.
RESOURCEFUL.
PAYLEEN, HOW'S THE SIGNAL BACK-TRACE GOING?
NOT MUCH DEBRIS LEFT. MENDERBOTS ARE UTILIZING MOST OF IT.
BUT THERE WAS DEFINITELY AN INCOMING SIGNAL RIGHT BEFORE THE BLAST.
TOO DEGRADED TO TRACK, THOUGH.

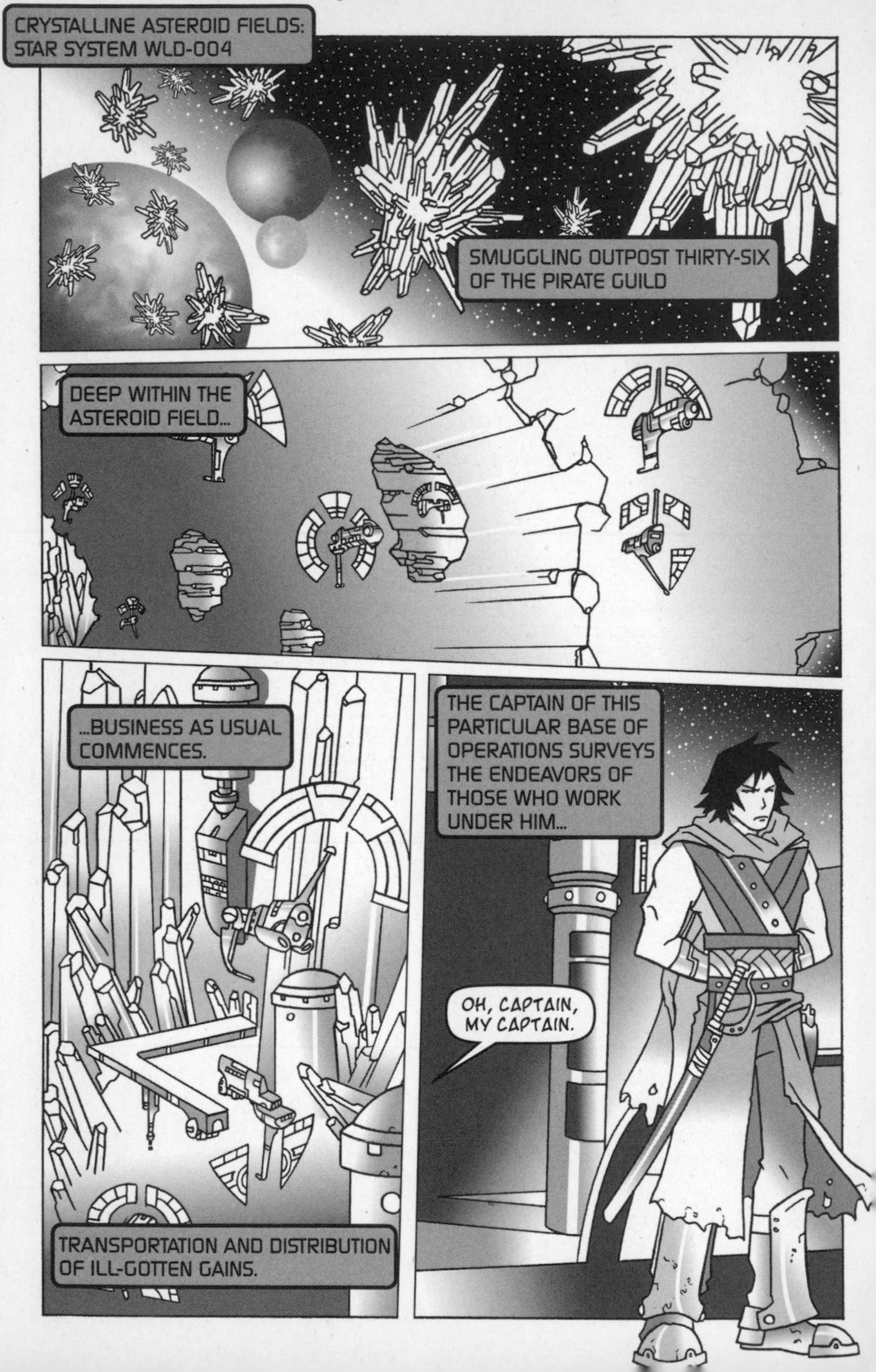
CRYSTALLINE ASTEROID FIELDS: STAR SYSTEM WLD-004
SMUGGLING OUTPOST THIRTY-SIX OF THE PIRATE GUILD
DEEP WITHIN THE ASTEROID FIELD...
...BUSINESS AS USUAL COMMENCES.
TRANSPORTATION AND DISTRIBUTION OF ILL-GOTTEN GAINS.
THE CAPTAIN OF THIS PARTICULAR BASE OF OPERATIONS SURVEYS THE ENDEAVORS OF THOSE WHO WORK UNDER HIM...
OH, CAPTAIN, MY CAPTAIN.

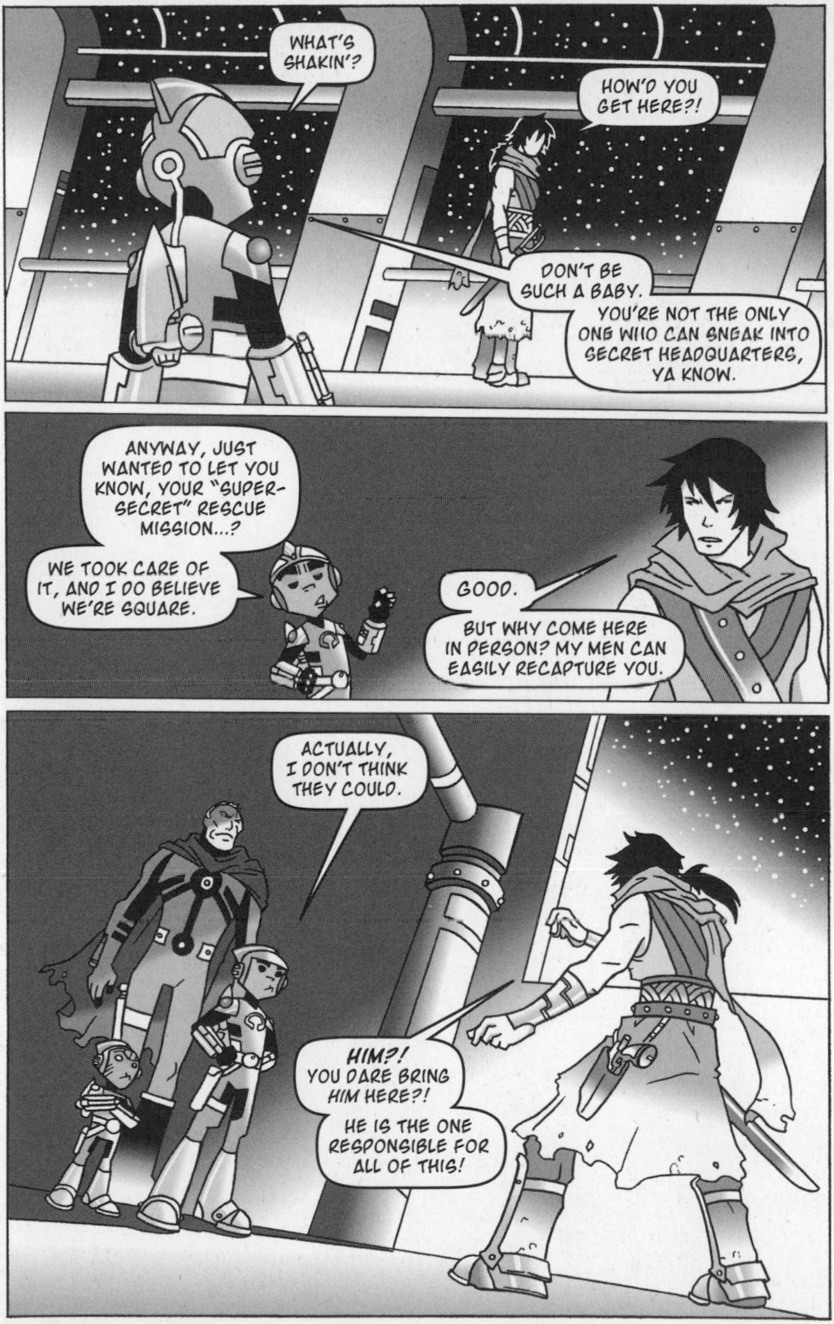
WHAT'S SHAKIN'?
HOW'D YOU GET HERE?!
DON'T BE SUCH A BABY.
YOU'RE NOT THE ONLY ONE WHO CAN SNEAK INTO SECRET HEADQUARTERS, YA KNOW.
ANYWAY, JUST WANTED TO LET YOU KNOW, YOUR "SUPER-SECRET" RESCUE MISSION...?
WE TOOK CARE OF IT, AND I DO BELIEVE WE'RE SQUARE.
GOOD.
BUT WHY COME HERE IN PERSON? MY MEN CAN EASILY RECAPTURE YOU.
ACTUALLY, I DON'T THINK THEY COULD.
HIM?! YOU DARE BRING HIM HERE?!
HE IS THE ONE RESPONSIBLE FOR ALL OF THIS!

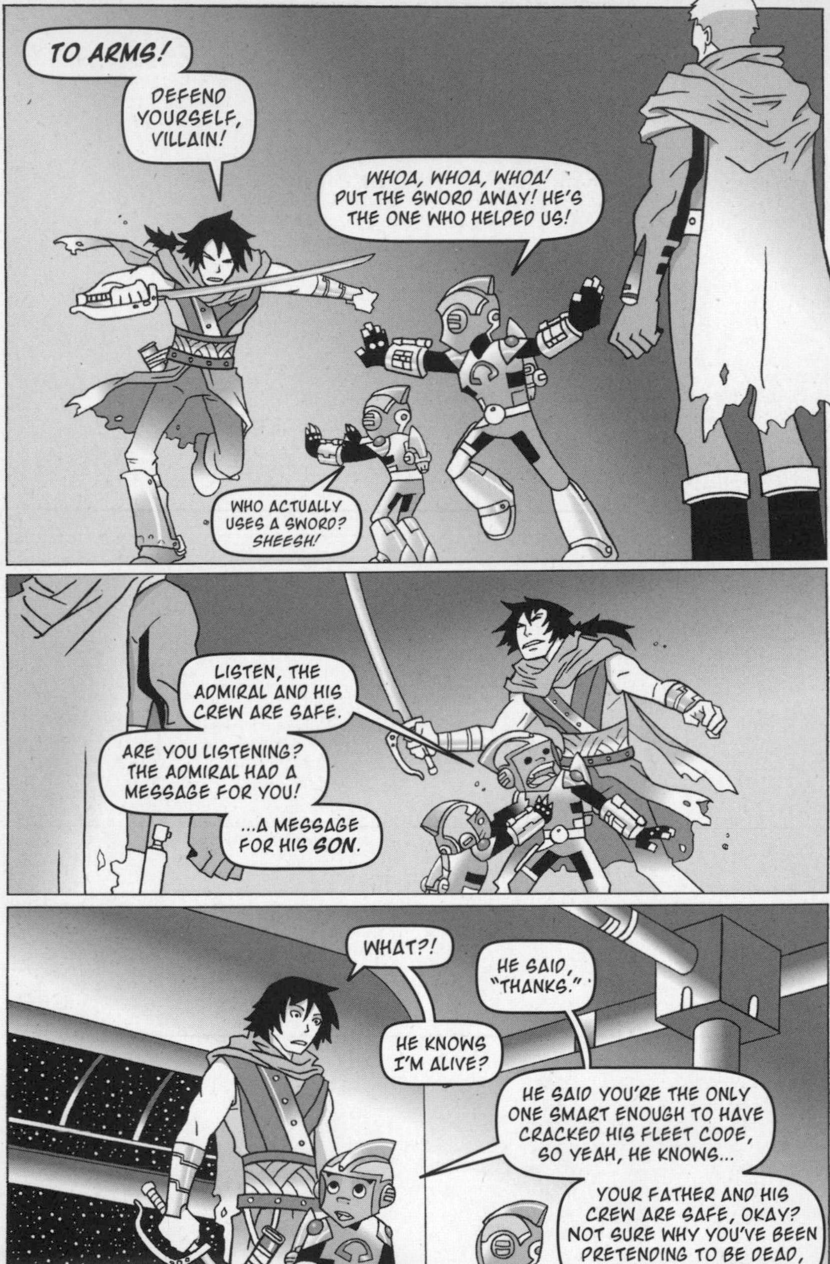
TO ARMS!
DEFEND YOURSELF, VILLAIN!
WHOA, WHOA, WHOA! PUT THE SWORD AWAY! HE'S THE ONE WHO HELPED US!
WHO ACTUALLY USES A SWORD? SHEESH!
LISTEN, THE ADMIRAL AND HIS CREW ARE SAFE.
ARE YOU LISTENING? THE ADMIRAL HAD A MESSAGE FOR YOU!
...A MESSAGE FOR HIS SON.
WHAT?!
HE SAID, "THANKS."
HE KNOWS I'M ALIVE?
HE SAID YOU'RE THE ONLY ONE SMART ENOUGH TO HAVE CRACKED HIS FLEET CODE, SO YEAH, HE KNOWS...
YOUR FATHER AND HIS CREW ARE SAFE, OKAY? NOT SURE WHY YOU'VE BEEN PRETENDING TO BE DEAD, BUT THAT'S YOUR BIZ.

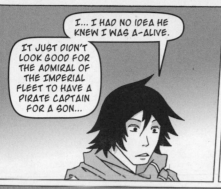

I... I HAD NO IDEA HE KNEW I WAS A-ALIVE.

IT JUST DIDN'T LOOK GOOD FOR THE ADMIRAL OF THE IMPERIAL FLEET TO HAVE A PIRATE CAPTAIN FOR A SON...

MAYBE HE KNEW IT WOULDN'T LOOK GOOD IF A PIRATE CAPTAIN HAD AN IMPERIAL ADMIRAL FOR A DAD.

LOOK, IN ANSWER TO YOUR EARLIER QUESTION, I'M HERE 'CAUSE IT'S THE RIGHT THING, AND AS A BONUS, YOU AND YOUR POP OWE ME A FAVOR.

OH, REALLY...? WHAT DO I OWE YOU FOR, NOW?

HEY, I'M PROVIDING YOU WITH YOUR VERY OWN STRIKE FORCE COMMANDER AND PERSONAL BODYGUARD!

HE KINDA NEEDS A JOB.

HE WAS FRAMED, AFTER ALL, AND DID SAVE YOUR DAD.

FINE, HE'S HIRED.

ANYTHING ELSE, YOUR PUSHINESS?

WELL, SINCE YOU ASKED...

WE KINDA NEED A RIDE BACK TO THE OFFICE!

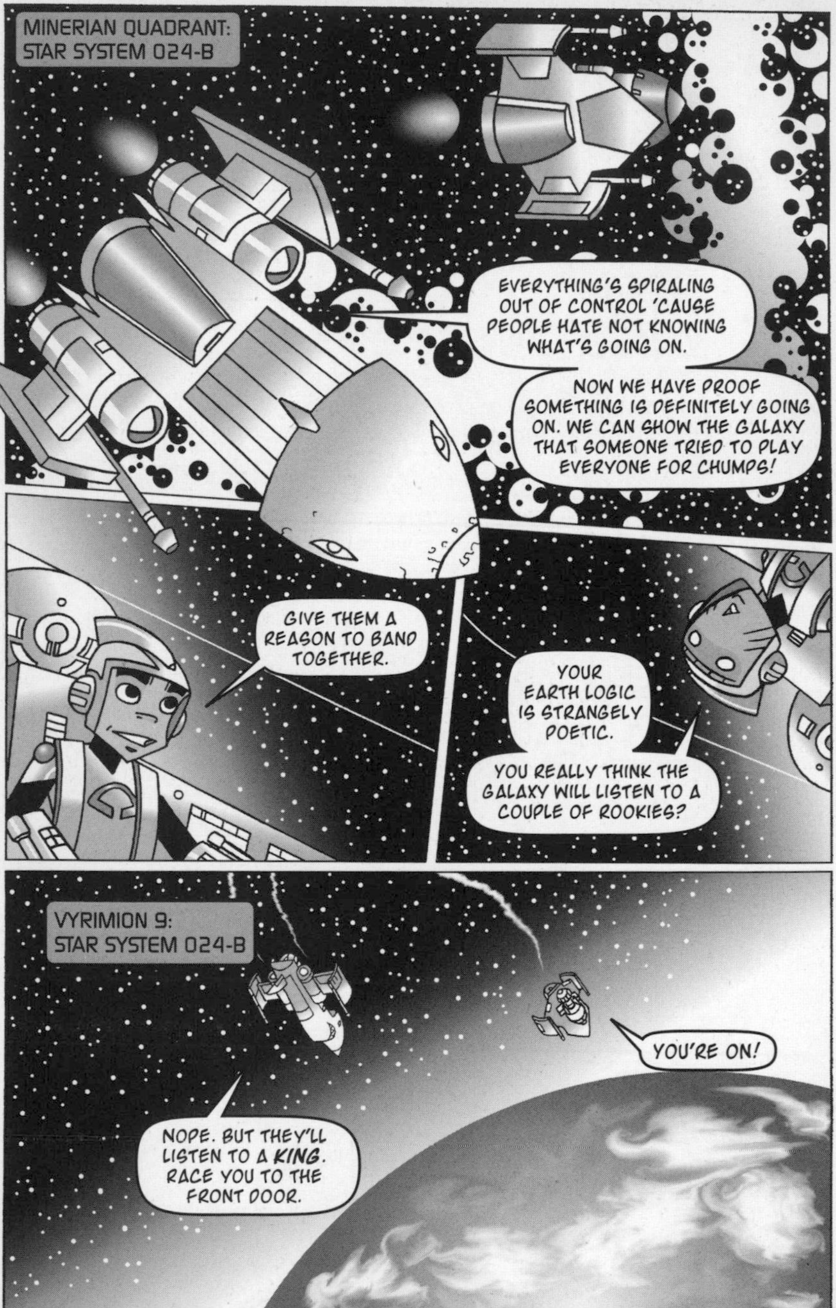
MINERIAN QUADRANT: STAR SYSTEM 024-B
EVERYTHING'S SPIRALING OUT OF CONTROL 'CAUSE PEOPLE HATE NOT KNOWING WHAT'S GOING ON.
NOW WE HAVE PROOF SOMETHING IS DEFINITELY GOING ON. WE CAN SHOW THE GALAXY THAT SOMEONE TRIED TO PLAY EVERYONE FOR CHUMPS!
GIVE THEM A REASON TO BAND TOGETHER.
YOUR EARTH LOGIC IS STRANGELY POETIC.
YOU REALLY THINK THE GALAXY WILL LISTEN TO A COUPLE OF ROOKIES?
VYRIMION 9: STAR SYSTEM 024-B
NOPE. BUT THEY'LL LISTEN TO A *KING*. RACE YOU TO THE FRONT DOOR.
YOU'RE ON!

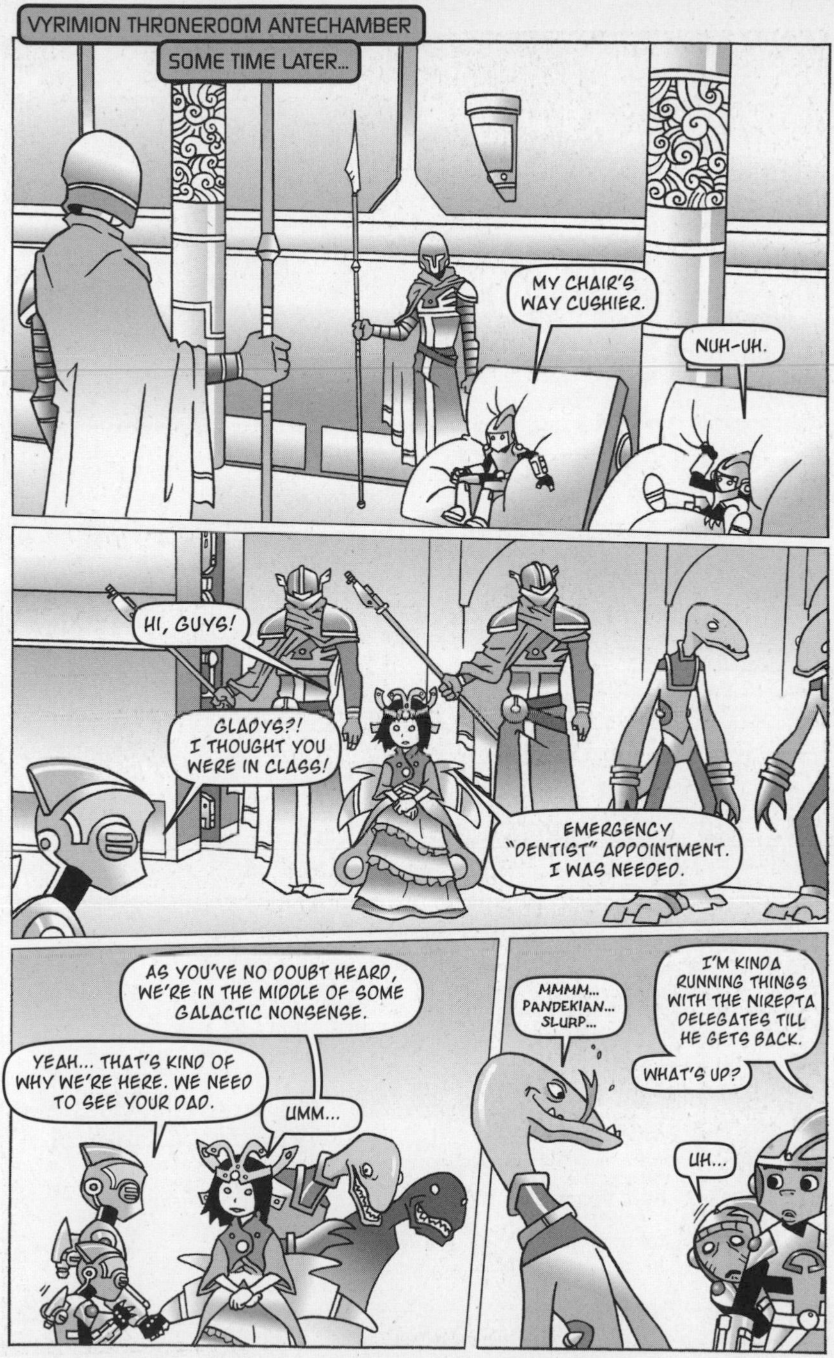
VYRIMION THRONEROOM ANTECHAMBER
SOME TIME LATER...
MY CHAIR'S WAY CUSHIER.
NUH-UH.
HI, GUYS!
GLADYS?! I THOUGHT YOU WERE IN CLASS!
EMERGENCY "DENTIST" APPOINTMENT. I WAS NEEDED.
AS YOU'VE NO DOUBT HEARD, WE'RE IN THE MIDDLE OF SOME GALACTIC NONSENSE.
YEAH... THAT'S KIND OF WHY WE'RE HERE. WE NEED TO SEE YOUR DAD.
UMM...
MMMM... PANDEKIAN... SLURP...
I'M KINDA RUNNING THINGS WITH THE NIREPTA DELEGATES TILL HE GETS BACK.
WHAT'S UP?
UH...

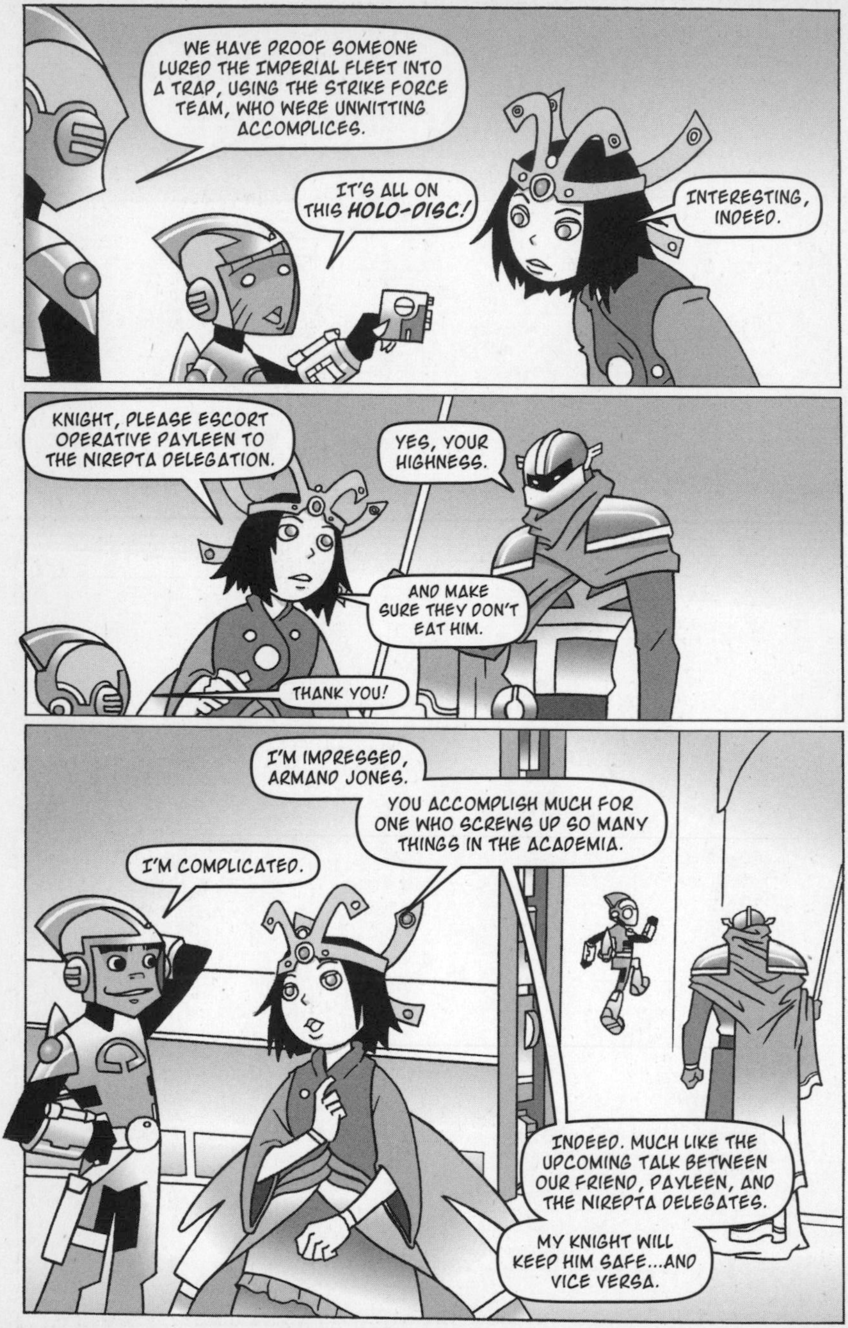
WE HAVE PROOF SOMEONE LURED THE IMPERIAL FLEET INTO A TRAP, USING THE STRIKE FORCE TEAM, WHO WERE UNWITTING ACCOMPLICES.
IT'S ALL ON THIS HOLO-DISC!
INTERESTING, INDEED.
KNIGHT, PLEASE ESCORT OPERATIVE PAYLEEN TO THE NIREPTA DELEGATION.
YES, YOUR HIGHNESS.
AND MAKE SURE THEY DON'T EAT HIM.
THANK YOU!
I'M IMPRESSED, ARMAND JONES.
YOU ACCOMPLISH MUCH FOR ONE WHO SCREWS UP SO MANY THINGS IN THE ACADEMIA.
I'M COMPLICATED.
INDEED. MUCH LIKE THE UPCOMING TALK BETWEEN OUR FRIEND, PAYLEEN, AND THE NIREPTA DELEGATES.
MY KNIGHT WILL KEEP HIM SAFE...AND VICE VERSA.

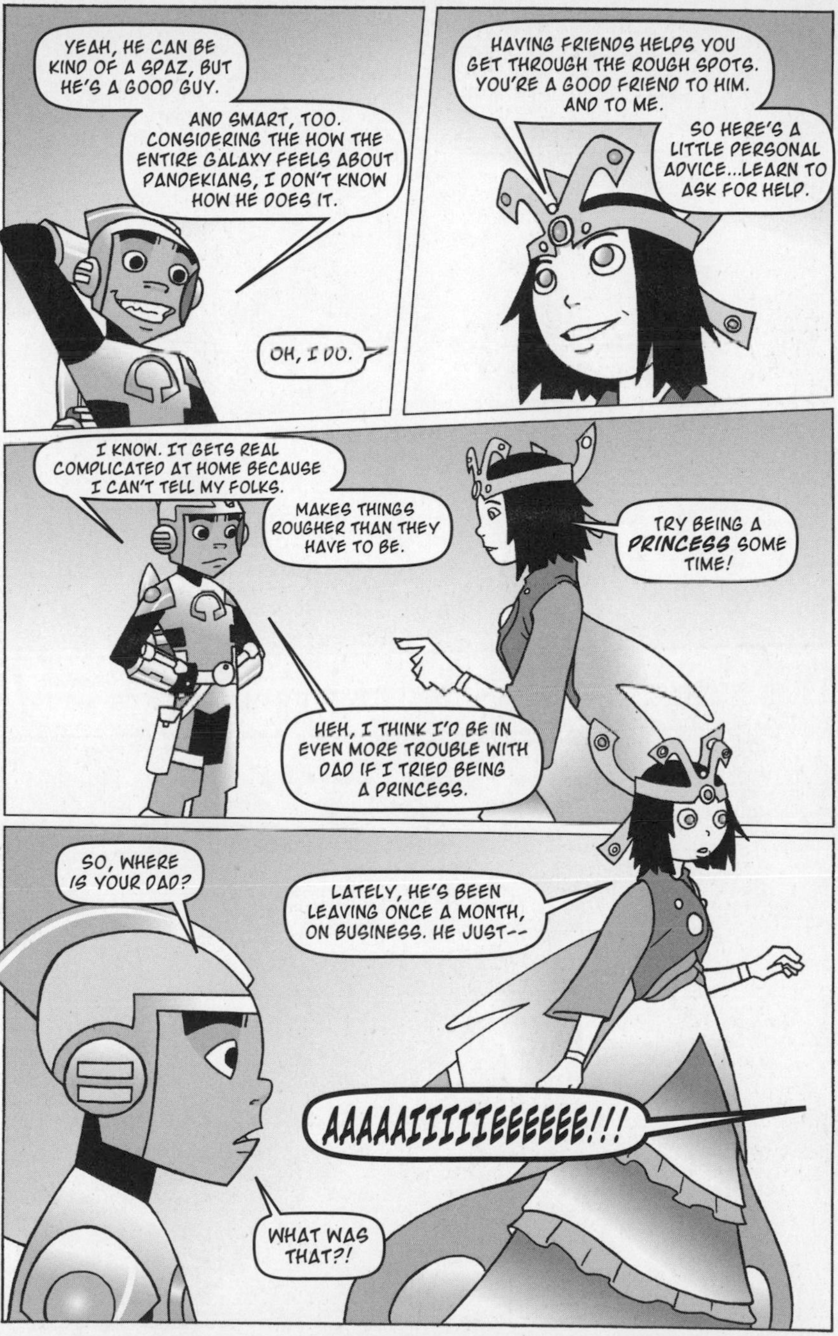
YEAH, HE CAN BE KIND OF A SPAZ, BUT HE'S A GOOD GUY.
AND SMART, TOO. CONSIDERING THE HOW THE ENTIRE GALAXY FEELS ABOUT PANDEKIANS, I DON'T KNOW HOW HE DOES IT.
OH, I DO.
HAVING FRIENDS HELPS YOU GET THROUGH THE ROUGH SPOTS. YOU'RE A GOOD FRIEND TO HIM. AND TO ME.
SO HERE'S A LITTLE PERSONAL ADVICE...LEARN TO ASK FOR HELP.
I KNOW. IT GETS REAL COMPLICATED AT HOME BECAUSE I CAN'T TELL MY FOLKS.
MAKES THINGS ROUGHER THAN THEY HAVE TO BE.
TRY BEING A PRINCESS SOME TIME!
HEH, I THINK I'D BE IN EVEN MORE TROUBLE WITH DAD IF I TRIED BEING A PRINCESS.
SO, WHERE IS YOUR DAD?
LATELY, HE'S BEEN LEAVING ONCE A MONTH, ON BUSINESS. HE JUST--
AAAAAIIIIIEEEEEEE!!!
WHAT WAS THAT?!

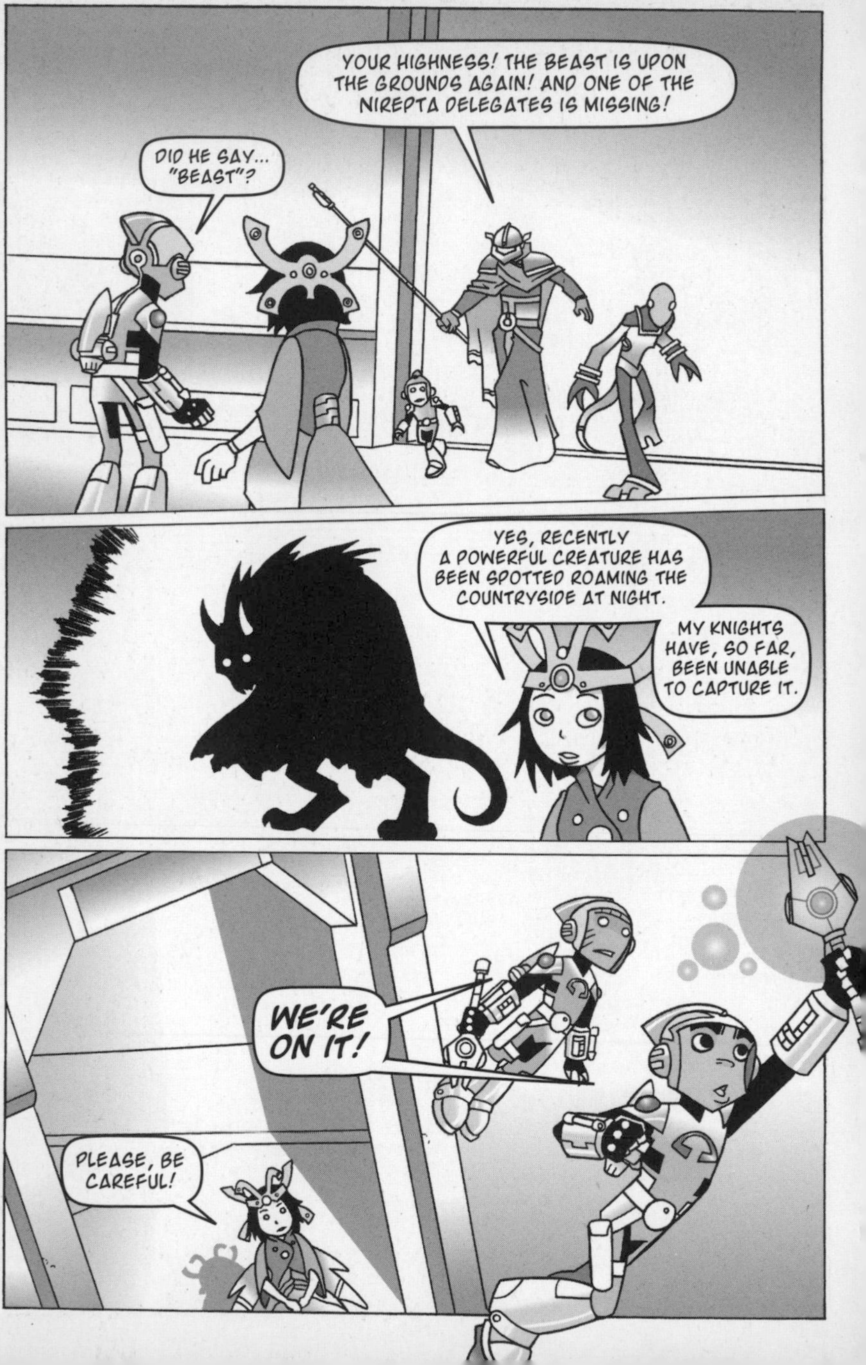
DID HE SAY... "BEAST"?
YOUR HIGHNESS! THE BEAST IS UPON THE GROUNDS AGAIN! AND ONE OF THE NIREPTA DELEGATES IS MISSING!
YES, RECENTLY A POWERFUL CREATURE HAS BEEN SPOTTED ROAMING THE COUNTRYSIDE AT NIGHT.
MY KNIGHTS HAVE, SO FAR, BEEN UNABLE TO CAPTURE IT.
WE'RE ON IT!
PLEASE, BE CAREFUL!

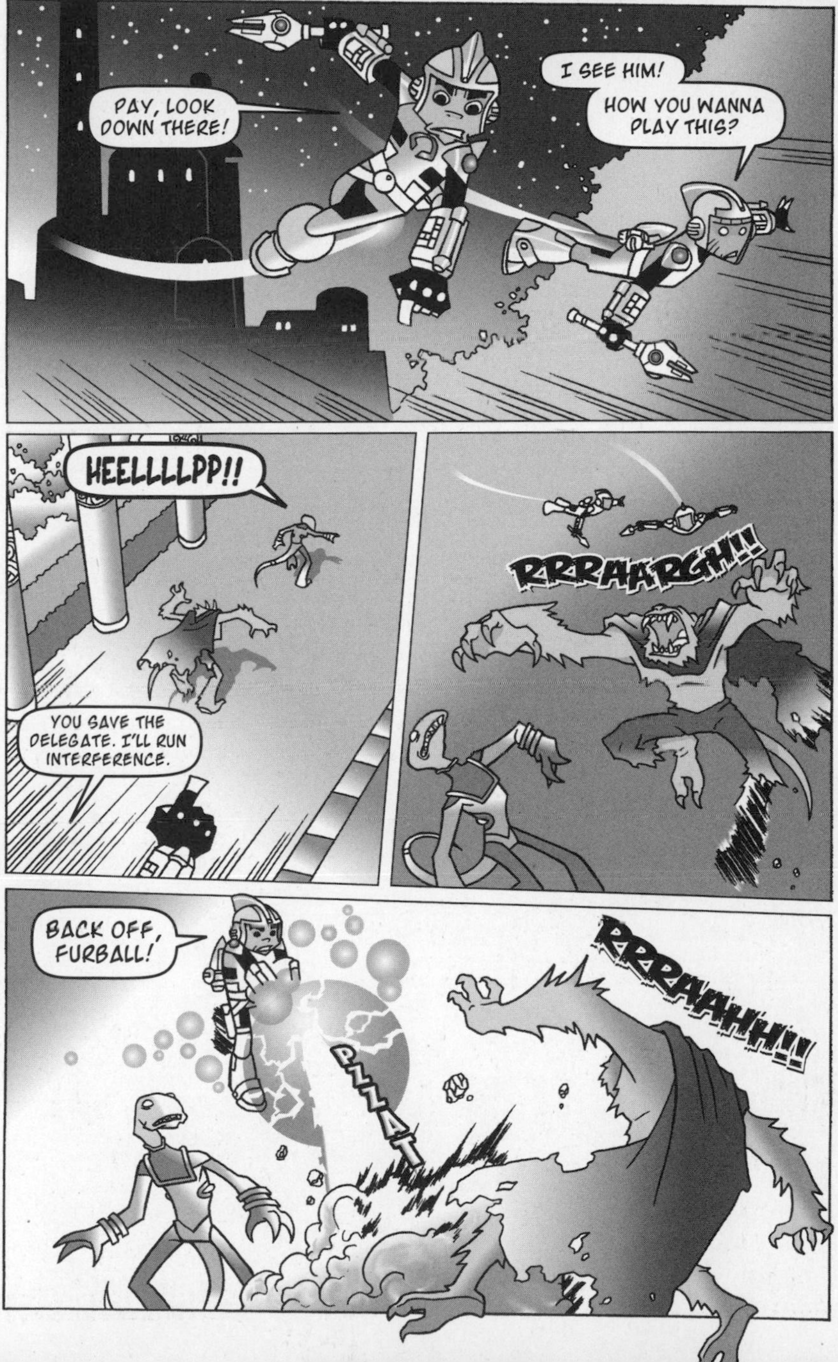
PAY, LOOK DOWN THERE!
I SEE HIM!
HOW YOU WANNA PLAY THIS?
HEELLLLPP!!
YOU SAVE THE DELEGATE. I'LL RUN INTERFERENCE.
RRRAARGH!!
BACK OFF, FURBALL!
PZZAT
RRRAAAHHH!!

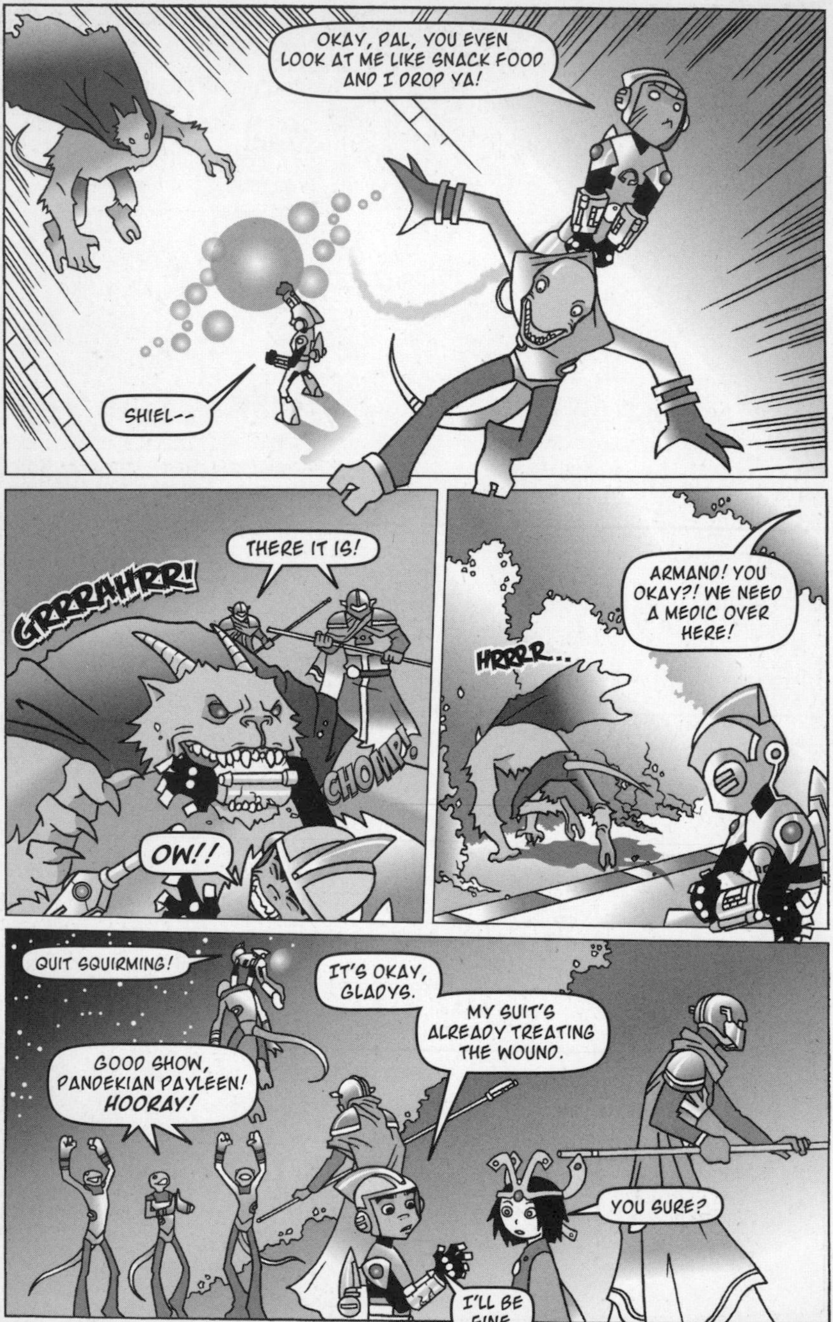
OKAY, PAL, YOU EVEN LOOK AT ME LIKE SNACK FOOD AND I DROP YA!
SHIEL--
THERE IT IS!
GRRRAHRR!
CHOMP!
OW!!
ARMAND! YOU OKAY?! WE NEED A MEDIC OVER HERE!
HRRRR...
QUIT SQUIRMING!
IT'S OKAY, GLADYS.
MY SUIT'S ALREADY TREATING THE WOUND.
GOOD SHOW, PANDEKIAN PAYLEEN! HOORAY!
YOU SURE?
I'LL BE FINE.

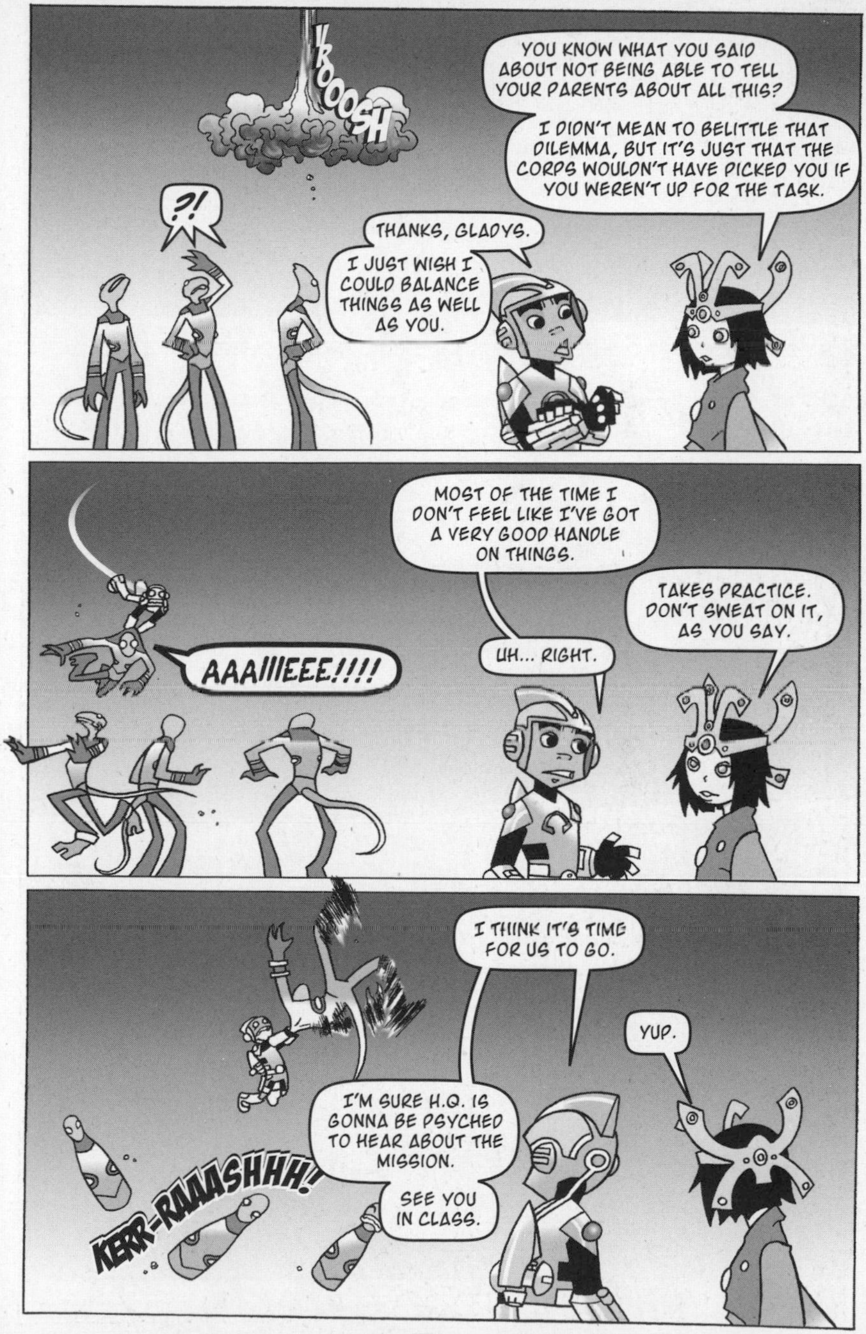
VROOOSH
YOU KNOW WHAT YOU SAID ABOUT NOT BEING ABLE TO TELL YOUR PARENTS ABOUT ALL THIS?
I DIDN'T MEAN TO BELITTLE THAT DILEMMA, BUT IT'S JUST THAT THE CORPS WOULDN'T HAVE PICKED YOU IF YOU WEREN'T UP FOR THE TASK.
?!
THANKS, GLADYS.
I JUST WISH I COULD BALANCE THINGS AS WELL AS YOU.
MOST OF THE TIME I DON'T FEEL LIKE I'VE GOT A VERY GOOD HANDLE ON THINGS.
TAKES PRACTICE. DON'T SWEAT ON IT, AS YOU SAY.
AAAIIIEEE!!!!
UH... RIGHT.
I THINK IT'S TIME FOR US TO GO.
YUP.
I'M SURE H.Q. IS GONNA BE PSYCHED TO HEAR ABOUT THE MISSION.
SEE YOU IN CLASS.
KERR-RAAASHHH!

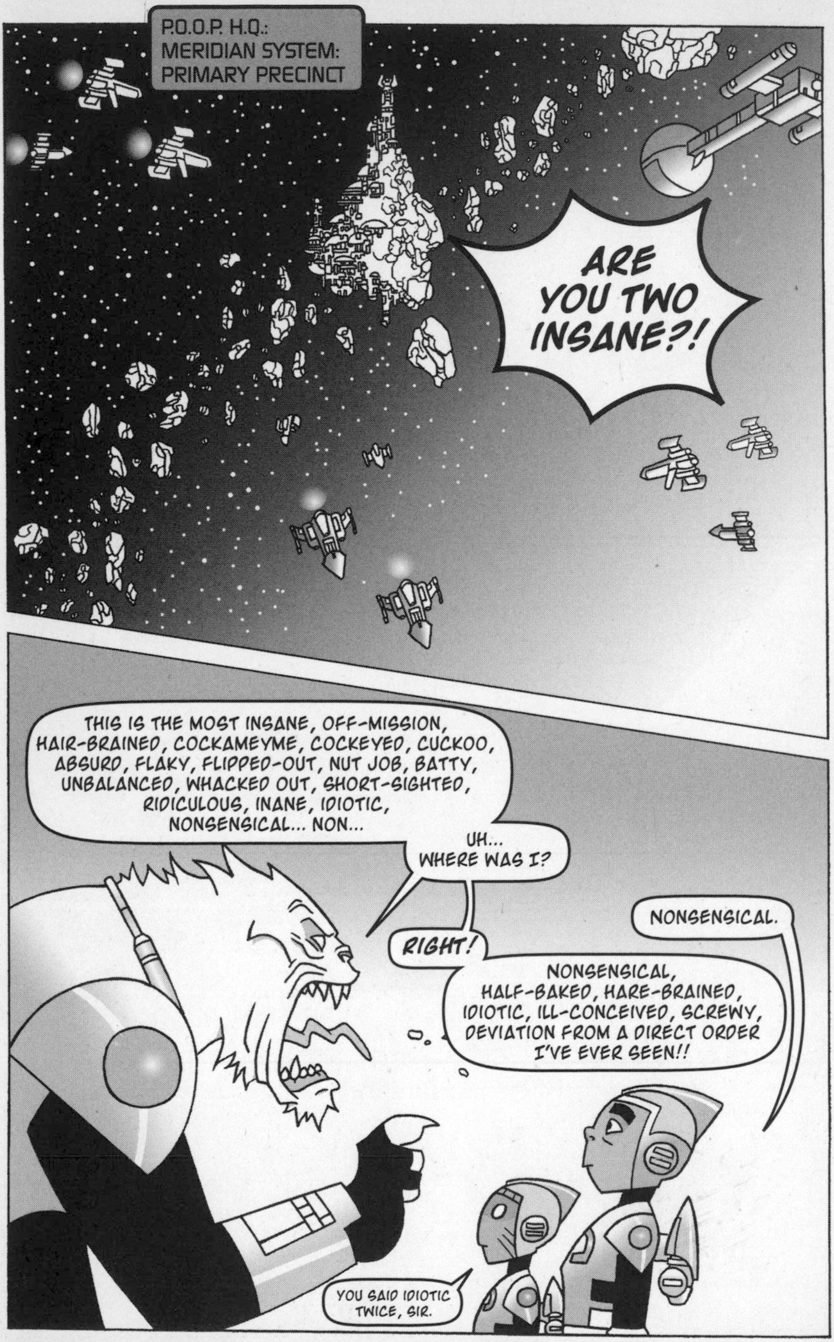
P.O.O.P. H.Q.: MERIDIAN SYSTEM: PRIMARY PRECINCT
ARE YOU TWO INSANE?!
THIS IS THE MOST INSANE, OFF-MISSION, HAIR-BRAINED, COCKAMEYME, COCKEYED, CUCKOO, ABSURD, FLAKY, FLIPPED-OUT, NUT JOB, BATTY, UNBALANCED, WHACKED OUT, SHORT-SIGHTED, RIDICULOUS, INANE, IDIOTIC, NONSENSICAL... NON...
UH... WHERE WAS I?
NONSENSICAL.
RIGHT!
NONSENSICAL, HALF-BAKED, HARE-BRAINED, IDIOTIC, ILL-CONCEIVED, SCREWY, DEVIATION FROM A DIRECT ORDER I'VE EVER SEEN!!
YOU SAID IDIOTIC TWICE, SIR.

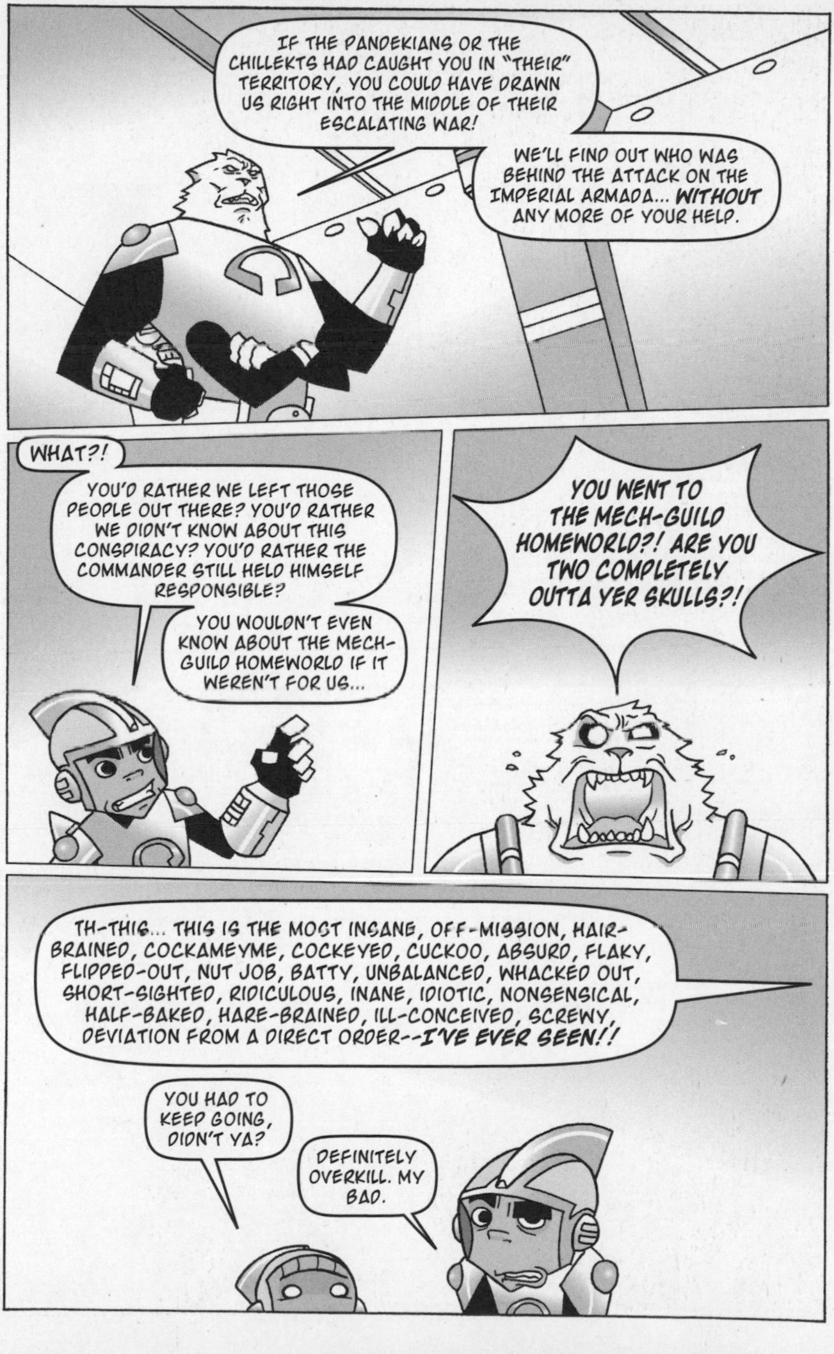
IF THE PANDEKIANS OR THE CHILLEKTS HAD CAUGHT YOU IN "THEIR" TERRITORY, YOU COULD HAVE DRAWN US RIGHT INTO THE MIDDLE OF THEIR ESCALATING WAR!
WE'LL FIND OUT WHO WAS BEHIND THE ATTACK ON THE IMPERIAL ARMADA... **WITHOUT** ANY MORE OF YOUR HELP.
WHAT?!
YOU'D RATHER WE LEFT THOSE PEOPLE OUT THERE? YOU'D RATHER WE DIDN'T KNOW ABOUT THIS CONSPIRACY? YOU'D RATHER THE COMMANDER STILL HELD HIMSELF RESPONSIBLE?
YOU WOULDN'T EVEN KNOW ABOUT THE MECH-GUILD HOMEWORLD IF IT WEREN'T FOR US...
YOU WENT TO THE MECH-GUILD HOMEWORLD?! ARE YOU TWO COMPLETELY OUTTA YER SKULLS?!
TH-THIS... THIS IS THE MOST INSANE, OFF-MISSION, HAIR-BRAINED, COCKAMEYME, COCKEYED, CUCKOO, ABSURD, FLAKY, FLIPPED-OUT, NUT JOB, BATTY, UNBALANCED, WHACKED OUT, SHORT-SIGHTED, RIDICULOUS, INANE, IDIOTIC, NONSENSICAL, HALF-BAKED, HARE-BRAINED, ILL-CONCEIVED, SCREWY, DEVIATION FROM A DIRECT ORDER--***I'VE EVER SEEN!!***
YOU HAD TO KEEP GOING, DIDN'T YA?
DEFINITELY OVERKILL. MY BAD.

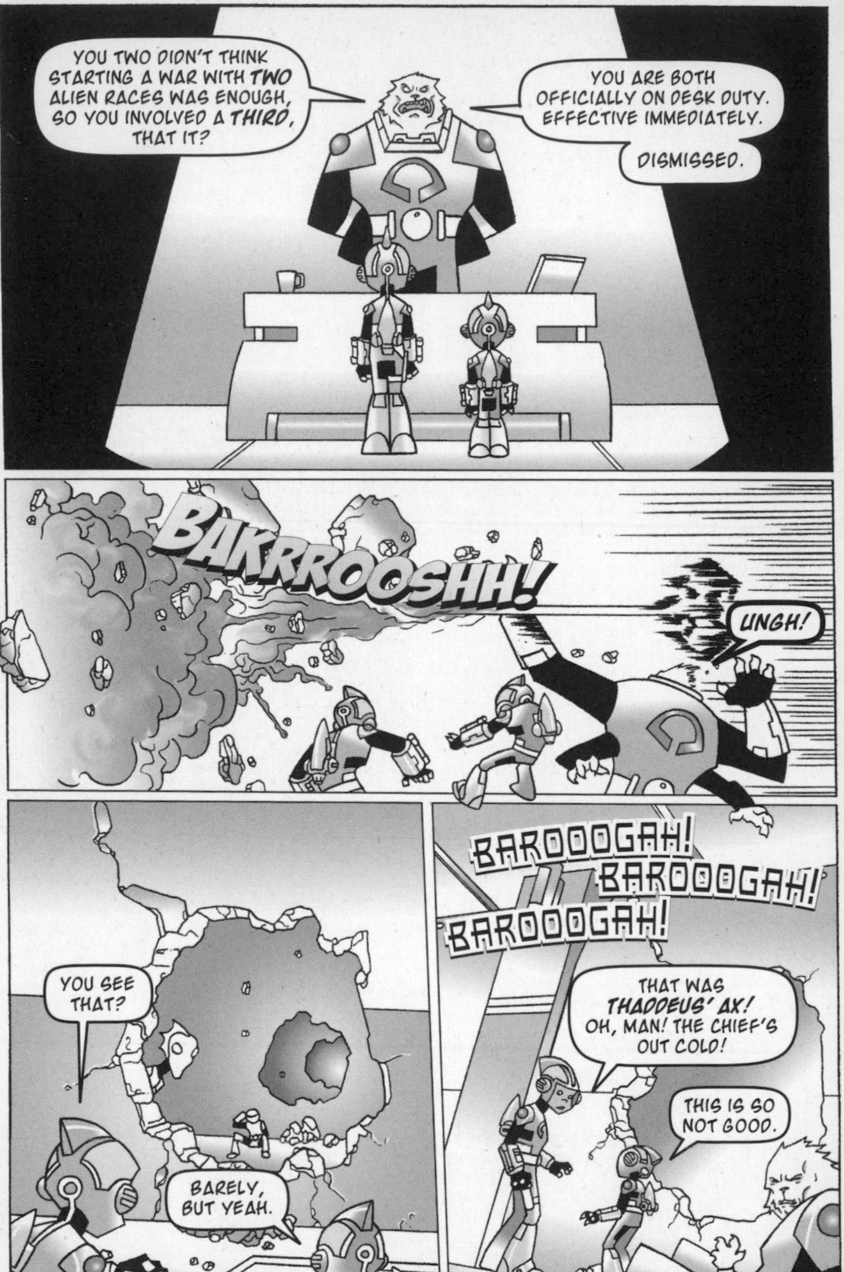
YOU TWO DIDN'T THINK STARTING A WAR WITH **TWO** ALIEN RACES WAS ENOUGH, SO YOU INVOLVED A **THIRD**, THAT IT?
YOU ARE BOTH OFFICIALLY ON DESK DUTY. EFFECTIVE IMMEDIATELY.
DISMISSED.
BAKRROOSHH!
UNGH!
YOU SEE THAT?
BARELY, BUT YEAH.
BAROOOGAH! BAROOOGAH! BAROOOGAH!
THAT WAS **THADDEUS' AX!** OH, MAN! THE CHIEF'S OUT COLD!
THIS IS SO NOT GOOD.

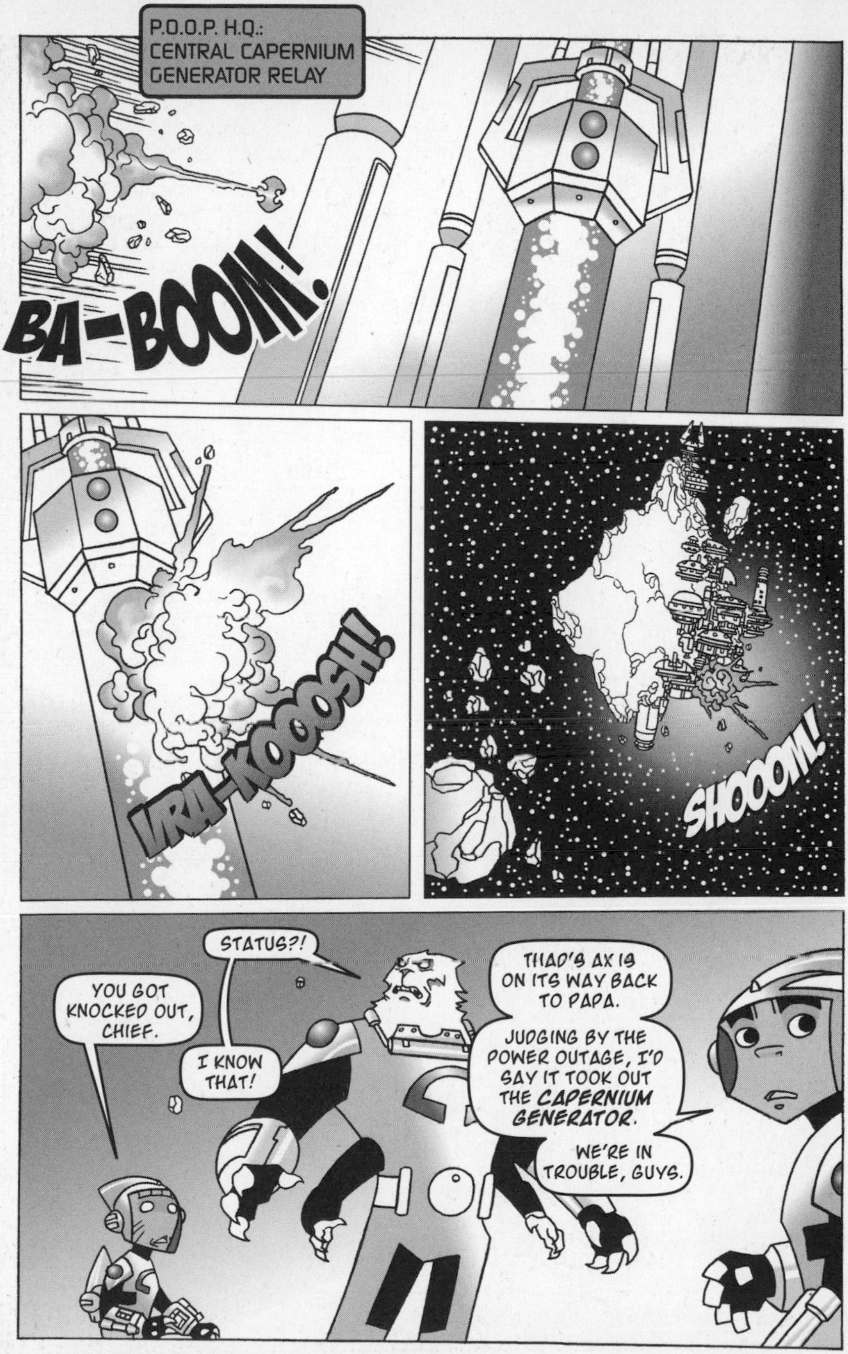
P.O.O.P. H.Q.:
CENTRAL CAPERNIUM
GENERATOR RELAY
BA-BOOM!
VRA-KOOOSH!
SHOOOM!
STATUS?!
YOU GOT KNOCKED OUT, CHIEF.
I KNOW THAT!
THAD'S AX IS ON ITS WAY BACK TO PAPA.
JUDGING BY THE POWER OUTAGE, I'D SAY IT TOOK OUT THE CAPERNIUM GENERATOR.
WE'RE IN TROUBLE, GUYS.

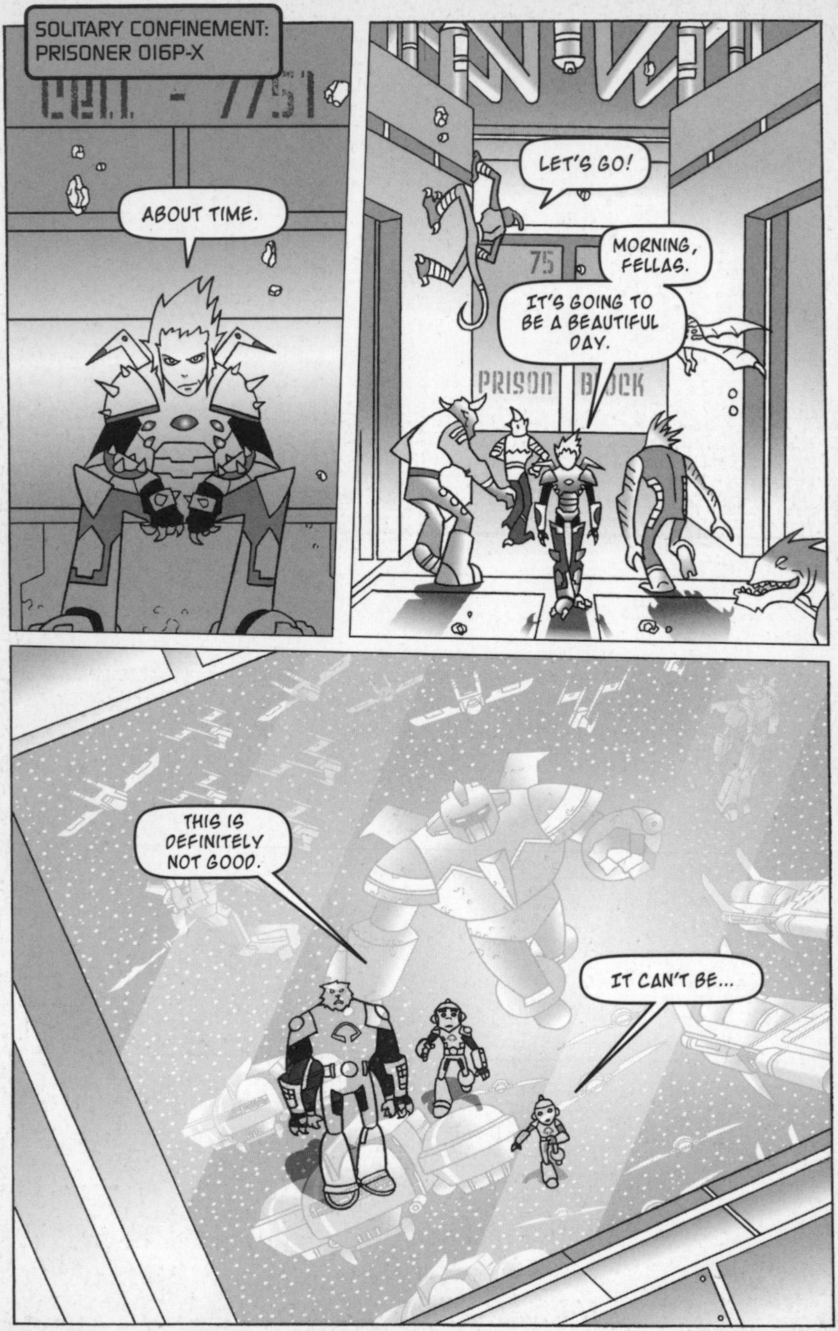
SOLITARY CONFINEMENT: PRISONER 016P-X
ABOUT TIME.
LET'S GO!
MORNING, FELLAS.
IT'S GOING TO BE A BEAUTIFUL DAY.
THIS IS DEFINITELY NOT GOOD.
IT CAN'T BE...

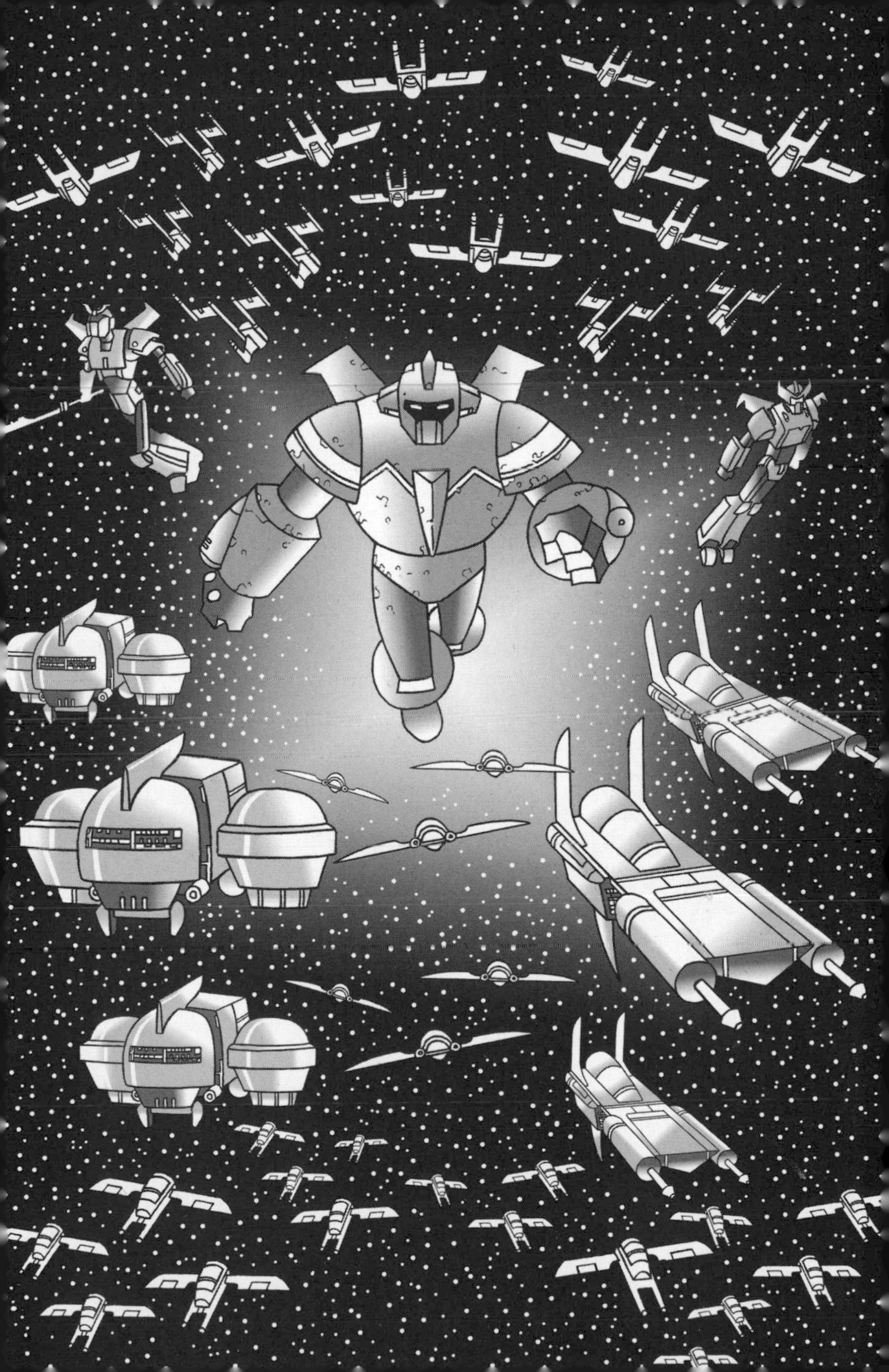

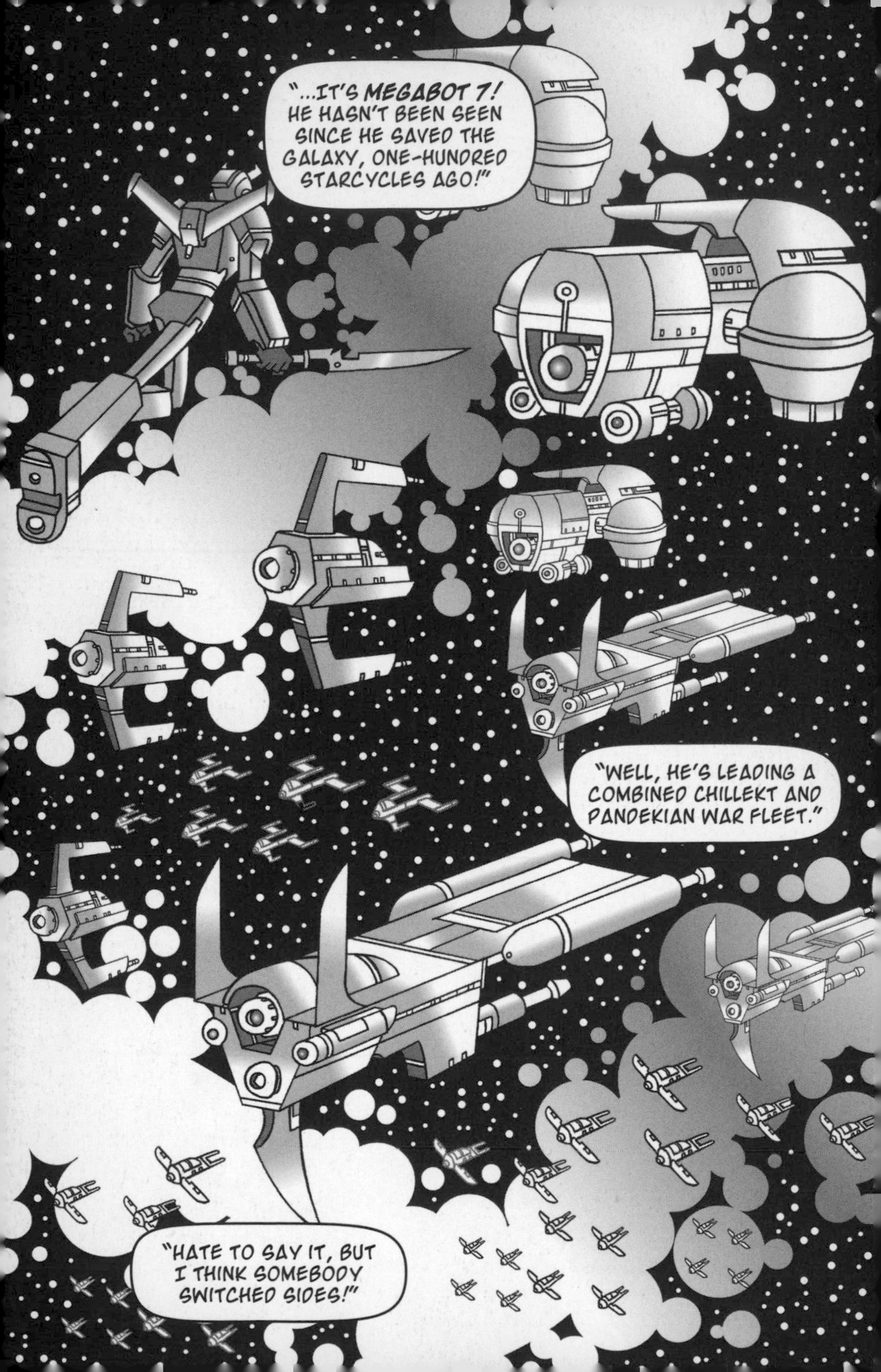
"...IT'S MEGABOT 7! HE HASN'T BEEN SEEN SINCE HE SAVED THE GALAXY, ONE-HUNDRED STARCYCLES AGO!"
"WELL, HE'S LEADING A COMBINED CHILLEKT AND PANDEKIAN WAR FLEET."
"HATE TO SAY IT, BUT I THINK SOMEBODY SWITCHED SIDES!"

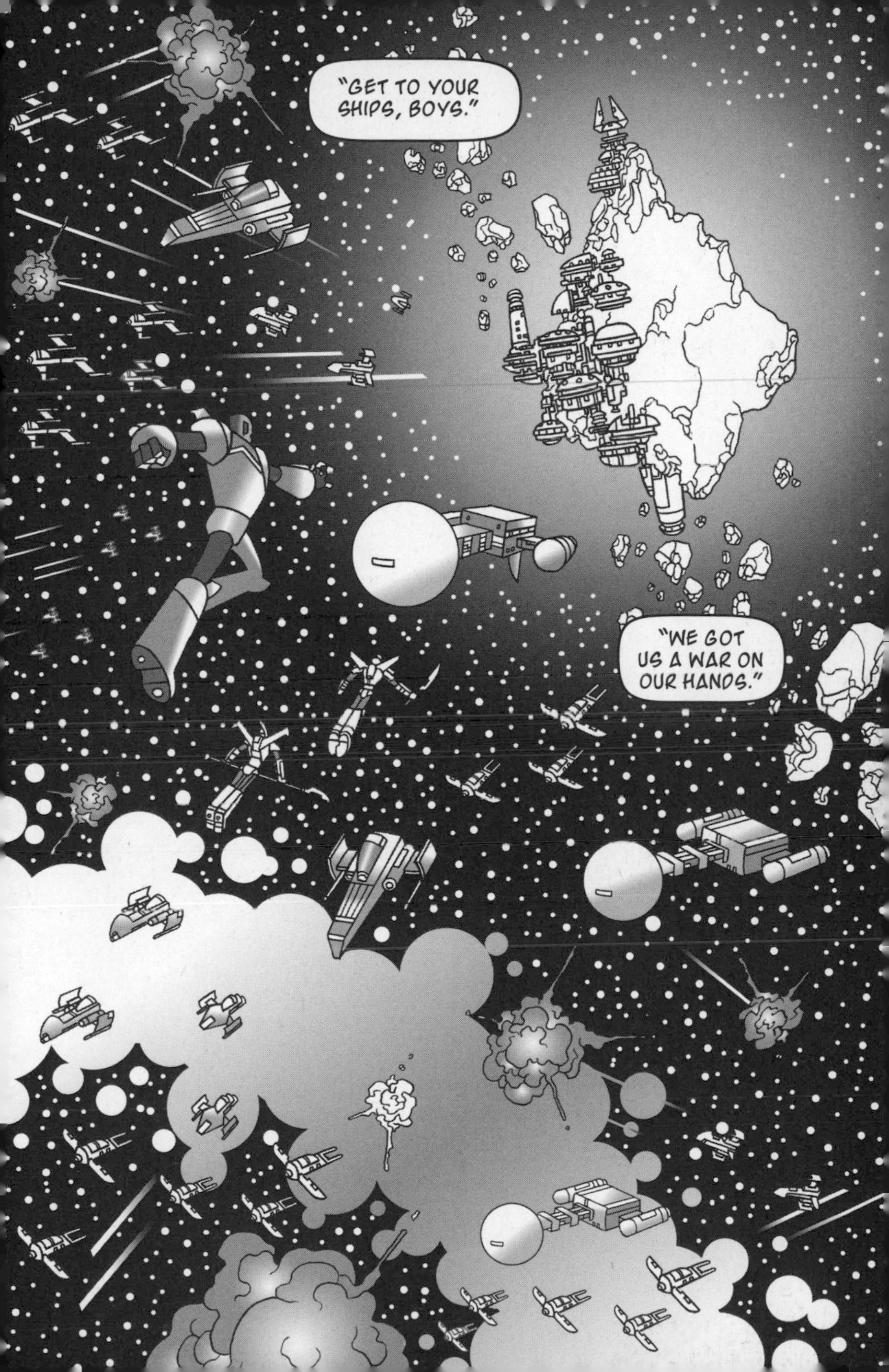
"GET TO YOUR SHIPS, BOYS."
"WE GOT US A WAR ON OUR HANDS."

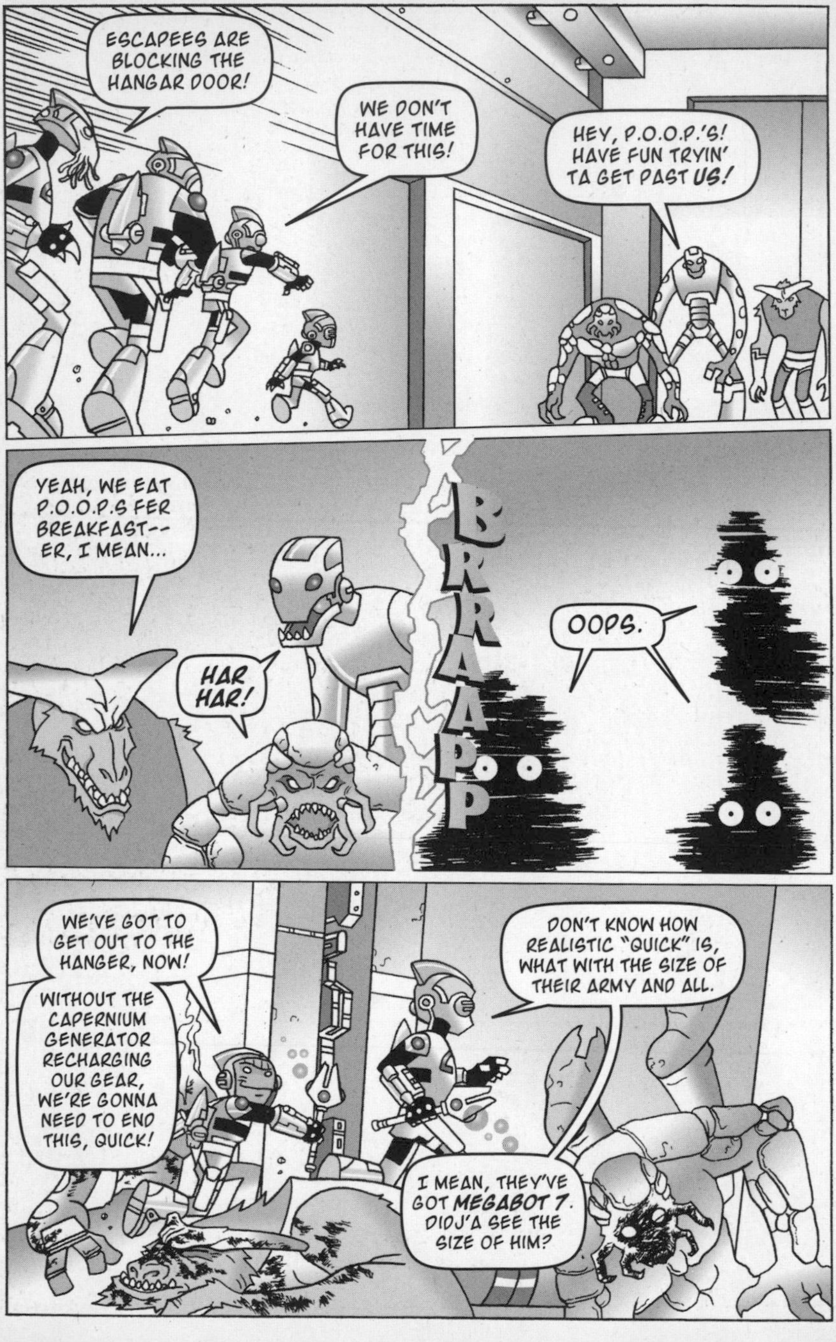
ESCAPEES ARE BLOCKING THE HANGAR DOOR!
WE DON'T HAVE TIME FOR THIS!
HEY, P.O.O.P.'S! HAVE FUN TRYIN' TA GET PAST **US**!
YEAH, WE EAT P.O.O.P.S FER BREAKFAST-- ER, I MEAN...
HAR HAR!
BRRAAPP
OOPS.
WE'VE GOT TO GET OUT TO THE HANGER, NOW!
WITHOUT THE CAPERNIUM GENERATOR RECHARGING OUR GEAR, WE'RE GONNA NEED TO END THIS, QUICK!
DON'T KNOW HOW REALISTIC "QUICK" IS, WHAT WITH THE SIZE OF THEIR ARMY AND ALL.
I MEAN, THEY'VE GOT **MEGABOT 7**. DIDJ'A SEE THE SIZE OF HIM?

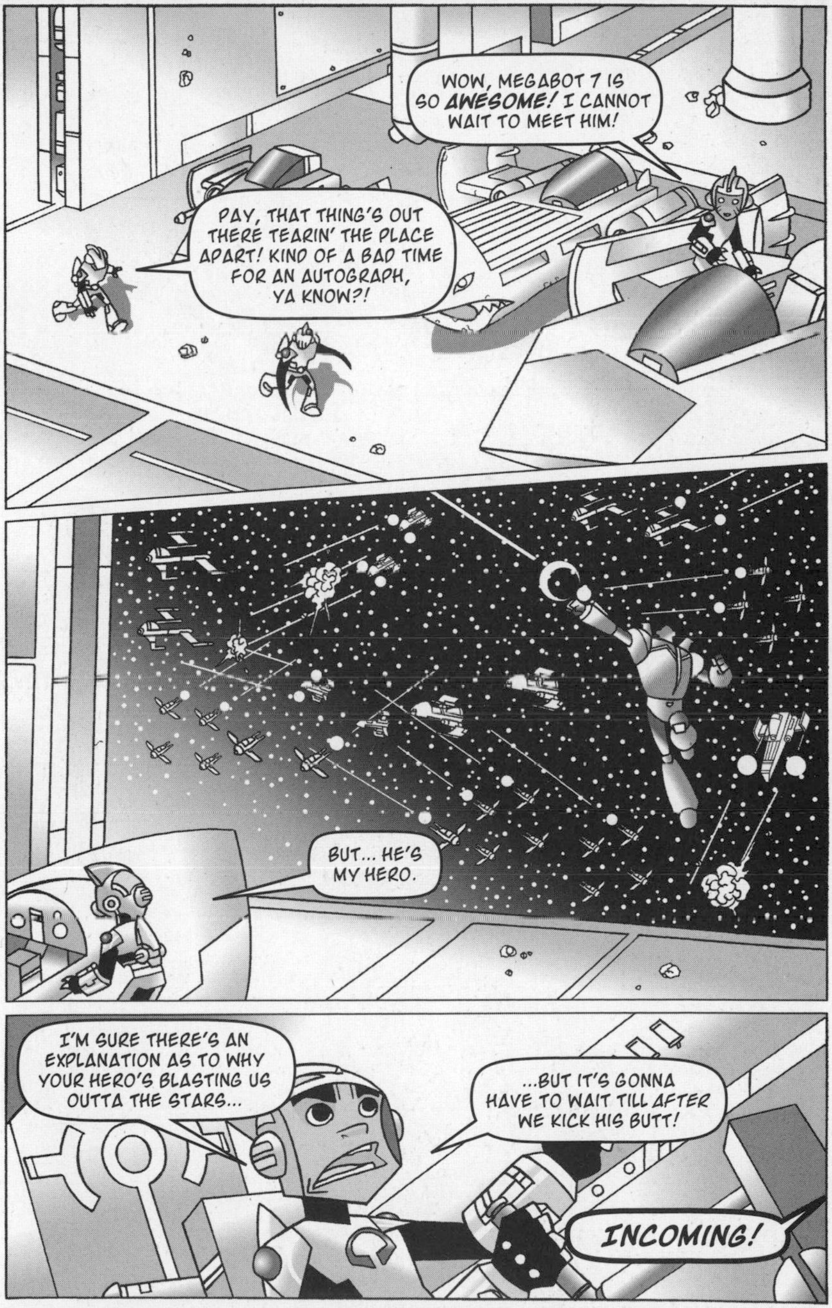
WOW, MEGABOT 7 IS SO AWESOME! I CANNOT WAIT TO MEET HIM!
PAY, THAT THING'S OUT THERE TEARIN' THE PLACE APART! KIND OF A BAD TIME FOR AN AUTOGRAPH, YA KNOW?!
BUT... HE'S MY HERO.
I'M SURE THERE'S AN EXPLANATION AS TO WHY YOUR HERO'S BLASTING US OUTTA THE STARS...
...BUT IT'S GONNA HAVE TO WAIT TILL AFTER WE KICK HIS BUTT!
INCOMING!

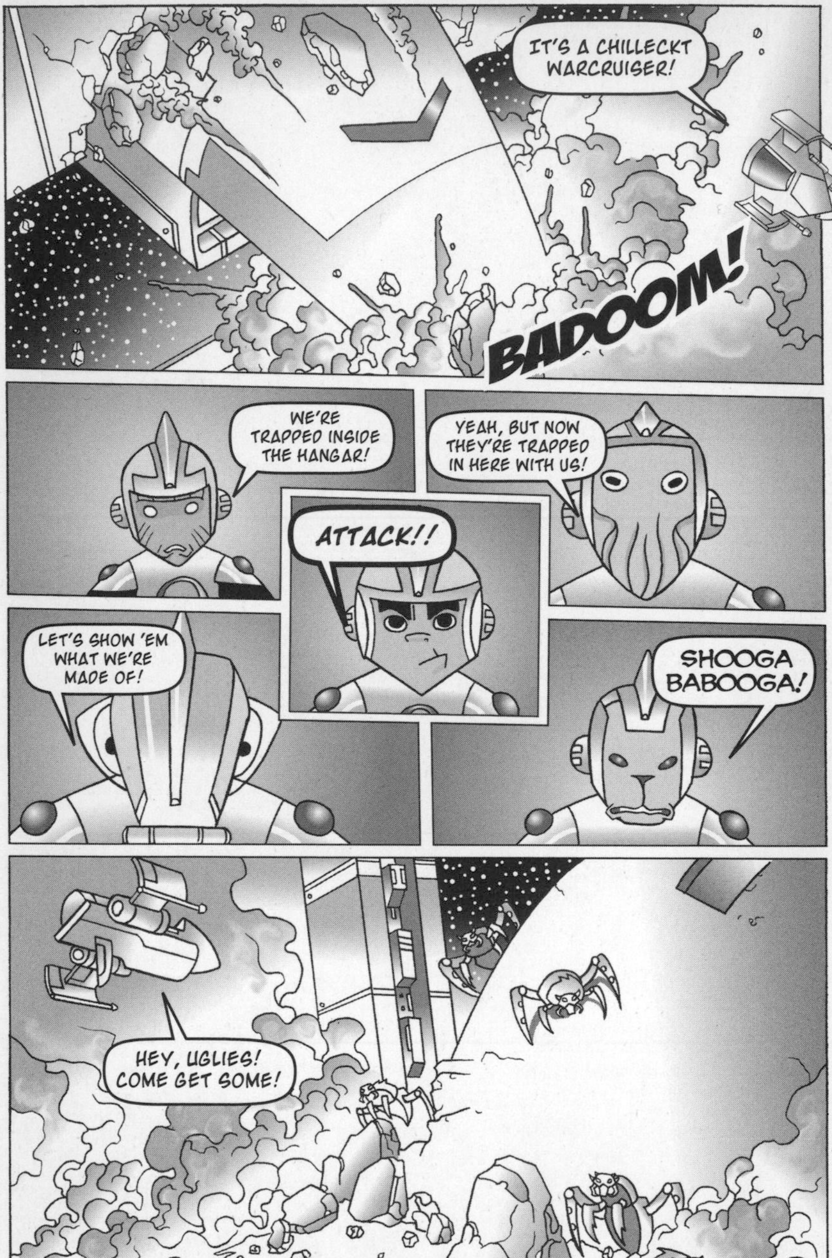
IT'S A CHILLECKT WARCRUISER!
BADOOM!
WE'RE TRAPPED INSIDE THE HANGAR!
YEAH, BUT NOW THEY'RE TRAPPED IN HERE WITH US!
ATTACK!!
LET'S SHOW 'EM WHAT WE'RE MADE OF!
SHOOGA BABOOGA!
HEY, UGLIES! COME GET SOME!

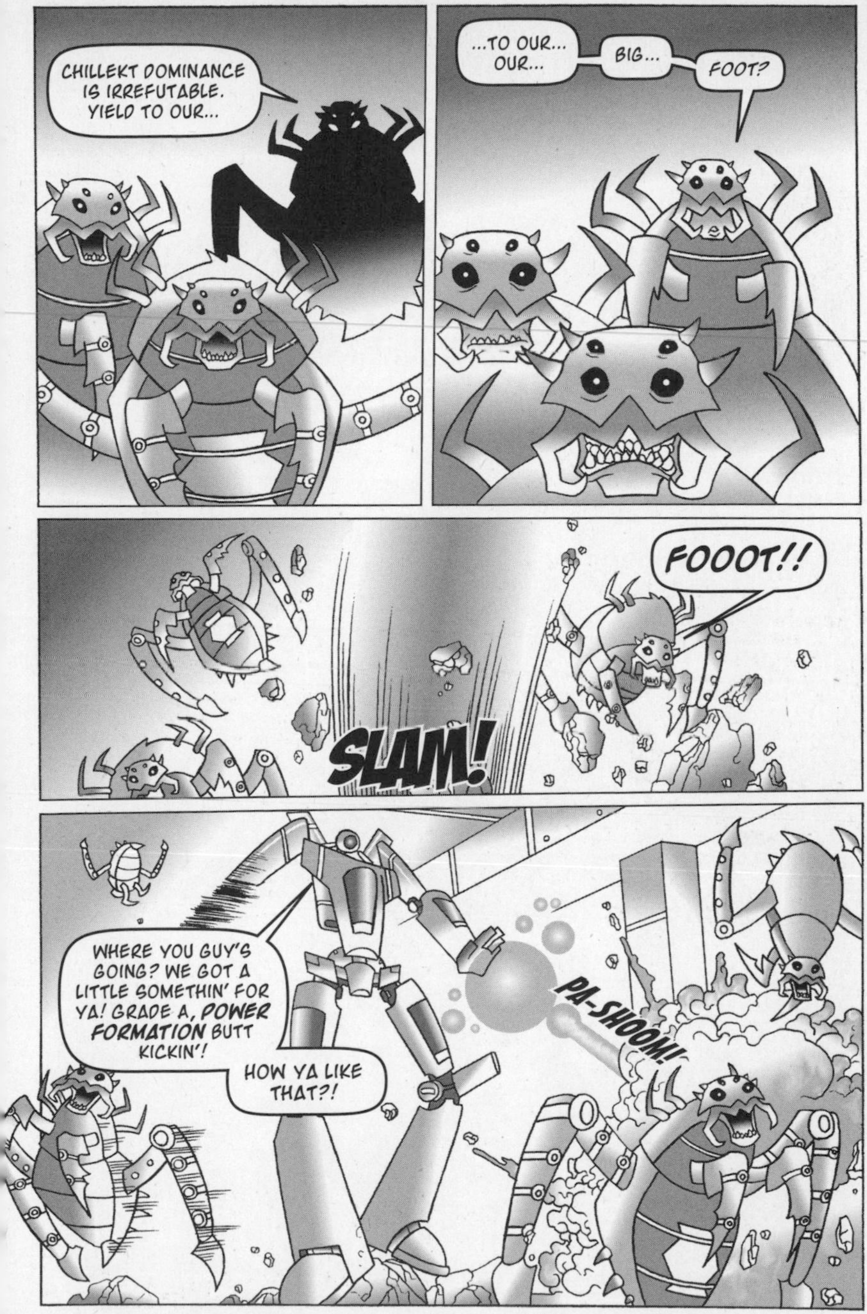
CHILLEKT DOMINANCE IS IRREFUTABLE. YIELD TO OUR...
...TO OUR... OUR...
BIG...
FOOT?
FOOOT!!
SLAM!
WHERE YOU GUY'S GOING? WE GOT A LITTLE SOMETHIN' FOR YA! GRADE A, POWER FORMATION BUTT KICKIN'!
HOW YA LIKE THAT?!
PA-SHOOM!

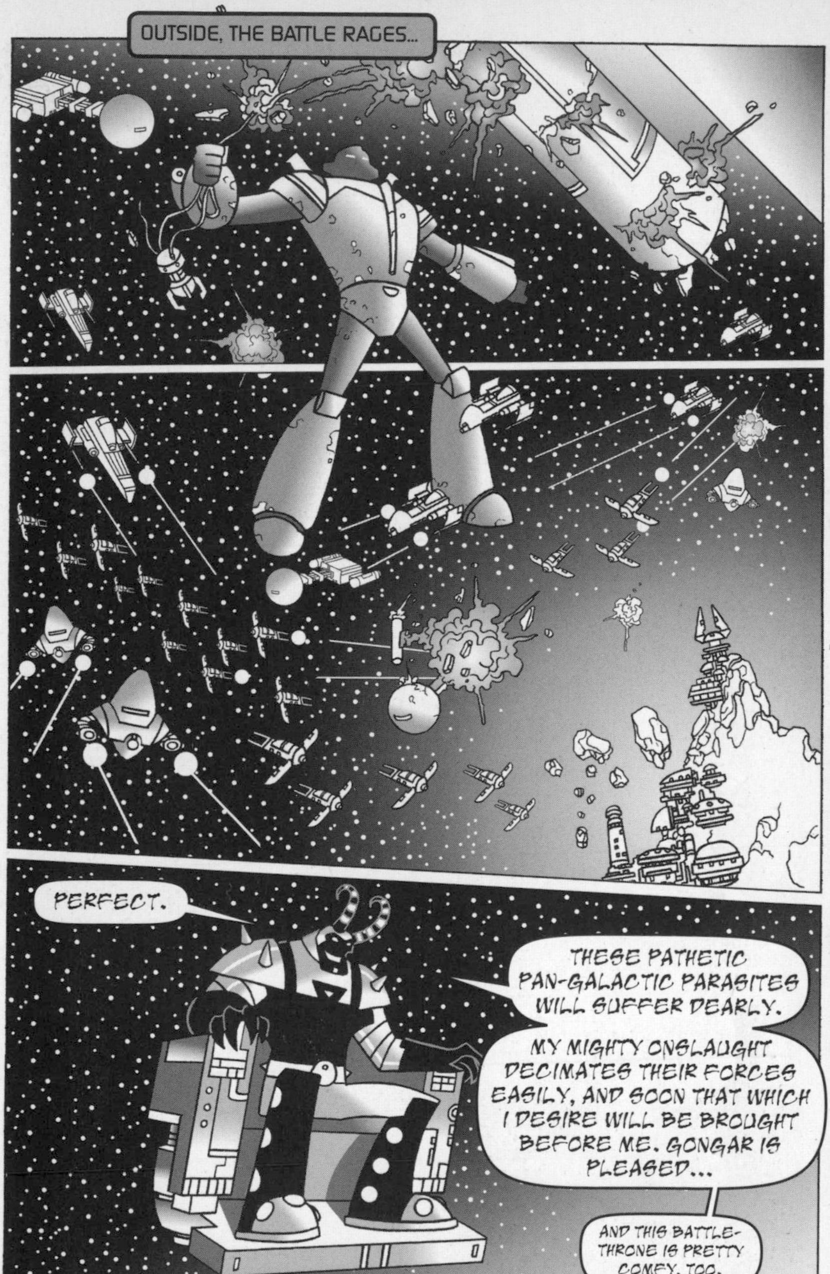
OUTSIDE, THE BATTLE RAGES...
PERFECT.
THESE PATHETIC PAN-GALACTIC PARASITES WILL SUFFER DEARLY.
MY MIGHTY ONSLAUGHT DECIMATES THEIR FORCES EASILY, AND SOON THAT WHICH I DESIRE WILL BE BROUGHT BEFORE ME. GONGAR IS PLEASED...
AND THIS BATTLE-THRONE IS PRETTY COMFY, TOO.

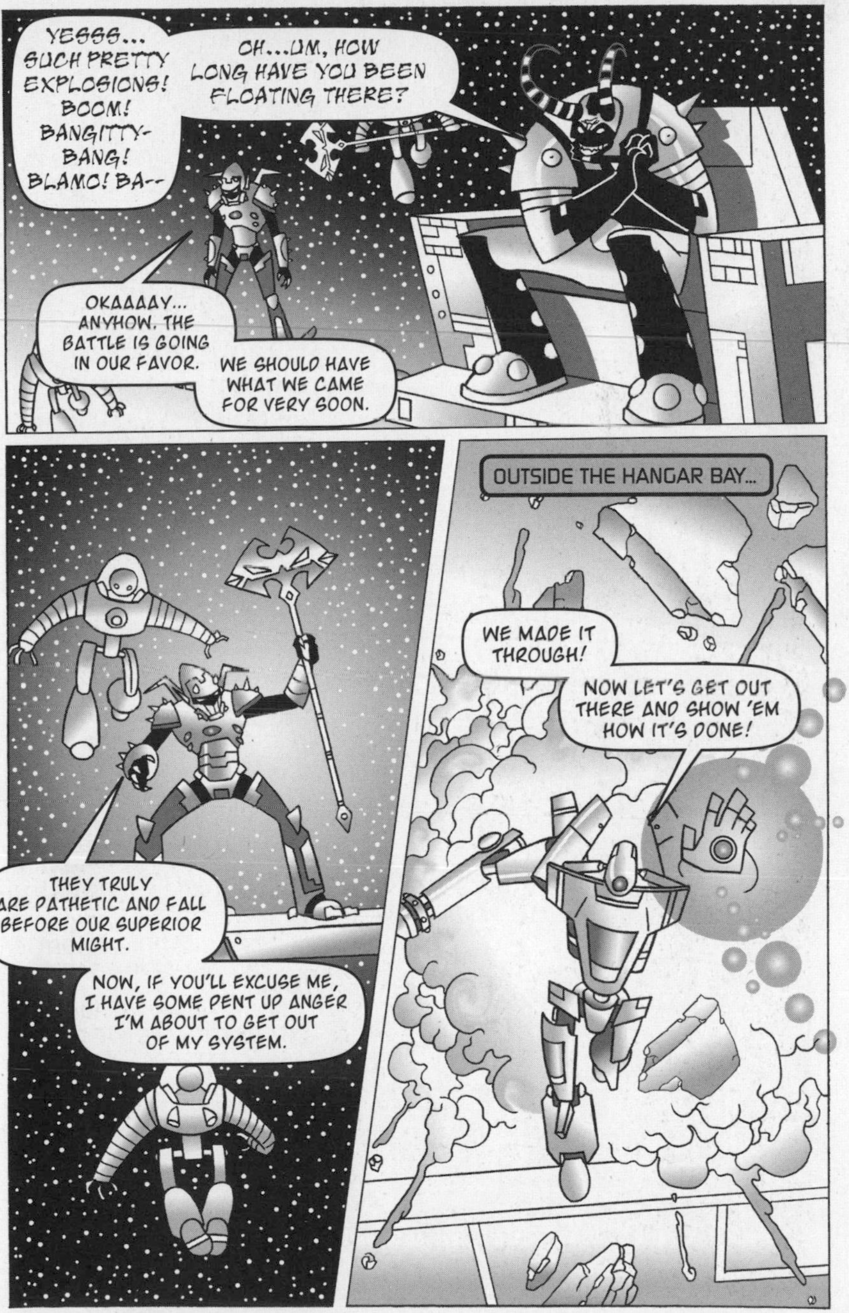
YESSS... SUCH PRETTY EXPLOSIONS! BOOM! BANGITTY-BANG! BLAMO! BA--
OH...UM, HOW LONG HAVE YOU BEEN FLOATING THERE?
OKAAAAY... ANYHOW. THE BATTLE IS GOING IN OUR FAVOR.
WE SHOULD HAVE WHAT WE CAME FOR VERY SOON.
THEY TRULY ARE PATHETIC AND FALL BEFORE OUR SUPERIOR MIGHT.
NOW, IF YOU'LL EXCUSE ME, I HAVE SOME PENT UP ANGER I'M ABOUT TO GET OUT OF MY SYSTEM.
OUTSIDE THE HANGAR BAY...
WE MADE IT THROUGH!
NOW LET'S GET OUT THERE AND SHOW 'EM HOW IT'S DONE!

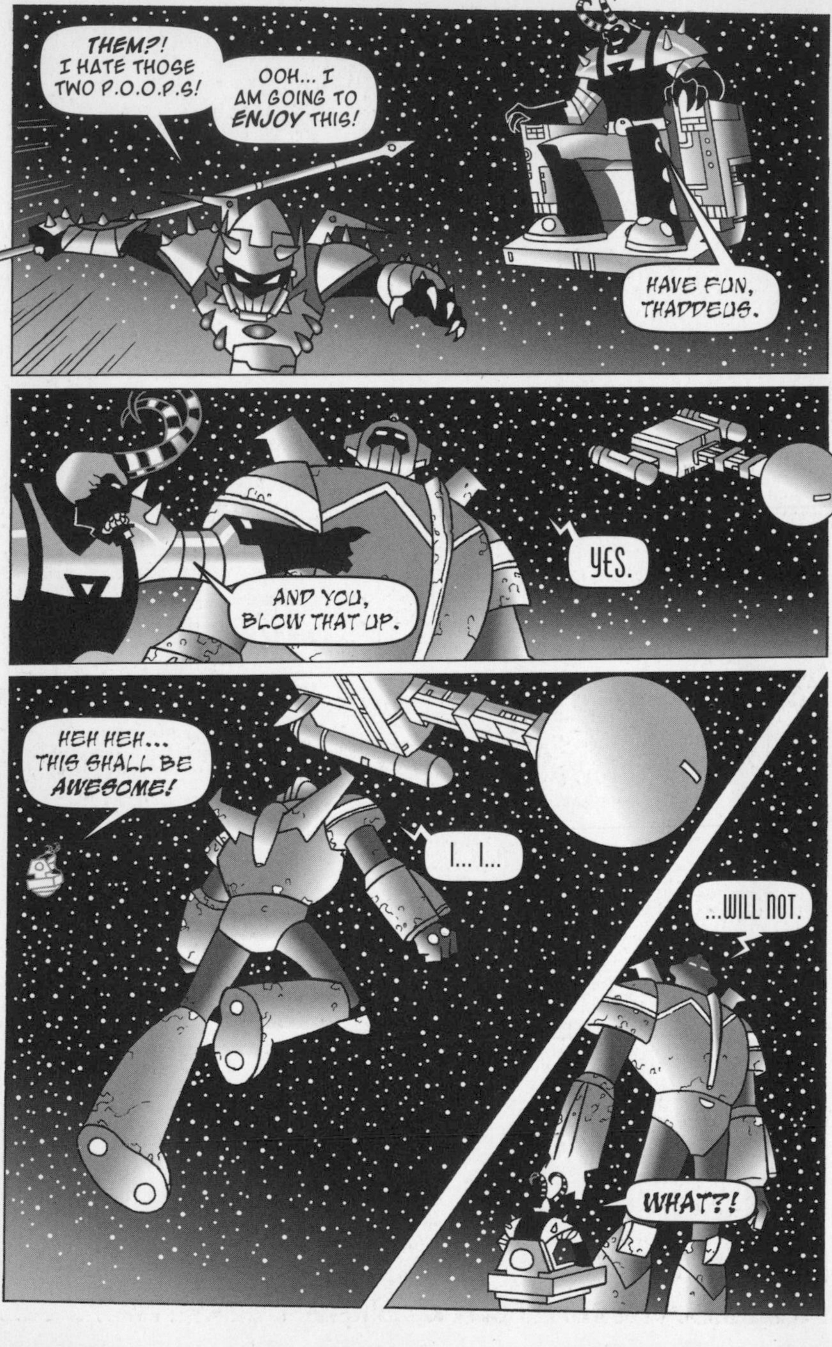
THEM?! I HATE THOSE TWO P.O.O.P.S!
OOH... I AM GOING TO ENJOY THIS!
HAVE FUN, THADDEUS.
AND YOU, BLOW THAT UP.
YES.
HEH HEH... THIS SHALL BE AWESOME!
I... I...
...WILL NOT.
WHAT?!

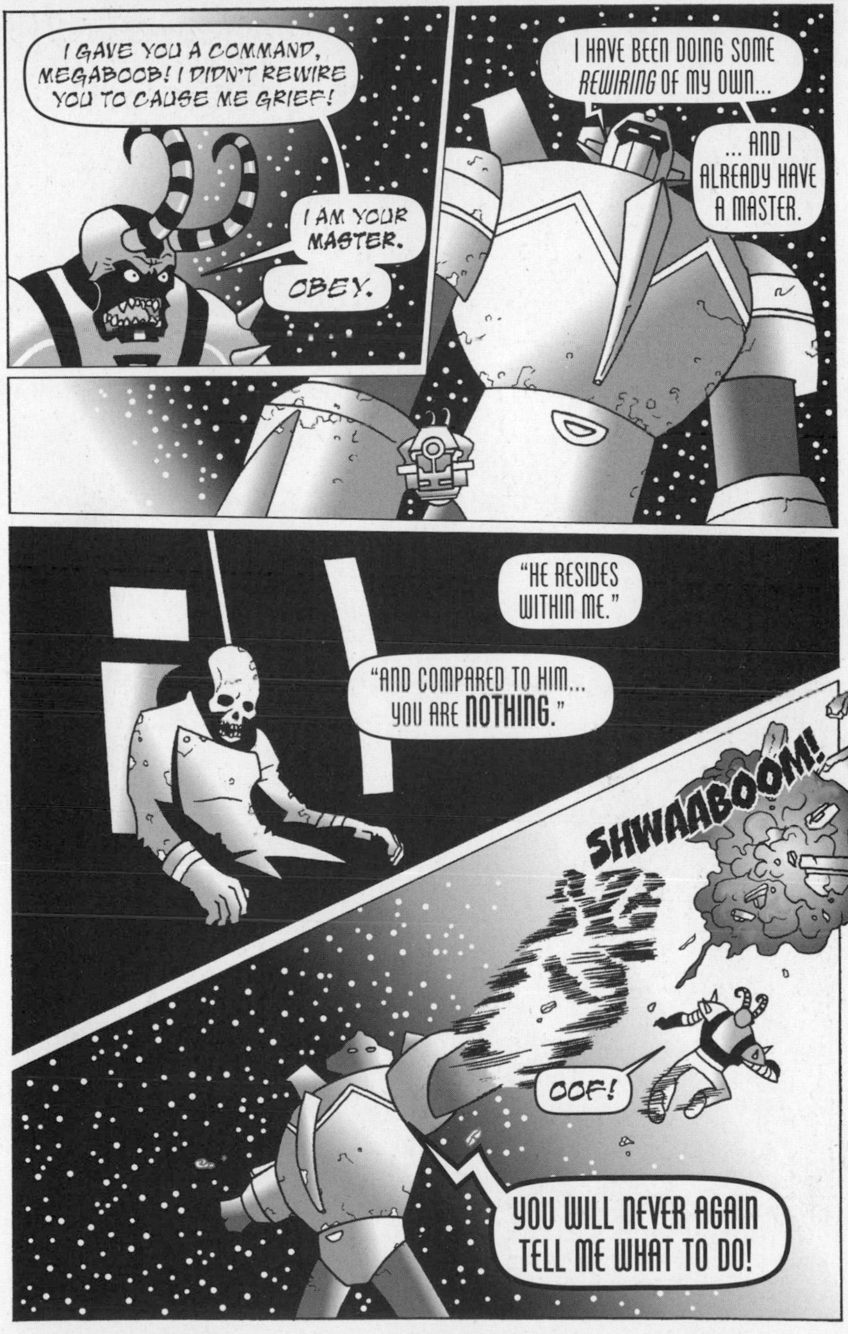

I GAVE YOU A COMMAND, MEGABOOB! I DIDN'T REWIRE YOU TO CAUSE ME GRIEF!
I AM YOUR MASTER.
OBEY.
I HAVE BEEN DOING SOME *REWIRING* OF MY OWN...
... AND I ALREADY HAVE A MASTER.
"HE RESIDES WITHIN ME."
"AND COMPARED TO HIM... YOU ARE **NOTHING**."
SHWAABOOM!
OOF!
YOU WILL NEVER AGAIN TELL ME WHAT TO DO!

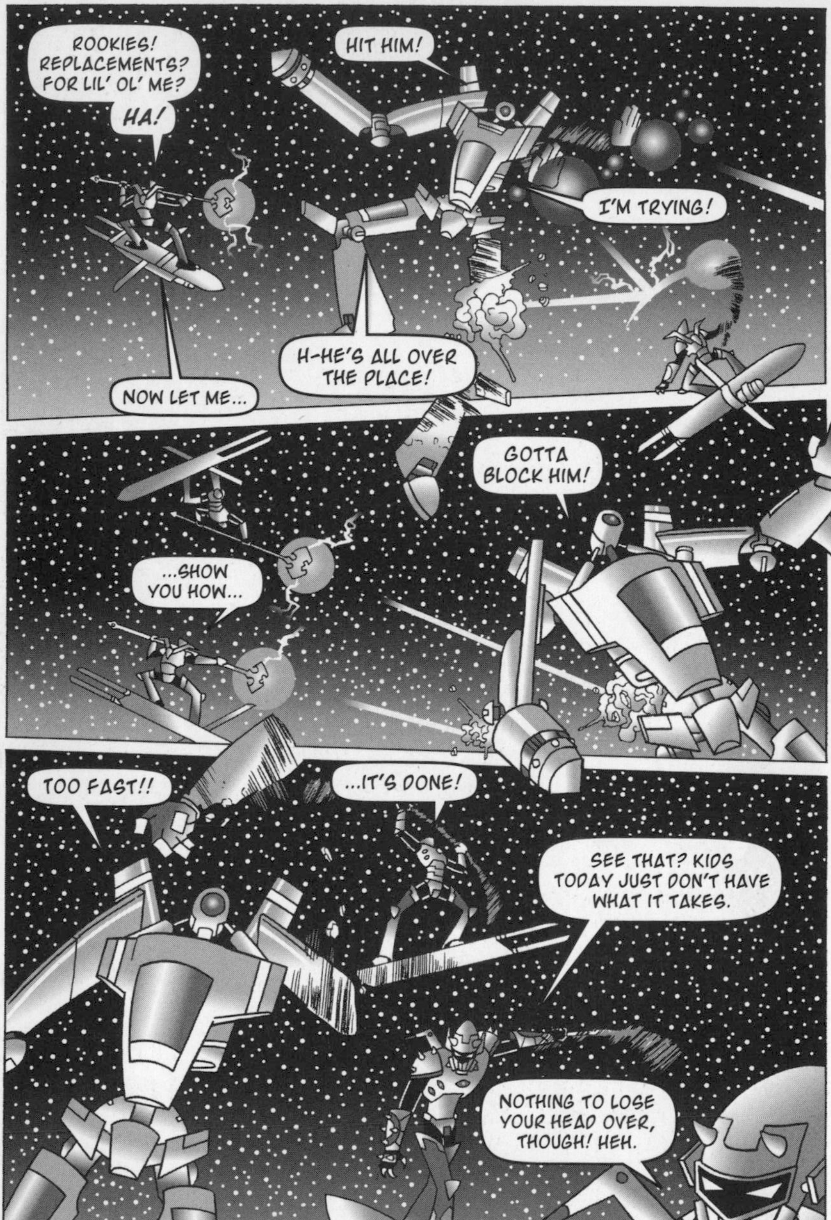
ROOKIES! REPLACEMENTS? FOR LIL' OL' ME?
HA!
HIT HIM!
I'M TRYING!
NOW LET ME...
H-HE'S ALL OVER THE PLACE!
GOTTA BLOCK HIM!
...SHOW YOU HOW...
TOO FAST!!
...IT'S DONE!
SEE THAT? KIDS TODAY JUST DON'T HAVE WHAT IT TAKES.
NOTHING TO LOSE YOUR HEAD OVER, THOUGH! HEH.

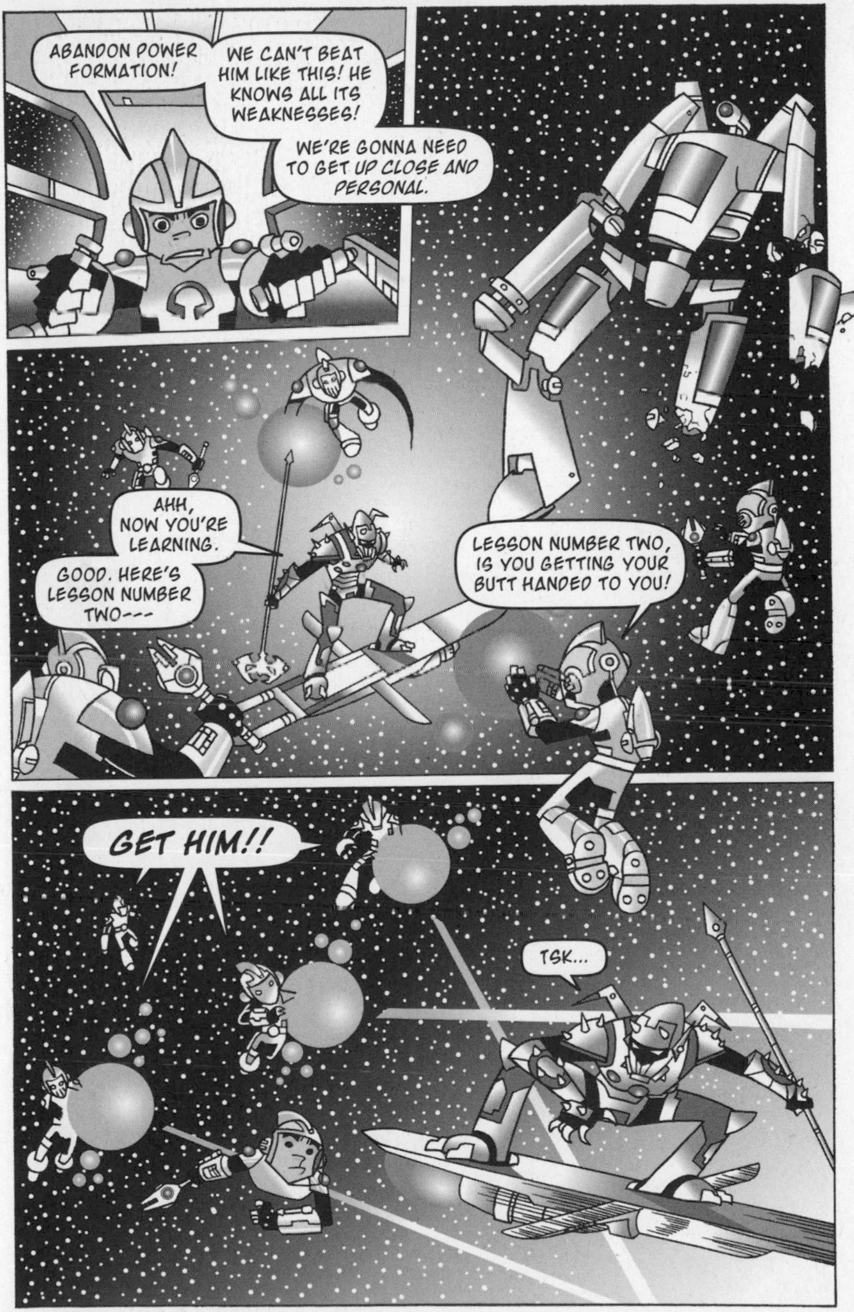
ABANDON POWER FORMATION!
WE CAN'T BEAT HIM LIKE THIS! HE KNOWS ALL ITS WEAKNESSES!
WE'RE GONNA NEED TO GET UP CLOSE AND PERSONAL.
AHH, NOW YOU'RE LEARNING.
GOOD. HERE'S LESSON NUMBER TWO---
LESSON NUMBER TWO, IS YOU GETTING YOUR BUTT HANDED TO YOU!
GET HIM!!
TSK...

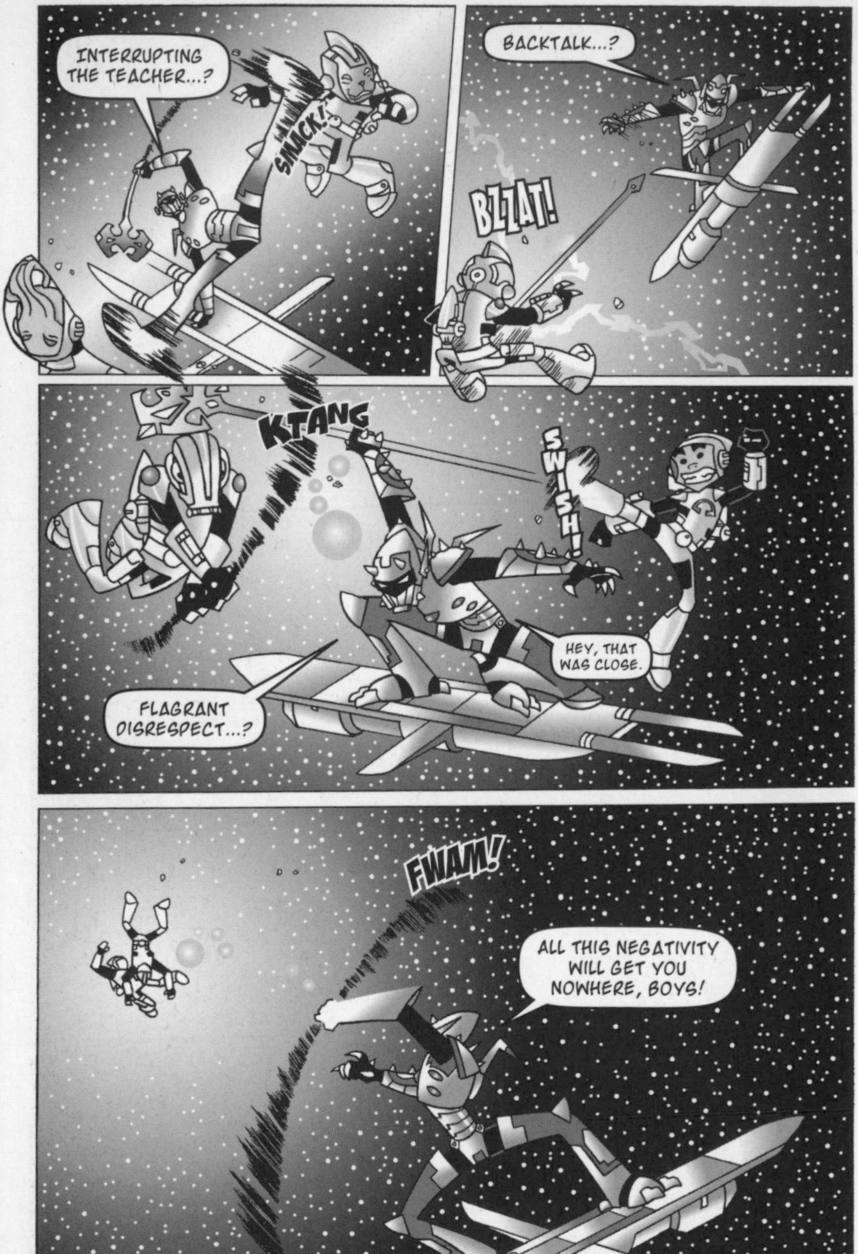
INTERRUPTING THE TEACHER...?
SMACK!
BACKTALK...?
BZZAT!
KTANG
SWISH!
HEY, THAT WAS CLOSE.
FLAGRANT DISRESPECT...?
FWAM!
ALL THIS NEGATIVITY WILL GET YOU NOWHERE, BOYS!

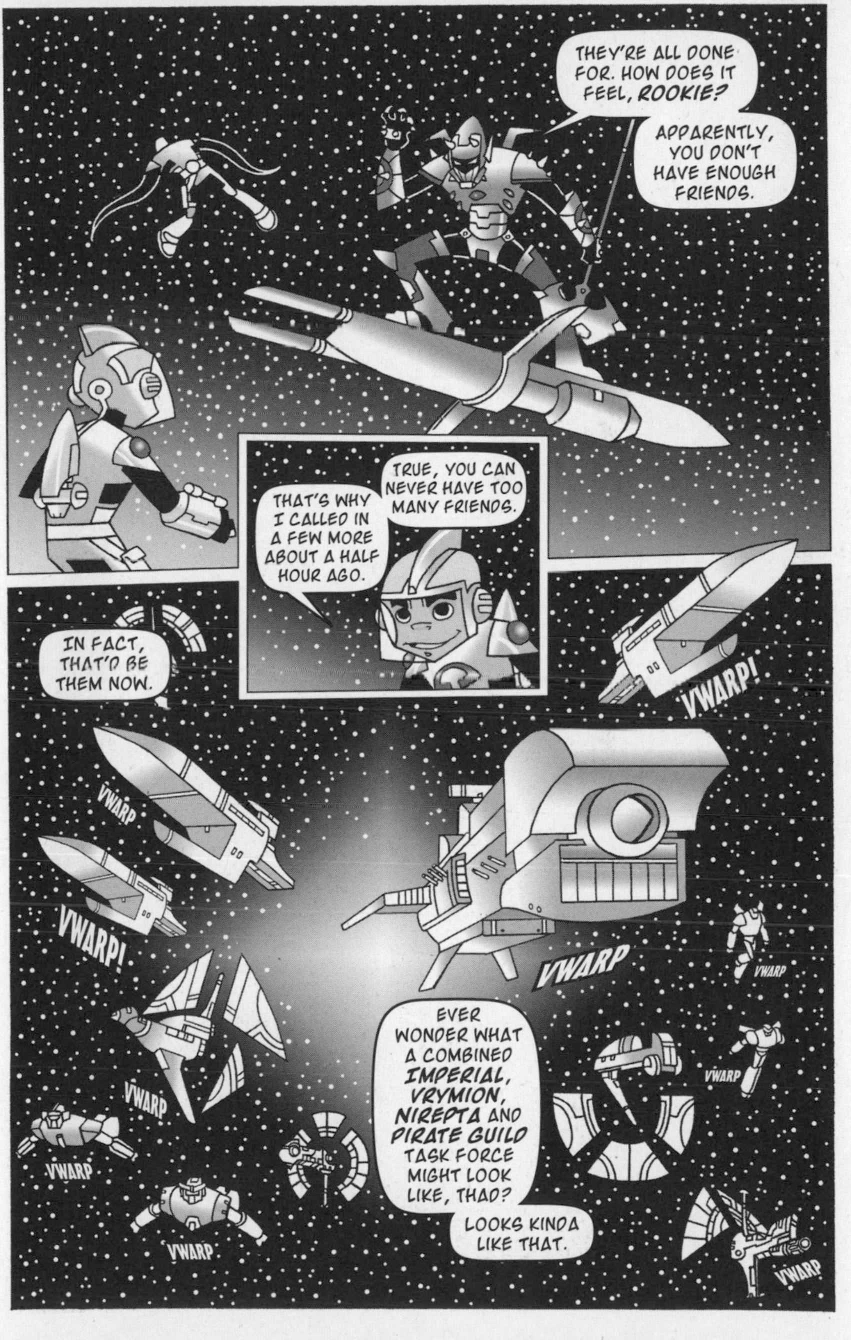
THEY'RE ALL DONE FOR. HOW DOES IT FEEL, *ROOKIE?*
APPARENTLY, YOU DON'T HAVE ENOUGH FRIENDS.
TRUE, YOU CAN NEVER HAVE TOO MANY FRIENDS.
THAT'S WHY I CALLED IN A FEW MORE ABOUT A HALF HOUR AGO.
IN FACT, THAT'D BE THEM NOW.
VWARP!
VWARP
VWARP!
VWARP
VWARP
VWARP
VWARP
VWARP
EVER WONDER WHAT A COMBINED *IMPERIAL, VRYMION, NIREPTA* AND *PIRATE GUILD* TASK FORCE MIGHT LOOK LIKE, THAD?
VWARP
LOOKS KINDA LIKE THAT.
VWARP
VWARP

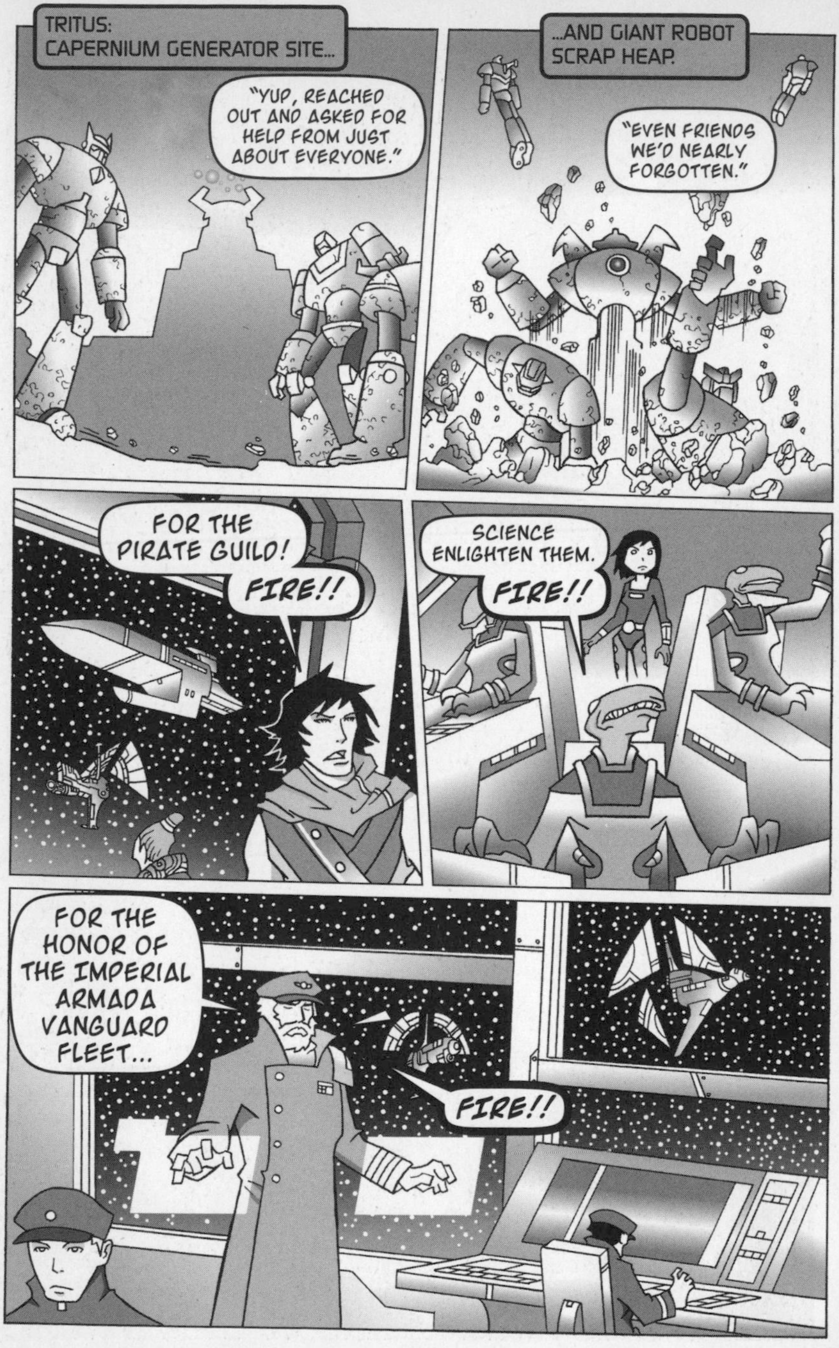
TRITUS:
CAPERNIUM GENERATOR SITE...
"YUP, REACHED OUT AND ASKED FOR HELP FROM JUST ABOUT EVERYONE."
...AND GIANT ROBOT SCRAP HEAP.
"EVEN FRIENDS WE'D NEARLY FORGOTTEN."
FOR THE PIRATE GUILD!
FIRE!!
SCIENCE ENLIGHTEN THEM.
FIRE!!
FOR THE HONOR OF THE IMPERIAL ARMADA VANGUARD FLEET...
FIRE!!

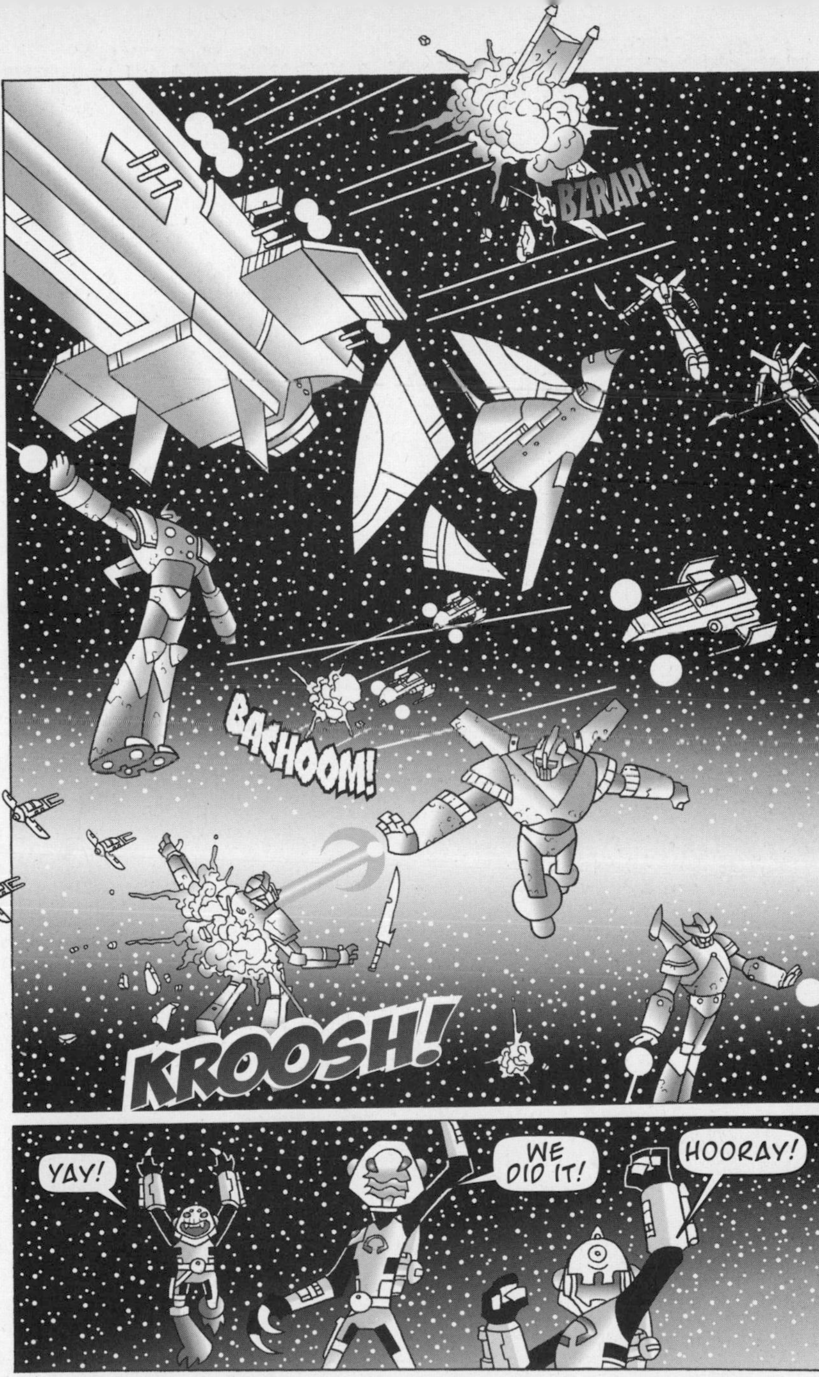
BZRAP!
BACHOOM!
KROOSH!
YAY!
WE DID IT!
HOORAY!

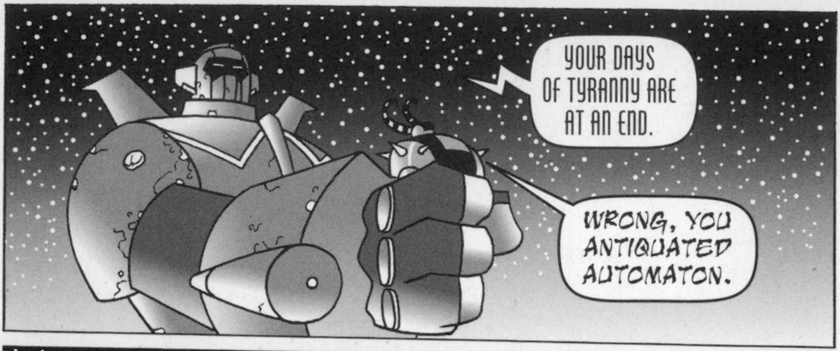
YOUR DAYS OF TYRANNY ARE AT AN END.
WRONG, YOU ANTIQUATED AUTOMATON.

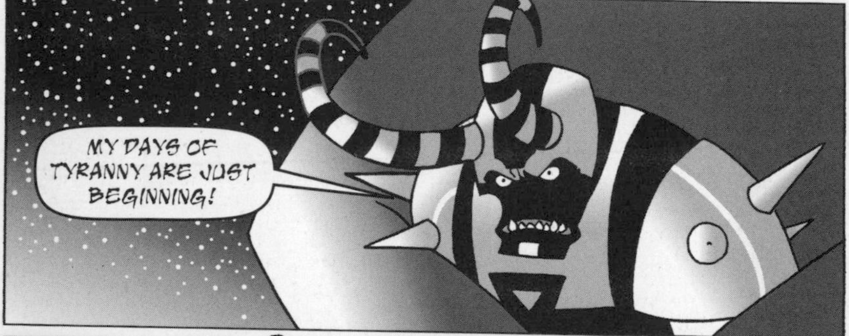
MY DAYS OF TYRANNY ARE JUST BEGINNING!

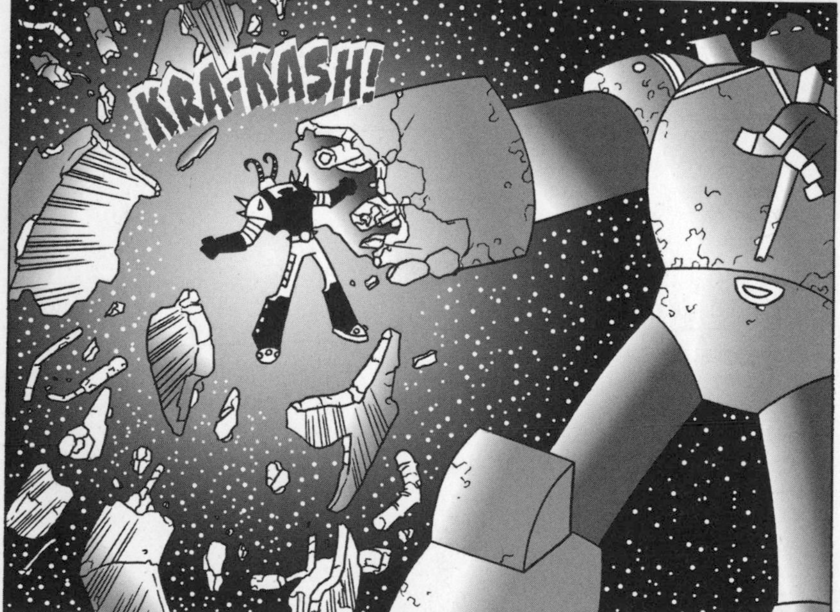
KRA-KASH!

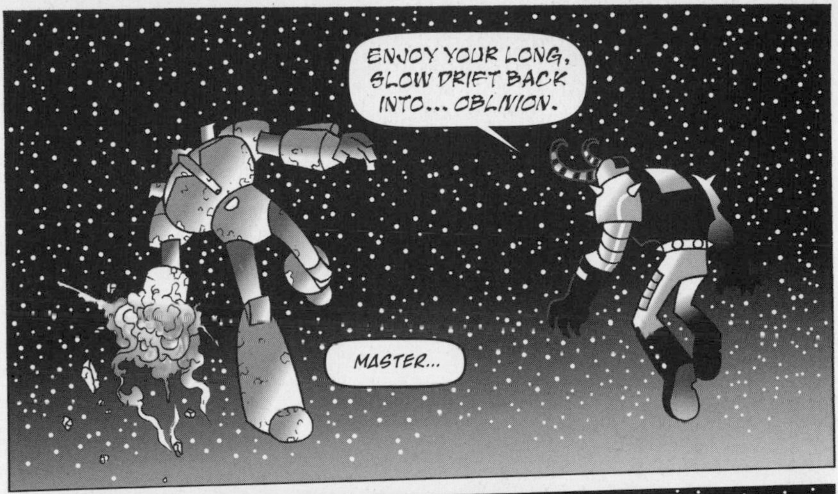
ENJOY YOUR LONG, SLOW DRIFT BACK INTO... OBLIVION.
MASTER...

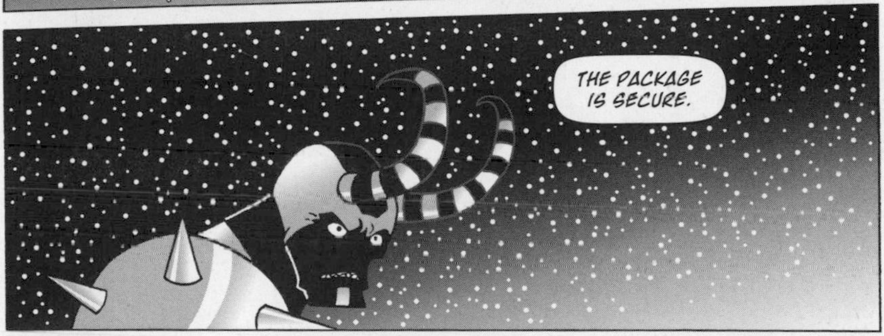
THE PACKAGE IS SECURE.

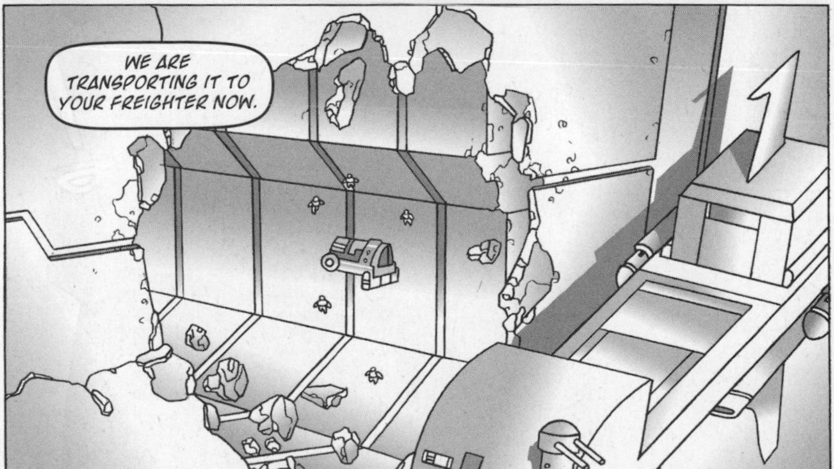
WE ARE TRANSPORTING IT TO YOUR FREIGHTER NOW.

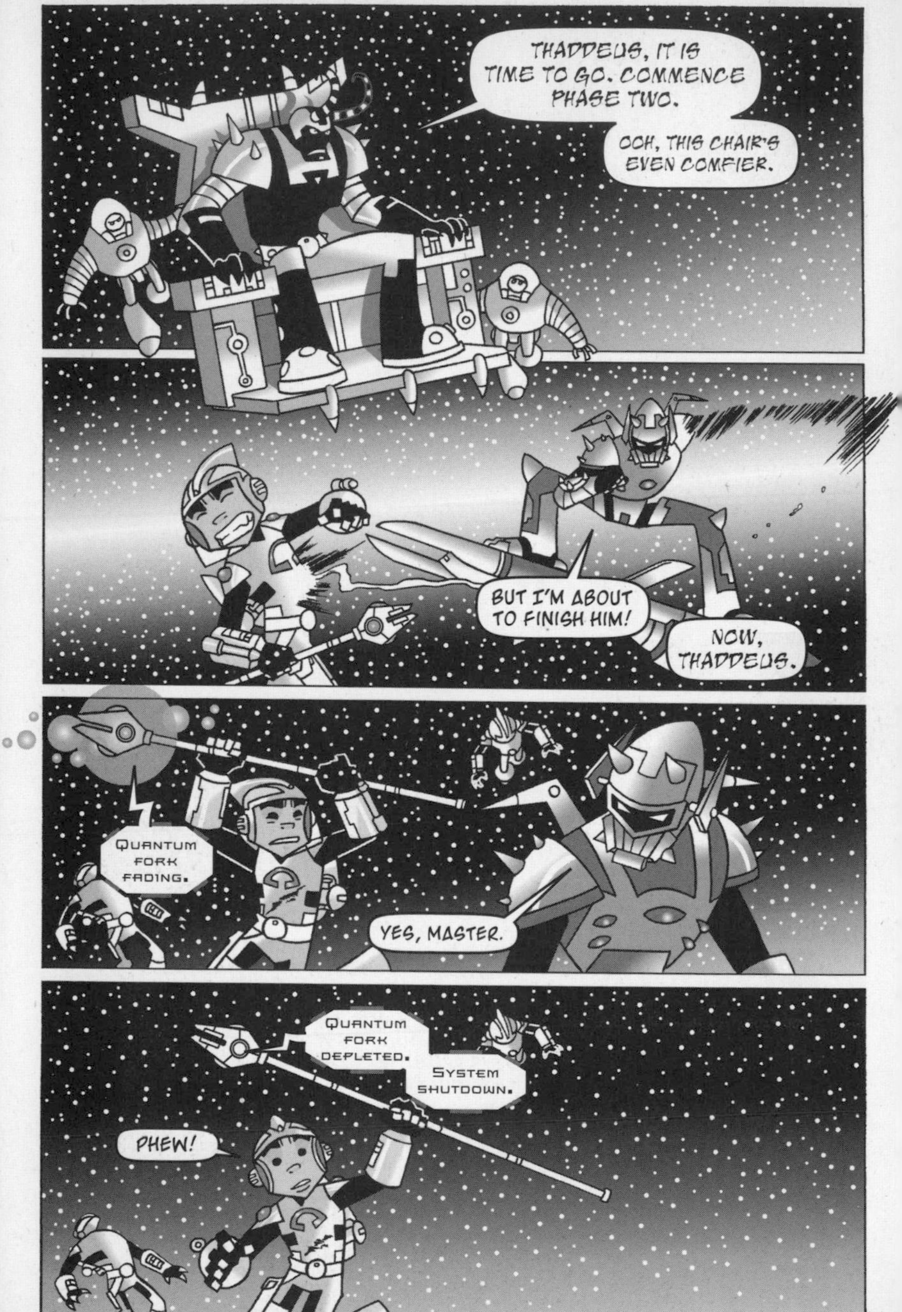
THADDEUS, IT IS TIME TO GO. COMMENCE PHASE TWO.
OOH, THIS CHAIR'S EVEN COMFIER.
BUT I'M ABOUT TO FINISH HIM!
NOW, THADDEUS.
QUANTUM FORK FADING.
YES, MASTER.
QUANTUM FORK DEPLETED.
SYSTEM SHUTDOWN.
PHEW!

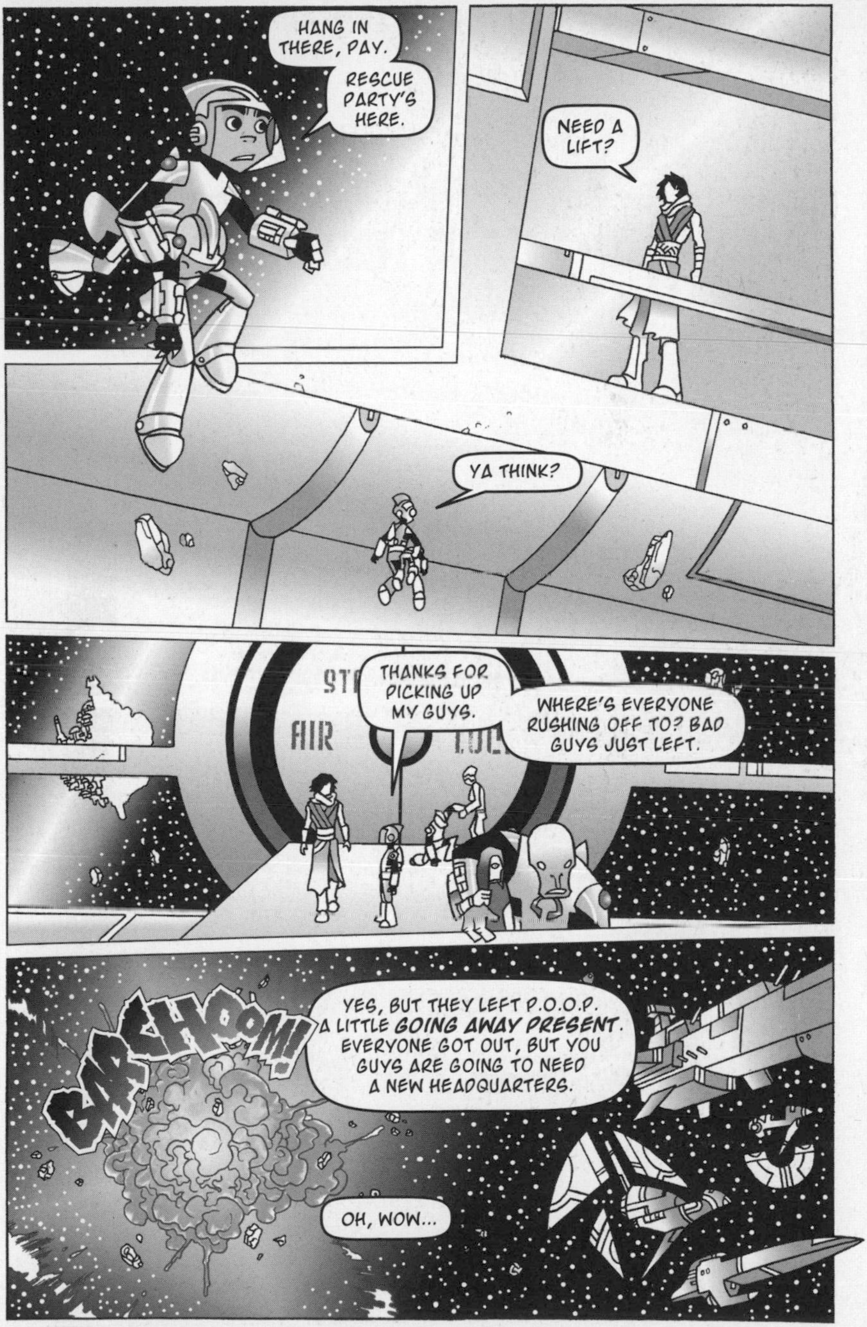
HANG IN THERE, PAY.
RESCUE PARTY'S HERE.
NEED A LIFT?
YA THINK?
STA
AIR LOC
THANKS FOR PICKING UP MY GUYS.
WHERE'S EVERYONE RUSHING OFF TO? BAD GUYS JUST LEFT.
BA-CHOOM!
YES, BUT THEY LEFT P.O.O.P. A LITTLE GOING AWAY PRESENT. EVERYONE GOT OUT, BUT YOU GUYS ARE GOING TO NEED A NEW HEADQUARTERS.
OH, WOW...

EPILOGUE:
NOBODY SAID IT'D BE EASY...

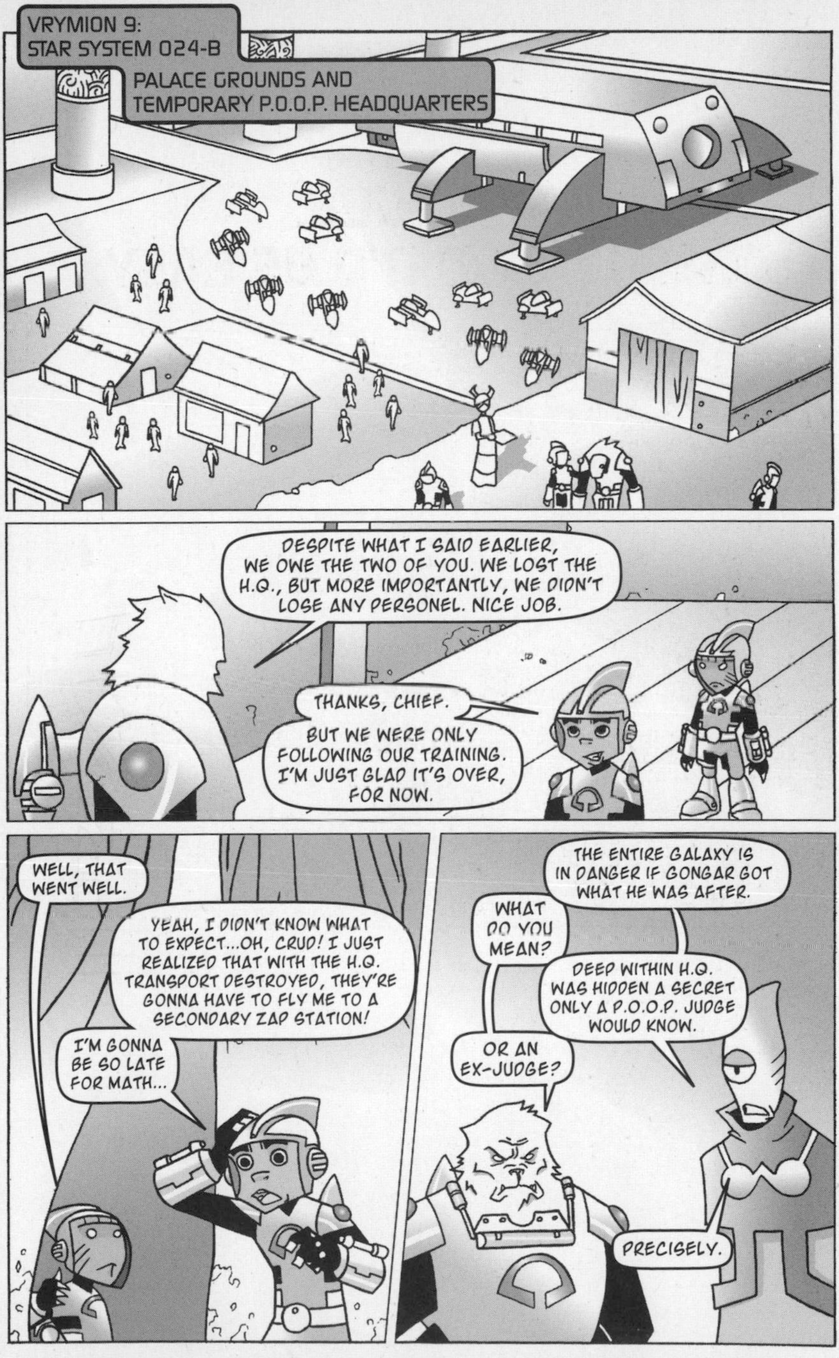
VRYMION 9: STAR SYSTEM 024-B
PALACE GROUNDS AND TEMPORARY P.O.O.P. HEADQUARTERS
DESPITE WHAT I SAID EARLIER, WE OWE THE TWO OF YOU. WE LOST THE H.Q., BUT MORE IMPORTANTLY, WE DIDN'T LOSE ANY PERSONEL. NICE JOB.
THANKS, CHIEF.
BUT WE WERE ONLY FOLLOWING OUR TRAINING. I'M JUST GLAD IT'S OVER, FOR NOW.
WELL, THAT WENT WELL.
YEAH, I DIDN'T KNOW WHAT TO EXPECT...OH, CRUD! I JUST REALIZED THAT WITH THE H.Q. TRANSPORT DESTROYED, THEY'RE GONNA HAVE TO FLY ME TO A SECONDARY ZAP STATION!
I'M GONNA BE SO LATE FOR MATH...
THE ENTIRE GALAXY IS IN DANGER IF GONGAR GOT WHAT HE WAS AFTER.
WHAT DO YOU MEAN?
DEEP WITHIN H.Q. WAS HIDDEN A SECRET ONLY A P.O.O.P. JUDGE WOULD KNOW.
OR AN EX-JUDGE?
PRECISELY.

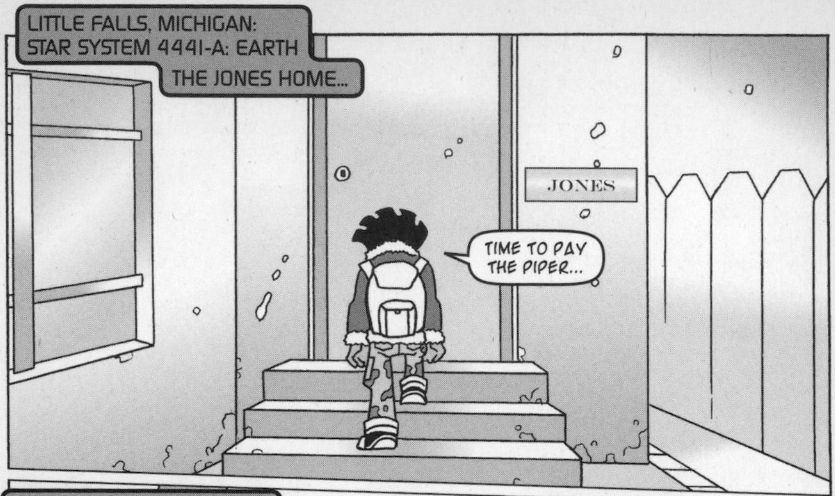
LITTLE FALLS, MICHIGAN: STAR SYSTEM 4441-A: EARTH
THE JONES HOME...
JONES
TIME TO PAY THE PIPER...
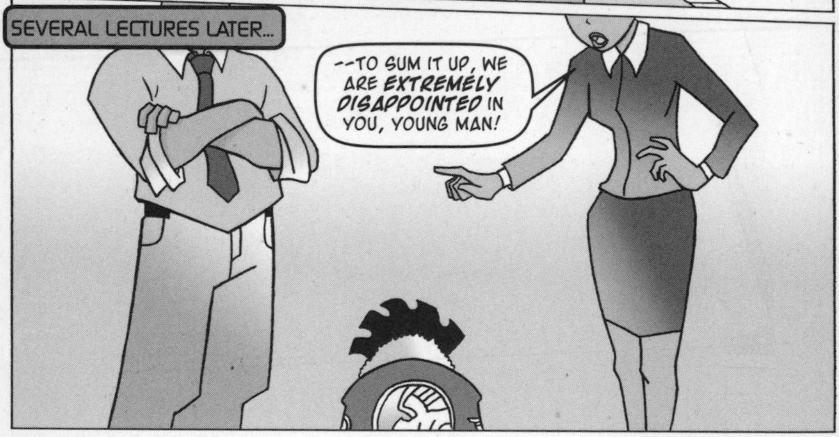
SEVERAL LECTURES LATER...
--TO SUM IT UP, WE ARE EXTREMELY DISAPPOINTED IN YOU, YOUNG MAN!
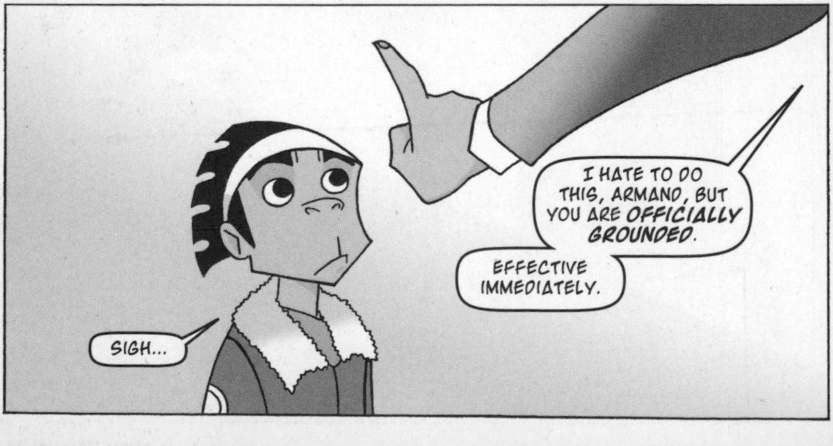
I HATE TO DO THIS, ARMAND, BUT YOU ARE OFFICIALLY GROUNDED.
EFFECTIVE IMMEDIATELY.
SIGH...

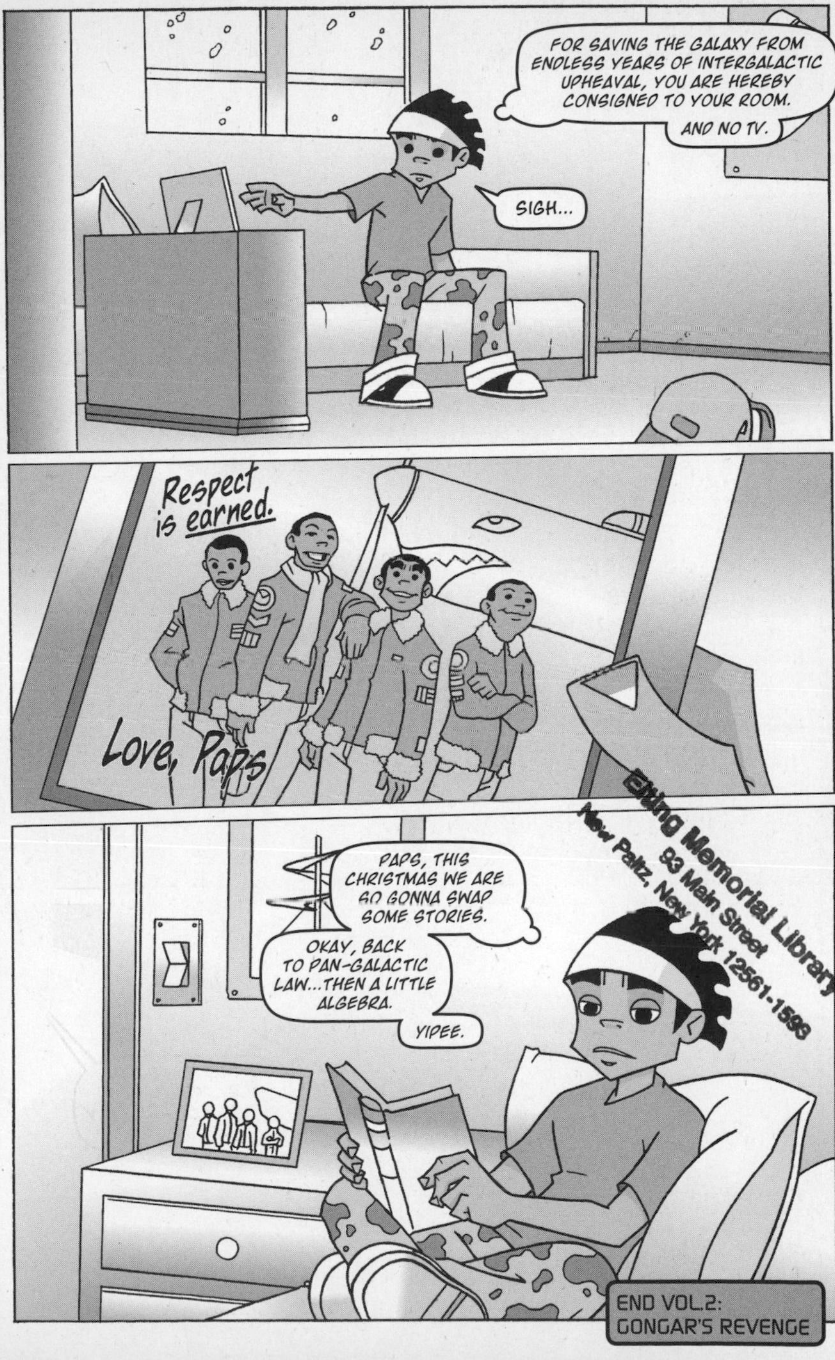
FOR SAVING THE GALAXY FROM ENDLESS YEARS OF INTERGALACTIC UPHEAVAL, YOU ARE HEREBY CONSIGNED TO YOUR ROOM.
AND NO TV.
SIGH...
Respect is earned.
Love, Paps
PAPS, THIS CHRISTMAS WE ARE SO GONNA SWAP SOME STORIES.
OKAY, BACK TO PAN-GALACTIC LAW...THEN A LITTLE ALGEBRA.
YIPEE.
END VOL.2: GONGAR'S REVENGE

NEXT TIME IN

Well, it looks like Armand might finally be getting the hang of juggling his P.O.O.P. duties with his school commitments. Now, if he could just find time to sleep, he'd be all set!

Although, getting a good night's sleep won't be easy, not with the knowledge that Gongar's still out there on the loose. But what Armand doesn't know is that Gongar stole a mysterious item from the H.Q. just before destroying the facility.

What is it that could have been worth all-out intergalactic war to steal? And why is it of such concern to the P.O.O.P. High Command? Whatever it is, Armand and Payleen will be there to meet the challenge head on!

BE HERE FOR THE NEXT EXCITING INSTALLMENT OF ZAPT!

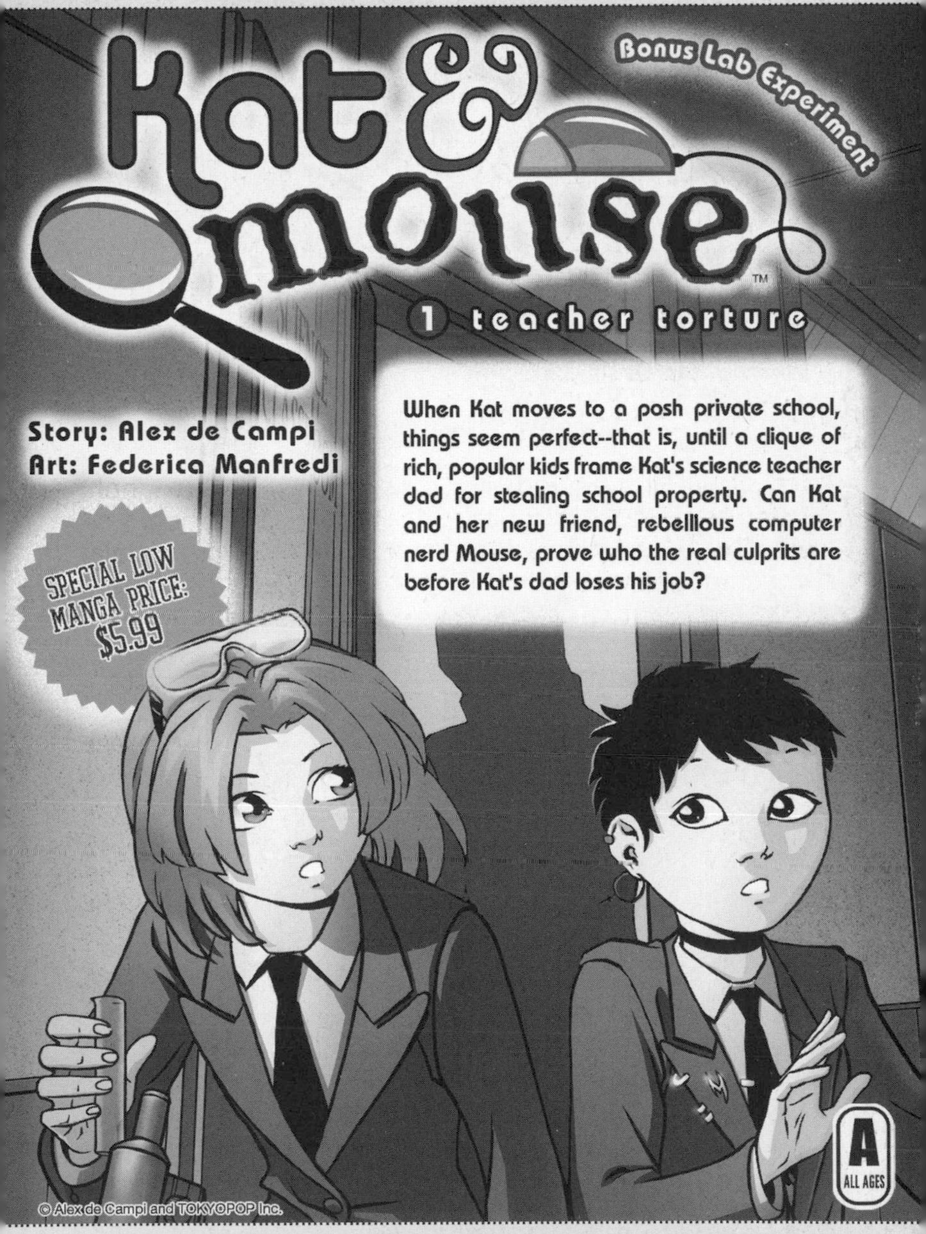
Kat & Mouse™
Bonus Lab Experiment
1 teacher torture
Story: Alex de Campi
Art: Federica Manfredi
When Kat moves to a posh private school, things seem perfect--that is, until a clique of rich, popular kids frame Kat's science teacher dad for stealing school property. Can Kat and her new friend, rebelllous computer nerd Mouse, prove who the real culprits are before Kat's dad loses his job?
SPECIAL LOW MANGA PRICE: $5.99
A
ALL AGES
© Alex de Campi and TOKYOPOP Inc.

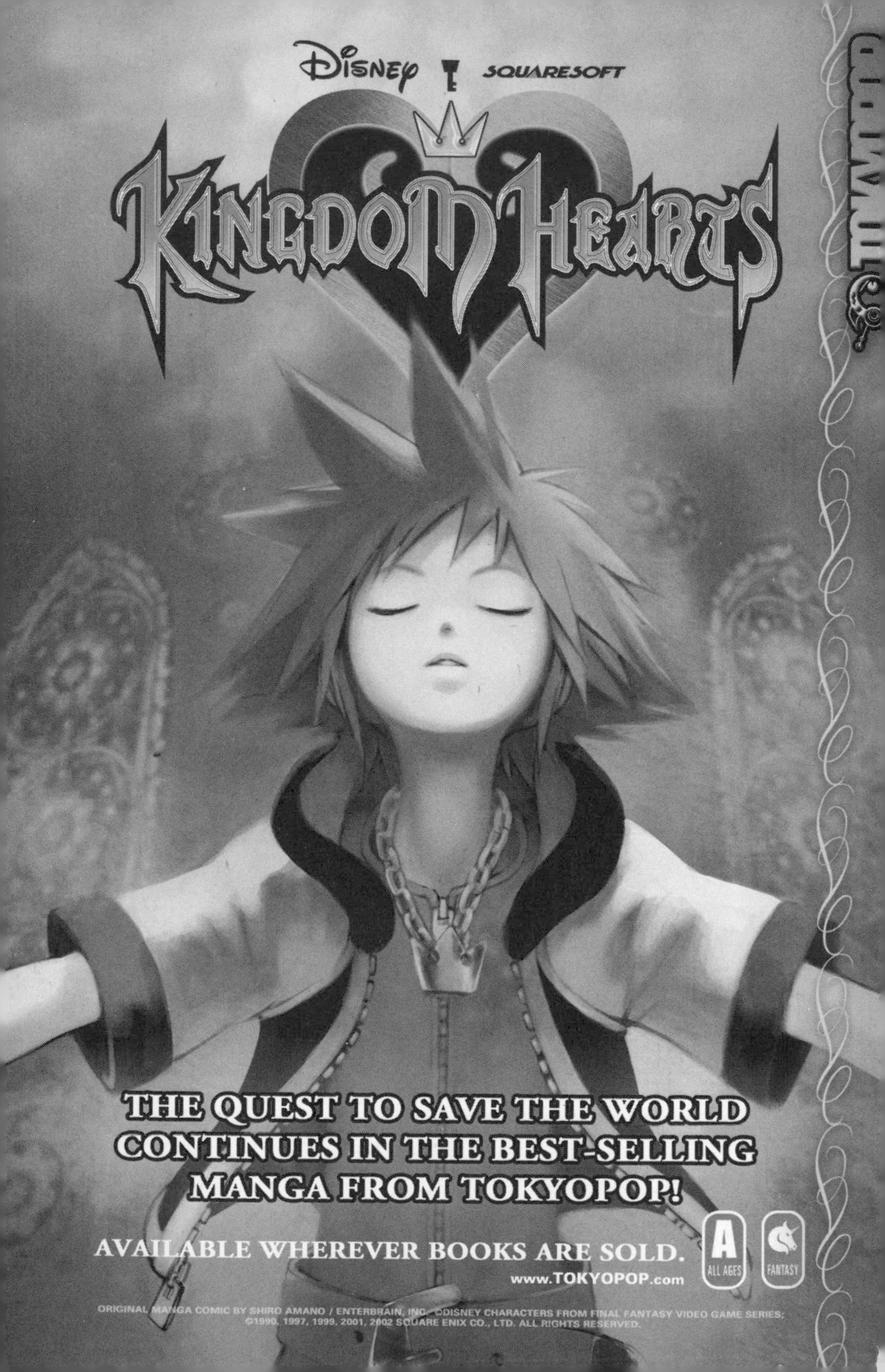
DISNEY SQUARESOFT
KINGDOM HEARTS
TOKYOPOP
THE QUEST TO SAVE THE WORLD CONTINUES IN THE BEST-SELLING MANGA FROM TOKYOPOP!
AVAILABLE WHEREVER BOOKS ARE SOLD.
www.TOKYOPOP.com
A ALL AGES
FANTASY
ORIGINAL MANGA COMIC BY SHIRO AMANO / ENTERBRAIN, INC. ©DISNEY CHARACTERS FROM FINAL FANTASY VIDEO GAME SERIES; ©1990, 1997, 1999, 2001, 2002 SQUARE ENIX CO., LTD. ALL RIGHTS RESERVED.